THE MALT *in* OUR STARS

THE MALT *in* OUR STARS

SARAH
FOX

KENSINGTON BOOKS
www.kensingtonbooks.com

KENSINGTON BOOKS are published by

Kensington Publishing Corp.
119 West 40th Street
New York, NY 10018

All Kensington titles, imprints, and distributed lines are available at special quantity discounts for bulk purchases for sales promotion, premiums, fund-raising, educational, or institutional use. Special book excerpts or customized printings can also be created to fit specific needs. For details, write or phone the office of the Kensington Special Sales Manager: Attn. Special Sales Department. Kensington Publishing Corp, 119 West 40th Street, New York, NY 10018. Phone: 1-800-221-2647.

Library of Congress Card Catalogue Number: 2020939640

Kensington and the K logo Reg. U.S. Pat. & TM Off.

ISBN-13: 978-1-4967-1870-9
ISBN-10: 1-4967-1870-4
First Kensington Hardcover Edition: December 2020

ISBN-13: 978-1-4967-1873-0 (ebook)
ISBN-10: 1-4967-1873-9 (ebook)

10 9 8 7 6 5 4 3 2 1

Printed in the United States of America

THE MALT *in* OUR STARS

Chapter 1

Shady Creek Manor was an impressive sight to behold. The three-story stone building sat in the middle of several acres of neatly trimmed lawn, immaculately kept gardens, and serene woodland. The clear blue sky made the scene even more spectacular. I cracked my car window open as I followed the long driveway, breathing in the heavenly scent of the spring air. The smell of flowers and freshly cut grass buoyed my already good mood, and I soaked in the warmth from the sun shining through the driver's-side window.

Instead of following the branch of the driveway that looped around a fountain to the front door of the manor, I drove along another arm, past the hotel to a parking lot beyond a row of trees that prevented the parked cars and cement from spoiling the view from the front of the property. The lot was only half full, and as I pulled into a free spot my nerves danced a little jig. I was about to meet one of my favorite authors, Linnea Bliss.

When I climbed out of my car, I smoothed down the skirt of my green dress and tucked an errant strand of red hair behind my ear. I wanted to be as professional as possible and I was determined not to fangirl when I met the author. Not too much, anyway. Still, as I headed across the parking lot, I had to take a deep breath to settle my still-dancing nerves. I reached the edge of the parking lot and was about to walk along a pathway that led around to the front of the manor when the sound of hushed but angry voices reached my ears.

I paused, seeking out the owners of the voices. A second later I spotted Brad Honeywell, one of the manor's owners, outside a rear door of the hotel. He was in the midst of an argument with a twenty-something woman with dark brown hair cut in a sleek, short bob with blunt bangs. Although I'd never formally met Brad, I knew him by sight since he came to my pub, the Inkwell, on occasion. The young woman with him was a complete stranger to me, however. I couldn't hear what the two of them were arguing about, but just as I was going to continue on my way, the young woman took a step back from Brad.

"Stay away from me!" she fumed.

Before Brad had a chance to say anything in response, she spun on her heel and disappeared into the manor, almost slamming the door behind her. Still agitated, Brad ran a hand through his thinning dark hair.

I didn't want him to catch me gawking, so I quickly set off along the pathway. I couldn't help but wonder what was going on between Brad and the young woman. It wasn't any of my business, but I was curious by nature and couldn't stop a list of possibilities from scrolling through my mind. I brought those thoughts to an abrupt halt when I reached the front of the manor.

Although I'd glimpsed the hotel while driving past on a few occasions, I'd never been inside, or even this close. Built in the first half of the twentieth century by a wealthy man named Edwin Vallencourt, the manor was originally a private mansion. According to local stories, Vallencourt had entertained other wealthy and sometimes famous figures and had thrown legendary parties at his extravagant home. After his death, his heirs had been unable to afford to keep the massive property and it had changed hands several times over the years.

Almost a decade ago, Brad Honeywell and his wife, Gemma, had purchased the property and restored the manor to its former glory before opening it as a hotel. It was the fanciest and most expensive place to stay in the small town of Shady Creek, Vermont, and I was almost as eager to get a look inside as I was to meet Linnea Bliss.

A short flight of wide stone steps led up to the elegant double doors. When I stepped into the spacious lobby, I had to pause on the threshold to take in the beautiful sight before me. A crystal chandelier hung from the high ceiling, but it was almost unnecessary at the moment, with all the daylight streaming in through the large windows. I couldn't spot a speck of dirt on the white marble floors, and the tasteful antique furnishings allowed me to feel as though I'd momentarily stepped back in time, until I noticed the computer on the reception desk.

On my left and next to a leafy potted plant was a settee so gorgeous that I wished I could have it for my own, even though it probably would have looked out of place in the cozy little apartment I called home. It had a beautifully carved crest and legs, and was upholstered with cream fabric. It likely cost more than all my furniture put together.

When I first entered the lobby, the reception desk to my right was unmanned, but as the door drifted shut, Brad Honeywell strode toward me. I experienced a brief moment of apprehension until he directed a welcoming smile my way. Most likely he was unaware that I'd witnessed him arguing with someone minutes earlier.

"Good morning and welcome to Shady Creek Manor," Brad said. "It's Sadie, isn't it?"

"That's right," I replied. "I'm here to meet with Linnea Bliss and her assistant."

"Yes, of course," a woman's voice chimed in. Gemma Honeywell entered the lobby through an arched doorway that appeared to lead to a sitting room. She wore a light gray pantsuit with a silk blouse, and her curly fair hair was tied back in a fancy twist. "We're all very excited to have such a famous author staying here at the manor."

"And I'm excited to meet her," I said.

Gemma introduced herself, since we'd never officially met, and told me she'd call Marcie Kent, Linnea's assistant, and let her know that I'd arrived.

I took the opportunity to try out the beautiful settee. I half expected it to be uncomfortable because of its formal appearance, but that wasn't the case. Perhaps it wasn't quite as comfy as my couch, but it was still a nice place to sit.

While I waited, Gemma had a hushed conversation on the phone behind the reception desk. I twisted one of the rings on my right hand, butterflies circling around each other in my stomach. Gemma was still on the phone when a woman in jeans and a flannel shirt with rolled up sleeves appeared in the lobby. She had cropped brown hair and carried a toolbox. I'd seen her at my pub and around town a few times. If I remembered correctly, her name was Jan and she had her own plumbing business.

As soon as Brad spotted her, he hurried out from behind the reception desk.

"Problem all fixed?" he asked.

"As good as new," Jan replied.

"Excellent. I'll write you a check." Brad ushered her down a hallway that led toward the back of the manor.

Gemma hung up the phone and smiled at me. "Ms. Kent asked that you meet her and Ms. Bliss in the parlor for tea. I'll show you the way."

Thanking her, I followed her through the archway into the sitting room. Although, *parlor* seemed like a much more suitable term. The room was bigger than my whole apartment and it reminded me of sitting rooms I'd seen in British movies featuring grand estates from days gone by. The rugs alone probably cost a fortune, never mind the ornate furnishings. The artwork on the walls might not have been created by the grand masters, but each piece was still gorgeous.

A marble fireplace was the focal point along one wall, while the opposite wall featured a row of arched windows, currently shaded with sheer curtains to filter out some of the bright sunlight. At the far end of the room, four chairs sat tucked beneath a round table covered in a white cloth.

Gemma nodded at the table. "If you'd like to take a seat, I'll be serving tea shortly."

"Thank you," I managed to say, even though most of my attention was taken up by my beautiful surroundings.

As distracted as I was, I tried to collect myself. I didn't want to seem scatterbrained when Linnea arrived. That didn't take long. I hadn't yet had a chance to pull out a chair from the table when footsteps drew my gaze to the doorway.

I recognized Linnea Bliss right away. I'd seen her picture many times online and on the dust jackets of her best-selling romantic suspense novels. She was in her late fifties, slightly plump, with gray streaks in her brown hair. Her warm smile put me immediately at ease.

"You must be Sadie Coleman." She offered me her hand. "Such a pleasure to meet you."

"You as well." I smiled as I shook her hand.

The woman who'd come into the room behind Linnea stepped forward.

"And this is my assistant, Marcie Kent," Linnea said. "I know the two of you have spoken on the phone."

I'd talked to Marcie a few times as we'd arranged for Linnea to come to Shady Creek to give a talk and sign books at my literary-themed pub. I'd never seen her picture before, though, and I had to catch myself quickly to mask my surprise at the fact that she was the woman I'd seen arguing with Brad behind the hotel.

We exchanged pleasantries and the three of us settled at the table, Gemma appearing a moment later with a tea cart. She set a teapot and cups on the table along with cream and sugar and a tiered plate that held scones and little cakes.

"I'm so happy you decided to come to Shady Creek," I said to Linnea once Gemma had left.

"It was Marcie's idea," Linnea said. "And since the book I'm currently writing is set in Vermont, I thought it would be a great way to soak in the local atmosphere and add authenticity to my writing."

"I can't wait to read it." I tried to keep my excitement at least somewhat under control, but there was still a good deal of enthusiasm behind my words. "I've read and loved everything you've written."

"Thank you, dear. That's a lovely thing to say."

"It's the absolute truth," I assured her before turning to Marcie. "Have you been to Shady Creek before?"

Since it was Marcie's idea to add the town to the end of Linnea's latest book tour, I was curious if she had a connection to the area. Although Shady Creek was a small town, it was popular with tourists, especially during leaf-peeping season, and I wondered if she'd vacationed here in the past.

Her reply quickly dispelled that idea. "I haven't, but I read about the town and Edwin Vallencourt while doing some research for Linnea. It sounded like such a nice place and I knew Linnea was hoping to make a trip to Vermont before she finished writing her book."

"I'm so glad you chose Shady Creek for your visit, and the Inkwell," I said to both of them.

Linnea added strawberry jam to a scone. "I can't wait to get a look at your pub. It sounds so charming and the pictures I saw online are delightful."

"Thank you," I said, my smile probably outshining the sun.

As we drank our tea and snacked on the delicious cakes and scones, we chatted about the upcoming event at the Inkwell, going over some final details. We'd nearly covered everything when approaching footsteps drew our attention to the doorway. My surprise probably showed on my face when I realized that Eleanor Grimes was hurrying toward us, her expression determined and her eyes fixed on Linnea.

Eleanor ran the Shady Creek Museum and didn't exactly have the sweetest disposition. When I moved to town ten months ago, she had her eye on the beautiful old gristmill that housed the local pub, hoping the town would buy it so she could move her beloved museum into the space. She hadn't been happy when I'd purchased the building and business. I'd never actually spoken with her, but she'd sent an icy glare my way on more than one occasion.

"Ms. Bliss," Eleanor said as she approached, "I wonder if I could trouble you for a moment of your time. I'd like to speak to you about a cause very dear to my heart."

"This is Eleanor Grimes," I said by way of introduction. "She's in charge of the local museum."

Eleanor didn't so much as glance my way. Her bony hands clutched a book to her chest. I couldn't see much of the cover, but it didn't appear to be one of Linnea's novels.

She continued on as if I hadn't spoken. "One writer to another, I'm sure you'll understand—"

"Eleanor!" Gemma rushed into the room. When she reached our table, she lowered her voice, although we could all still hear her clearly. "I asked you to please *not* interrupt Ms. Bliss."

"Donations are vital to the continued operation of the Shady Creek Museum. Our history is the backbone of our community and—"

"Yes, yes." Gemma forced a smile that wasn't far off from

a grimace. "But Ms. Bliss doesn't want to hear about that right now."

She put an arm around Eleanor's thin shoulders and attempted to turn her away from the table.

Eleanor resisted and addressed Linnea again. "I brought you a copy of my book." She placed the volume on the table next to Linnea's plate.

I glanced at the cover. It was titled *Shady Creek: A History* and Eleanor's name was printed near the bottom in fancy script. I'd heard that she'd recently self-published a book about the town, but I hadn't seen a copy of it before today.

Marcie spoke up. "I've read that."

I'd never seen Eleanor smile before, but she did now.

"Have you?" She sounded ridiculously pleased. "Then I'm sure you appreciate—"

"In chapter nine you state that Edwin Vallencourt amassed his fortune through wholly legitimate business dealings and that the rumors about him earning money from shadier ventures are completely baseless."

Eleanor stood up straighter. "That's right."

"But in actual fact, there's plenty of documentation to back up those rumors," Marcie said, sounding a bit like a know-it-all. "Vallencourt had his fingers in several less-than-honorable pies and was heavily involved in bootlegging during Prohibition."

The remains of Eleanor's smile slipped away. She pursed her thin lips and her eyes hardened. "Those are all lies!"

"Historical facts, actually," Marcie countered, her cool demeanor a sharp contrast to Eleanor's growing fury.

"How dare you come to our town and spout such filth about one of Shady Creek's most revered citizens from the past! I'll have you know that—"

"Eleanor!" Gemma cut her off sharply, her forced smile long gone. "I apologize for the interruption," she said to us before turning Eleanor around and herding her from the room.

"Sorry," Marcie said to me and Linnea, although she didn't sound all that contrite. "It drives me crazy when people spread factual errors."

Linnea poured more tea into Marcie's cup. "There's no real harm done, dear."

I realized that my fingers had a painfully tight grip on the napkin lying across my lap. I hadn't expected such tension when I'd arrived for tea. Marcie and Linnea appeared to have already put the encounter behind them, so I tried to do the same. That wasn't easy when Eleanor's indignant protests could still be heard off in the distance. Eventually, however, her voice died away and we were left in peace.

Chapter 2

Fortunately, we met with no further interruptions and drew our meeting to a close shortly after we'd finished off the pot of tea. Aside from the one brief disturbance, our conversation had gone smoothly and pleasantly. I'd enjoyed spending time with Linnea, and Marcie as well, and I was now looking forward to the author's visit to the Inkwell more than ever. Plenty of townsfolk had expressed interest in hearing the author speak, and I knew many people planned to show up at the event the next day. The members of the Inkwell's romance book club would be in the audience and had told me they intended to show up as early as possible so they could claim the best seats.

Now that I'd met Linnea, I didn't have a single doubt that she'd be a hit with her fans. She was charming, engaging, and full of colorful stories. There wouldn't be one bored person in the audience. I was still a tiny bit nervous, simply because I desperately wanted the event to go off without a hitch, but mostly I was excited.

After saying goodbye in the lobby, Linnea and Marcie had gone up to their rooms, taking the broad, curving staircase to the next floor. Instead of heading for my car, I stopped in the lobby and glanced at the reception desk. There was no one behind it at the moment. I could hear voices in the distance but there was no one around to stop me from venturing deeper into the manor.

I wasn't planning to explore the entire hotel, even though I desperately wanted to. Getting a look at the lobby and parlor had only made me all the more eager to check out the rest of the place. I didn't want to annoy anyone, however, so I exercised restraint and bypassed the staircase. I wasn't going to leave without a little exploration, though.

Following a wide hallway that led toward the back of the hotel, I walked as quietly as possible in my high heels. An arched doorway to my right led to a dining room, where about a dozen hotel guests were sitting down to an early lunch. A few feet farther along, arched double doors stood open on my left. I was hoping I'd found the ballroom and I soon discovered that I had. The room I peeked into was large enough to host dozens of dancing couples with plenty of space to spare. The polished parquet floors gleamed in the sunlight that poured into the room through the numerous tall windows that lined the wall across from me. Two sets of French doors also let in streams of daylight and one set stood open, leading out onto a large patio.

The ballroom was empty at the moment, so I crept inside for a better look. An enormous crystal chandelier hung from the ornate plaster ceiling high above me. It was turned off at the moment, but I could imagine what it would look like lit up at night, each one of the dangling crystals sparkling and glittering. The rest of the light fixtures were wall sconces designed to look like old-fashioned gas lamps. At one end of the room, a balcony overlooked the dance floor and beneath it was a small stage, likely where live music would be played on the night of the May Day masquerade.

I hadn't yet lived in Vermont for a full year—I'd moved to

town during the summer—so I hadn't experienced Shady Creek's annual masquerade before. I'd heard it was not to be missed and I'd already purchased my ticket. I didn't have a mask yet, or a dress, for that matter, and I made a mental note to address those issues soon.

Movement outside the windows caught my eye and I realized that someone was out on the patio. When he turned so his profile was lit up by the sun, I crossed the ballroom to the open French doors.

"Hi, Judson," I greeted.

"Hey, Sadie," he said with a smile. "What brings you here?"

Judson was a regular patron at the Inkwell and was employed as the manor's gardener. He was in his mid-thirties and single, from what I'd heard. He wasn't, however, short on female attention. It was easy to see why so many women found him attractive. His eyes and his wavy hair were both the color of milk chocolate and he had a lean and well-toned physique from all his gardening work. I'd spoken to him several times at the pub and I found him to be a pleasant, easygoing guy.

"I had a meeting with Linnea Bliss and her assistant," I said in answer to his question.

"The famous author? She'll be at the pub tomorrow, right?"

"That's right. I'm hoping she'll be a hit."

"She probably will be. She seems nice."

"You've met her?"

"She stopped to talk to me this morning," he said. "She was out for a walk and I was weeding the flower beds out front. Some guests pretend I'm invisible and others look down their noses at me, but not her."

"She does seem nice," I agreed.

I watched as he grabbed a hose with a nozzle attachment and watered the colorful flowers growing in large stone pots on the patio.

"The gardens look amazing," I said. "You've done great work."

"Thanks. The Honeywells want everything to look even more immaculate than usual with the masquerade coming up. Hopefully they'll be as impressed as you are."

"I'm sure they will be."

Hearing a noise behind me, I glanced over my shoulder. A fair-haired woman in a gray dress and white apron rolled a housekeeping cart into the ballroom from the hallway. When she spotted me and Judson, she left her cart in the middle of the room and came out onto the patio. I recognized her as she stepped into the light.

I'd met Connie Archer two weeks earlier when she came by the Inkwell for lunch. Apparently, she was new to town. She was about forty years old and maybe a bit jaded, but she seemed nice enough.

"Hey, Connie," Judson said as she joined us.

I added my own greeting and she cracked a brief smile.

"Gorgeous day," she observed, her gaze going to the clear blue sky. "I'd much rather be out here than stuck inside."

"You're working here as a housekeeper?" I figured that was a safe guess, judging by her uniform and the cart she'd left inside.

"Yep. I'm supposed to get the walls washed in the ballroom before the interior decorator comes with her team to get the place ready for the masquerade."

"That seems like a big task," I said, not envying her.

She shrugged. "It's not really so bad. I don't need to clean every inch, just any smudges or dirt I find. How come you're here?"

I repeated what I'd told Judson about meeting with Linnea. "This is my first time at the manor, so I thought I'd take a peek at the ballroom."

Judson tugged on the hose and moved along the patio to water another set of flowerpots. "It's something, isn't it?"

"It really is."

"You should see the rest of the place," Connie said. "Fit for a queen, if you ask me. Must be nice."

I wasn't sure what she meant by that. "Staying here, you mean?"

"That too, but I meant the Honeywells. It took a lot of dosh to get this place turned into a hotel. Word is they inherited millions and that's how they were able to buy the place. The only thing I ever inherited was my glaucoma." She said it with a wry grin, softening the complaint.

Judson shut off the water. "If the Honeywells find the hidden treasure, they'll be even richer." He pulled off his work gloves and ran the back of one hand across his forehead.

"Hidden treasure?" I echoed, my curiosity piqued.

Connie rolled her eyes. "Not that story again."

"It's a good one," Judson said. "That's why everyone likes to repeat it."

"What treasure?" I asked, eager for more information.

"You know this place was originally owned by Edwin Vallencourt, right?" Connie said.

When I nodded, Judson picked up the thread. "Rumor has it that he loved his secrets and stashed away some of his valuables before he died."

"But no one's ever found them?" I guessed.

"That's because there's nothing to find." Connie turned for the door. "I have to get back to work."

"Don't worry, Con," Judson called after her with a grin. "When I find the treasure, I'll give you a trinket or two."

She muttered something under her breath, but I didn't catch the words.

Judson laughed and pulled his gloves back on.

"Do you really think there's hidden treasure?" I asked him.

"Probably not," he admitted, "but it's fun to speculate." He grabbed the hose. "I'd better get back to work too. I'll see you at the pub sometime soon, Sadie."

"See you."

As he headed off around the corner of the manor, pulling the hose with him, I returned to the ballroom. The housekeeping cart still sat in the middle of the room, but Connie was nowhere to be seen. Since it was time for me to get back to the Inkwell, I resisted the temptation to explore more of the manor and instead set off for my car.

When I made my way onto the village green the next morning, my original plan was to cut across the northeast corner and make a direct line for the Village Bean, the local coffee shop. I'd had a cup of coffee with my bowl of oatmeal an hour earlier, but now I had a hankering for a mocha latte and the Village Bean had the best lattes around.

As eager as I was to get my first taste of mocha deliciousness, my steps slowed when I reached the grassy village green. Signs of spring were all around me and, not for the first time, I was almost taken aback by the incredible beauty of the town I now called home. The white bandstand in the middle of the green had recently received a fresh coat of paint, and hanging baskets bursting with colorful flowers hung from each of the old-fashioned lampposts lining the streets around the green. Many of the storefronts around the square also had hanging baskets or flowerpots flanking their doors, and all around me birds chirped and sang.

Pulling my phone from my purse, I turned my back on the green and snapped a photo of my beloved pub, which also doubled as my home. Housed in a renovated grist mill, the pub and the apartment above it practically oozed charm and character. The stone building had red-trimmed windows and a bright red water wheel. With the lush green forest and the bold blue sky as a backdrop, the pub made for an eye-catching sight. I planned to post the photo on the Inkwell's Instagram account, but that would have to wait for the moment.

I resumed my progress over to the corner of Sycamore Street, where the Village Bean was located. I lingered for a minute or two as I chatted with the coffee shop's owner, Nettie Jo, but then I took a seat by one of the windows and pulled out my phone again. Once I had the picture of the Inkwell posted on social media, I checked my email and text messages. Marcie hadn't contacted me to cancel the event last-minute, much to my relief. Not that I'd expected her to, but I'd had an unsettling dream that Linnea had suddenly decided to leave Shady Creek and set sail for Tahiti.

When I set down my phone, I sat back and tried to relax. For the first time since my arrival, I studied the other customers in the coffee shop. I smiled at a woman who walked past me with a coffee and muffin in hand, heading for a free table at the back of the shop. I recognized a couple of faces, but the other customers were strangers. Some of them might have been tourists, but the man and woman sitting three tables away from me didn't look like they were on a relaxing vacation.

The woman appeared to be a little older than my age of thirty and had her straight black hair cut in an asymmetrical bob. Her high-heeled boots, skinny jeans, and leather jacket probably cost more than my entire wardrobe. Her companion was probably a few years younger than her and his curly hair was a shade lighter.

"You don't get it, Alex," the woman said to him, her face intense. "This is a test. Everything has to go perfectly or they'll think I'm not cut out for the job."

"Everything will be fine, Liv." He sounded unconcerned, but the tension in his jaw suggested that he wasn't as relaxed as he was trying to appear.

"Fine?" She practically spat the word out. "Our windshield got smashed!"

"And it's getting fixed," Alex said, his voice even. "Besides, this town is so small we can probably walk everywhere we need to go."

"In these heels?" With a frustrated sigh, the woman whipped out her phone and started tapping away at it, her thumbs little more than two blurs.

I finished off my latte and got up to leave. Listening to those two made it impossible for me to relax. It was time to get back to the Inkwell, anyway.

When I got to the pub, I swept my gaze around the main room, making sure everything looked perfect. I hoped Linnea would appreciate the rustic charm of the place, with its exposed wide plank floors and stone walls lined with my sizable book collection. Earlier that morning I'd set up an easel to hold a large sign advertising the event. I nudged the sign half an inch to the left before standing back to make sure it was perfectly centered.

"Please tell me you aren't going to start dusting again." Mel Costas, one of my employees, watched me from behind the bar, where she was setting out clean mugs and glasses. She wore her blue and blond hair in tousled spikes. The short style showed off her latest tattoo: a line of small birds in flight, curving around from the back of her neck to up behind her right ear.

"Of course not," I said, although I'd been thinking about grabbing my feather duster. I'd already dusted and cleaned everything three times over since we'd closed the Inkwell the night before, but my restless energy was making it hard to stay still. "But I'll have one last look at the Christie room."

"Everything's perfect," Mel called after me as I headed for one of the pub's two overflow rooms. "Just like it was an hour ago."

I could hear the smile in her voice and knew she was teasing. She was right, though. The room I'd named for Agatha Christie was spotless and all set up for the event, with rows of chairs facing one end of the room. I'd decided to have Linnea's talk in the Christie room to give it a cozier, more intimate feel. Plus, any customers who weren't taking part in the event wouldn't disrupt the talk or feel like they were intruding.

When I returned to the main part of the pub, I glanced at the clock. Linnea and Marcie would be arriving at any moment. A knock on the front door made me jump and my heart skipped a beat. I recovered quickly and hurried to greet my guests.

It was finally time for the Inkwell's first author visit.

Chapter 3

By the time the event got underway, every chair in the Christie room was occupied. There were many familiar faces in the crowd, including my aunt Gilda's, but also a few that were new to me. I was pleased to see that so many townsfolk were interested in coming to meet Linnea and hear her speak. The event had barely begun, but at least it was off to a good start.

After introducing our guest, I sat off to the side of the room, ready to step in if needed for any reason. Linnea had done dozens, if not hundreds, of these events over the years and was far more experienced with dealing with audiences than I was, but as the host I wanted to make sure everything stayed under control.

Linnea read a scene from her latest book, holding me and the rest of the audience captive with every word. I hadn't read *Midnight's Shadow* yet, but it was on my to-be-read pile. Now that I'd heard Linnea read from the first chapter, I vowed to bump it up to the top of the list.

After Linnea had finished reading and had spoken a bit about her journey to becoming a successful writer, I invited the audience to ask a few questions. Several hands shot up right away and another half hour zoomed by as Linnea answered the questions, keeping everyone entertained the whole way through.

I discreetly glanced at my phone and saw that it was time to wind down the question period. I didn't want to keep Linnea past the scheduled end time for her visit, and the plan was for her to sign books for a while after her talk.

"A few more questions and then we'll move on to the book signing," I announced to the room.

Linnea nodded at a woman in the third row who wanted to speak.

"I've heard that some literary writers are scornful of authors who write genre fiction," the woman said. "Is that true and have you ever encountered someone like that?"

"It's definitely true," Linnea said. "Although, I have to say, most of the writers I've met through the years are wonderful people. There's always a few in every bunch, though. And I've run into three or four of them over the years. I remember one conference I attended, shortly after I hit the *New York Times* bestseller list for the first time, where I ran into an author who was also a college professor. He clearly thought he was above everyone else, especially those who wrote genre fiction. Unfortunately for me, I ended up in an elevator with him on my way to a panel discussion. We started chatting and as soon as he found out that I wrote romantic suspense, he looked down his nose at me, sneered, and asked when I was going to write a *real* book."

Someone in the audience gasped and an outraged murmur ran through the crowd. I shared the general sentiment and would have been sorely tempted to give the man a piece of my mind if I'd been in Linnea's shoes.

"What did you say?" a woman in the front row asked.

"Maybe I should have bitten my tongue, but I told him,

'Probably right around the time you get down off your high horse.'"

The tone immediately changed in the room. A few people let out bursts of laughter while others congratulated Linnea and told her she'd said the right thing.

When everyone had calmed down, I addressed the room again. "Any further questions?"

A young woman's hand shot up. I knew her name was Karidee because I'd asked to see her ID when she arrived. I'd worried she was too young to be in the pub, but she'd turned twenty-one a few weeks ago.

"Do you think it's necessary to have a college degree in creative writing to become a successful author?" she asked.

"Absolutely not," Linnea said. "I enjoyed my years at college and got a lot out of it, but many talented and successful writers don't have writing degrees."

Karidee seemed relieved by that answer.

I stood up. "We've really enjoyed having you here, Linnea. Thank you so much for visiting Shady Creek and the Inkwell."

I clapped and everyone in the room joined in enthusiastically. A few minutes later, Linnea was seated at a table, a lineup snaking around the perimeter of the room as her fans waited eagerly to get her signature. A handful of people had come with one or two of Linnea's books, while others had purchased a copy of *Midnight's Shadow* from Marcie near the entrance to the Christie room. A couple of people were simply hoping to get the author to sign one of the free bookmarks Marcie had handed out at the beginning of the event.

"I'd say that was a success," I said quietly to Marcie as the line grew shorter.

"It went very well," Marcie agreed. "Thanks so much for allowing us to come here. Linnea and I were both really looking forward to spending some time in Vermont."

"It's my pleasure," I assured her. "Everyone's so thrilled that you chose our town for a visit."

I inched closer to the table where Linnea was sitting, signing a book for my friend Cordelia King. Cordelia thanked the author profusely and then turned my way, beaming as she hugged the book to her chest.

"This is so exciting!" she whispered as she passed by me on her way out of the Christie room.

Cordelia shared my enthusiasm for books and was a member of the Inkwell's mystery book club. She was a few years younger than me but we'd become good friends since we'd met last fall.

A man and woman headed out of the Christie room in Cordelia's wake. Karidee was next in line to have her book signed.

"It's so great to meet you," she enthused when she stood in front of Linnea. "I've been a fan for years."

"Thank you so much," Linnea said graciously as she signed Karidee's book. "It's lovely to meet you too."

"I was hoping to ask you—"

An excited squeal cut her off. Karidee's friend, who'd shown up for the event with her, practically shoved her out of the way as she moved in for her chance to meet Linnea. She babbled away excitedly as Linnea autographed her book.

Karidee hovered near the table, as if hoping for another chance to speak with Linnea.

Marcie brushed past me and approached the table. "Thank you so much for coming, ladies," she said to Karidee and her friend. "I'm afraid Linnea needs to be on her way now."

Karidee hesitated, but then Marcie walked the two young women toward the door. As Karidee passed me, she seemed disappointed. Fortunately, she was the only one I'd noticed who wasn't completely happy with their experience.

When just the three of us remained in the room, Linnea got up from her seat and clasped my hand in both of hers. "I had a wonderful time, Sadie. And your pub is so charming. I'm glad I had a chance to visit."

"I'm so glad you did too. It's really been a pleasure to have you here."

"I'd be delighted if you'd meet me for lunch tomorrow at the manor."

"Really?" I wanted to kick myself for not coming up with a more eloquent response.

Linnea laughed, but in a kind way. "Really."

"I'd love that," I said. "Thank you."

We arranged a time to meet at the manor and then I walked Marcie and Linnea to their car, parked in the small lot at the edge of the Inkwell's property. I waved as I watched them drive off along Creekside Road, so incredibly happy that the event had been such a success.

I didn't think my spirits could rise much higher, but I was pleased to see that several of the people who'd shown up for Linnea's talk had remained at the pub to have something to eat or drink. Other customers had arrived while the event was on and Mel was busy serving food, pulling pints, and mixing cocktails. I jumped in to help her and around midafternoon business slowed slightly, enough that I could take a short break to venture into the kitchen for a snack.

"How did things go with the author event?" Booker asked as I poured myself a cup of coffee.

Booker James was one of two chefs I'd hired to work at the Inkwell. He covered the day shifts and Teagan Trimble worked in the evenings. They'd both proved to be great additions to my small staff and had helped me create a menu of literary-themed foods that had been a hit with our customers.

"It was great," I said, unable to stop the smile that appeared on my face. "Linnea's very entertaining and everyone seemed to enjoy themselves."

"Good to hear."

I took a sip of my coffee and my stomach grumbled loudly. Booker laughed as my cheeks flushed. "Sounds like you didn't eat any lunch."

"I didn't have a spare moment until now."

"Nachos?" he suggested.

"Please." My stomach gave another rumble and my mouth watered in anticipation.

After I'd had my fill of nachos laden with warm cheese, black olives, peppers, guacamole, and salsa, I got back to work. I was in the middle of mixing up three Yellow Brick Road cocktails when Cordelia showed up for the second time that day. I waved to her before picking up my tray and delivering the drinks to three women who'd clearly just been on a shopping spree. They had several bags piled on the fourth chair at the table, all of them bearing the names of local stores.

I chatted with them for a minute and learned that they were tourists on a short vacation from Pennsylvania. They'd ordered food as well, and I made a quick trip to the kitchen to grab their appetizers. When I returned to the bar, Cordelia was perched on one of the stools.

"Can I get you anything?" I asked.

"To Be or Nacho Be," she said, without looking at a menu. "And a Milky Way Gargle Blaster. But the mocktail version, please. Gran won't be pleased if I'm tipsy when I get back to the inn."

Cordelia lived up the road from the Inkwell at the Creekside Inn, housed in a beautiful Queen Anne. Her grandmother, Grace King, owned and operated the inn, and Cordelia had moved back to Shady Creek after going to college so she could help out with the business. Cordelia was not only a fellow bibliophile but also a fellow redhead. Her hair, however, was crinkly while mine was straight.

"I had to get back to the inn right after I had my book

signed," Cordelia said as I mixed together root beer, cream, and vanilla for her mocktail. "But I came back as soon as I could. I wanted to tell you that I had the best time earlier. Linnea is amazing!"

"She really is great," I agreed. "I'm glad you had a good time."

"I can't wait to start reading *Midnight's Shadow*. I'm already hooked after hearing her read the opening pages."

"Me too." I set Cordelia's Milky Way Gargle Blaster on a coaster in front of her. "I'm hoping I can get some reading time in tomorrow."

While she sipped at her drink, I served a few other customers and then brought her platter of nachos out from the kitchen. Two men at the other end of the bar ordered pints of beer, but Mel was looking after that order so I took some more time to chat with Cordelia.

"How are things at the inn these days?" I asked.

"Great! Did I tell you about our new guests?"

"No. Tourists?"

Cordelia shook her head, her blue eyes bright with excitement. "The *Craft Nation* crew! They arrived yesterday. There's only three of them so far, but the show's host is supposed to arrive later today. I can't wait to meet him. He's so handsome!"

I understood the dreamy look in her eyes. I'd only ever watched a couple of episodes of *Craft Nation*, but the host, Jules Beamer, really was quite attractive.

"It's good to know they're finally filming the episode," I said.

Originally, it was supposed to happen in February, but a succession of delays had postponed the crew's arrival in Shady Creek.

Cordelia scooped guacamole onto a cheesy nacho. "I know. I was worried they wouldn't show up after everything that happened, but they're finally here. Three of them, anyway."

"When do they start filming?" I asked.

"They already have."

"Without Jules Beamer?"

Cordelia demolished another nacho before replying. "I think they're getting some shots of the brewery. Things they don't need the host for. That's what it sounded like, anyway. The woman in charge is Olivia Lo. I think she's the director. Anyway, she's so fashionable. You should have seen the boots she was wearing today. I'm sure there's no way I could afford a pair like that."

I thought back to my morning visit to the Village Bean. "Maybe I did see them. Is there a guy on the crew named Alex?"

"Alex Nevarez." She picked up another nacho piled high with toppings. "He's the cameraman."

"I saw the two of them at the coffee shop earlier. Those really were nice boots."

Cordelia sighed as she reached for her mocktail. "I guess it doesn't matter that I can't afford boots like that. I can't walk in high heels anyway. How do you do it?"

"Practice," I said. "I'm fine up to three inches, but anything higher than that and I worry too much about breaking an ankle."

I left Cordelia for a minute while I attended to some other customers. By the time I returned, she'd nearly finished her platter of nachos and her Milky Way Gargle Blaster.

"Grayson must be relieved that filming is finally underway," she said as she scooped up the last of the guacamole with one of the remaining nachos.

"He must be," I agreed with a twinge of disappointment. I wished I didn't have to assume that.

Grayson Blake owned the Spirit Hill Brewery, which was the focus of the *Craft Nation* episode. Although we hadn't started out on the best foot—I'd suspected him of committing murder and other crimes—our relationship had smoothed out to the point where I considered us to be friends. Unfortunately, he'd spent a lot of time out of town recently, so I hadn't had a chance to talk to him. I missed him, probably more than I should have, but maybe I'd see him soon. He'd most likely be in town while the *Craft Nation* crew was here.

That thought helped to ease my disappointment, and by the time Cordelia left the Inkwell moments later, I was back to floating on my cloud of happiness.

Chapter 4

Clouds rolled in the next morning, their dark color holding a threat of rain, but I didn't let that dampen my spirits. Mel would be opening the Inkwell at noon, since I'd likely be away for a couple of hours, so I didn't have to worry about the pub. All I had to do was enjoy my lunch with Linnea.

When I turned into the manor's long driveway, I lowered my window again so I could enjoy the sweet scent of the spring air. I spotted Marcie out on the lawn near one of the flower beds, talking with Judson. As I drove past them, Marcie placed a hand on Judson's arm and let out a tinkling laugh, the sound floating toward me on the breeze.

I continued on toward the parking lot, and when I glanced in my rearview mirror, Marcie was making her way across the lawn toward the manor. Like the day before, the parking lot was about half full. I pulled my white Toyota into a free spot next to a van with FINCH'S PLUMBING written across the side. It was Jan's van, most likely, although I'd never known her last name. Either she hadn't fixed yesterday's problem as well as she'd thought she had, or the manor had yet another plumbing issue needing attention.

As I climbed out of my car, a drop of rain hit the top of my head, quickly followed by another. I hadn't brought a coat, despite the dark sky, and I silently chided myself for that. I didn't want my dress to get soaked, so I grabbed my purse and hurried around to the front door. By the time I stepped inside the lobby, the rain was beating a steady rhythm against the paved driveway.

The lobby was empty when I shut the door behind me, but I could hear someone talking nearby. The closer I drew to the reception desk, the clearer the words became.

"I'd like to do an inventory of all the linens for the dining room. I'm going to order some new ones and I'd like to know how many tablecloths and napkins we need to replace. I thought we could work on that together."

I was pretty sure that was Gemma's voice.

"Of course," another woman said in response.

A second later Gemma and Connie emerged from the office behind the desk. Connie flashed me a brief smile before heading briskly down one of the hallways that led off the lobby.

Gemma smiled more brightly. "Hello again. You're here for lunch with Ms. Bliss?"

"That's right," I said.

"I think you'll find her in the dining room."

Almost before Gemma finished speaking, Marcie arrived in the lobby from the direction of the ballroom and dining room.

"Hi, Sadie," she greeted. She was slightly flushed, but her hair and clothes were dry. She must have made it back inside before the rain started. "Linnea is already in the dining room, if you'd like to go join her."

"Thank you," I said.

"I'll just—" Marcie's gaze shifted to one of the tall windows flanking the manor's double front doors. A flash of annoyance crossed her face. "Not again." She was already on her way out the front door when she called out over her shoulder, "Excuse me. There's something I need to take care of."

Instead of heading straight for the dining room, I moved closer to the window and peeked outside. Karidee stood at the base of the front steps, clutching a large handbag. Marcie stopped on the bottom step, blocking her way. The two seemed to be arguing and Marcie pointed emphatically down the driveway.

Karidee glared at her before saying something I couldn't hear. Then she spun around and stomped off through the rain. Marcie stayed standing on the steps, watching her go, as if wanting to make sure Karidee wouldn't turn back.

"The perils of fame, I suppose," Gemma said from behind the reception desk.

I'd almost forgotten she was there. "Sorry?"

"Ms. Kent caught that young woman trying to sneak up to Ms. Bliss's room yesterday. Can you believe her audacity?" She shook her head. "Some people are desperate to rub shoulders with the rich and famous."

The phone at the reception desk rang and Gemma answered it, so I didn't hang around in the lobby any longer. In the dining room, Linnea sat at a round table set for three. Four other tables in the room were occupied, one by a group of four, two by couples, and one by a woman about my age with blond hair that cascaded down her back in glossy waves.

"Sadie, it's so wonderful to see you again," Linnea said when I approached her table. "Please, sit down."

"Thanks again for inviting me." I pulled out a chair and settled into it. "And also for making yesterday's event such a hit."

"It was great fun and I'm delighted to have you here."

Marcie appeared in the doorway then, but most of my attention was focused elsewhere. The blond woman at the next table grabbed her handbag, donned a large pair of sunglasses, and jumped up from her table, all in one swift movement. She rushed from the dining room, leaving through a door near the one that led to the kitchen.

Marcie was making her way across the dining room toward us, and two others had entered the room on her heels. I recognized them a second later as Olivia Lo and Alex Nevarez from the *Craft Nation* film crew. Alex was dressed in dark jeans and a black sweater. Olivia wore high-heeled ankle boots and the same leather jacket as I'd seen her in before. Her red cashmere sweater provided a bright splash of color against her black pants and jacket.

"Sorry for the delay," Marcie said as she reached our table.

Across the room, Alex and Olivia claimed a table by one of the windows.

"No worries," Linnea said. "Will you join us?"

"I'm afraid not. I've got a migraine coming on, so I thought I'd lie down for a while."

"Of course, dear," Linnea said with sympathy. "Rest for as long as you need to."

Marcie took a step back. "Hopefully it won't get too bad. So nice to see you again, Sadie."

"You too," I said.

She flashed us a smile and then left the dining room.

"Poor thing," Linnea said quietly. "She gets terrible migraines, especially when the weather's changing."

A waiter dressed in black and white approached us, so I didn't say anything in response. Before long, we were dining on a delicious lunch of poached salmon in hollandaise sauce, asparagus, and herb roasted potatoes. Linnea had a glass of wine with her meal, but I settled for ice water since I'd be driving home.

At my request, Linnea expanded on the story she'd told the day before about how she'd become a writer. She'd always known she wanted to be an author, she said, ever since she was a little girl writing stories about her cat, Fluffy, and her pet turtle, Frankie.

"I've always loved books," I said, after sampling the salmon. "I've thought about trying to write one, but I doubt I have it in me. Filling three hundred pages with a story compelling enough to keep readers interested seems like such a daunting task."

"It isn't easy, but for me it's always the first page that's the most intimidating. After that I get into the swing of things and tend to forget about the world around me. As for not having it in you, you just might. You'll never know until you try."

"True," I conceded.

An idea struck me. The Inkwell currently hosted three book clubs. The newest one, for science fiction and fantasy books, was in its infancy. There had only been one meeting for that one so far, but up to this point all of the clubs had been a great success. I wondered if there would be any interest in a writing group as well. There could be monthly meetings at the Inkwell so members could encourage and help each other. I wasn't sure if I was ready to try my hand at writing a book—I had my hands full with the Inkwell—but others in town might be interested.

I tucked the thought away to consider later. For the moment, I wanted to enjoy my time with Linnea.

After we'd finished our main course, the waiter brought out our dessert. My eyes widened when he placed a generous slice of chocolate mousse cake in front of me.

"This looks incredible," I said, my mouth watering.

"It tastes even better," Linnea assured me. "I confess I already indulged in a slice last night after dinner. It's absolutely heavenly."

"I can't wait to taste it."

Linnea picked up her fork, so I did the same. When I took my first bite, I nearly sighed with happiness. The decadent layers of chocolate mousse and cake were divine. I tried to eat the dessert slowly, to make it last, but that was hard to do. Too soon, we'd both cleaned our plates.

I took a sip of the tea our waiter had brought along with our dessert, feeling full and content. I was about to comment on our excellent meal when hurried footsteps headed our way. When I realized who was approaching, I quickly set down my teacup, apprehension creeping over my skin.

Eleanor Grimes made a beeline for our table. Linnea gave her a pleasant smile and I was impressed by the fact that she didn't show any annoyance.

"It's Ms. Grimes, isn't it?" Linnea asked.

"*Mrs.* Grimes," Eleanor corrected. "My Elmer passed away thirteen years ago."

"I'm sorry to hear that."

"Yes, well . . ." Eleanor cleared her throat. "I've come across some rather concerning information and I thought you should know about it right away."

"What sort of information?" I asked, surprised. I'd thought Eleanor was there to make another attempt at getting a donation for the museum.

She ignored me, and the slight flare of her nostrils suggested that she wasn't pleased that I'd spoken to her.

"It's about your assistant," Eleanor continued.

"Marcie? What about her?" Linnea asked.

"I'm afraid she may not be who you think she is."

"Whatever do you mean by that?"

Eleanor leaned closer to the author and lowered her voice. "I have reason to doubt that she's of good character."

For the first time, a hint of annoyance showed on Linnea's face. "Nonsense. Marcie is a delightful young woman and a wonderful assistant. She's intelligent, kind, and someone I consider a friend."

"She has you fooled." Eleanor's tone had become belligerent. "She has a criminal past and shouldn't be trusted. I wouldn't believe a single word that comes out of her mouth."

"That's enough!" Linnea admonished. "I know all I need to know about Marcie and I won't sit here listening to you spouting lies about her."

"Oh, dear! I'm so sorry!" Gemma rushed over to us, her eyes wide with alarm. "I didn't see her come in. Is she bothering you?"

"*She* is standing right here," Eleanor fumed, her indignation almost palpable.

"She is bothering us, yes," Linnea said.

Eleanor pursed her lips and red splotches appeared on her cheeks. "I was merely trying to—"

Gemma put an arm around her and forced her toward the door. "I'm so sorry," she said to us over her shoulder.

"Unhand me!" Eleanor groused, but then she and Gemma were out of sight.

It took a second for me to recover from the encounter. "I'm sorry," I said when I found my voice.

"You've no need to apologize."

"I feel like her behavior reflects poorly on the town."

"It doesn't," Linnea said. "Please believe me. Everyone else I've met here has been wonderful."

"I really don't know what's up with her. I know she's not the most pleasant woman at the best of times, but that was downright strange." I wanted to ask Linnea if she knew what Eleanor had been hinting at, but I bit my tongue. I sensed that she wouldn't appreciate the question and I didn't want her opinion of me to sour.

Gemma reappeared, her cheeks flushed and her manner harried. "I'm so terribly sorry, Ms. Bliss. Mrs. Grimes has been banned from the premises now, and I promise to do everything I can to ensure she never bothers you again."

"I appreciate that," Linnea said, her kind smile back.

"Your meals are on the house."

"There's no need for that," Linnea protested.

"I insist. It's the least I can do."

After Linnea assured her that everything was now fine, Gemma left us to finish our tea.

Linnea poured more into each of our cups. "That was a somewhat more eventful meal than I'd anticipated."

I added a splash of cream to my tea. "Hopefully the rest of your stay in Shady Creek will be more peaceful."

"I have no doubt that it will be. I'm looking forward to a nice stretch of dedicated writing time. I enjoy book tours, but they do take time away from my writing projects."

"I imagine so. You must live a busy life."

"At times it's very busy, but I enjoy it. I'm living my dream."

We continued to chat as we finished our tea. Outside the windows, the rain poured down. I wasn't looking forward to leaving the manor. I'd most likely be soaked by the time I reached my car.

When we finished our tea, we left the dining room and walked together toward the lobby. Once again, there was no one behind the reception desk. Aside from the occasional noise coming from the dining room down the hall, the only sound to be heard in the lobby was the pattering of the rain outside.

"Did you bring an umbrella?" Linnea asked, watching the driving rain through the window.

"Unfortunately, no," I said.

"Maybe the Honeywells have one you could borrow. You'll get drenched if you go out there without one."

"I'll be all right," I assured her. "Maybe I can go out through a back door so I'll be closer to the parking lot."

"Good thinking."

I thanked her once again for inviting me to lunch. "I'll be diving into *Midnight's Shadow* very soon."

"I hope you'll enjoy it."

"I know I will," I said without a shred of doubt. "Enjoy the rest of your stay in Shady Creek."

"Thank you, dear. I plan to."

We were about to part ways there in the lobby when a spine-chilling scream brought us both to a halt.

Chapter 5

I stood frozen for a second or two before running to the door and out into the rain. The scream sounded like it had originated from out front of the manor. I wasn't the only one who thought so. As I burst out the door, Judson came tearing around the corner of the building. He skidded to a stop when he saw me and opened his mouth like he was about to ask what had happened. Before he formed any words, his eyes widened and he took off, running as if he were in a race for his life.

I descended the steps as quickly as I could in my high heels and chased after him. He dropped to his knees next to what looked like a heap of clothes on the paved walkway that ran along the front of the manor, bordered on one side by bushes and flowers and on the other by neatly trimmed grass. As I drew closer, horror tightened my chest and I found it hard to draw breath into my lungs.

I slowed my steps and put a hand to my chest as I gasped for air. I couldn't take my eyes off of what I'd thought was a heap of clothes. I could see now that it was a person. When I got three steps closer, I could see past Judson to get a closer look at the woman lying on the ground. I gasped for air again, letting out a strangled sound.

It was Marcie and she wasn't moving. Her left arm was bent at an unnatural angle and her eyes stared lifelessly up at the sky.

Judson brushed damp hair off of Marcie's forehead. His hand came away smeared with blood. He raised his eyes to mine and I could tell he was feeling the exact same horror and shock that was sending numbness through my body.

"She's dead," he said quietly, his words almost swallowed up by the rain driving down on the walkway.

I'd already known she was dead, but hearing him say the words brought tears to my eyes.

"What happened?" I asked, my voice sounding strained and unfamiliar.

Judson raised his gaze and I followed it with my own to an open window on the third floor of the manor.

"She must have fallen," he said.

"Sadie? What's going on?" Linnea called from the shelter of the covered front steps.

"Oh no," I whispered. I didn't want to be the one to break the news to Linnea.

Judson got to his feet and pulled a cell phone out of the back pocket of his jeans. "I'll call 911."

His hand trembled as he woke up the device.

I took a step backward, my gaze glued on Marcie. Those lifeless eyes . . .

I closed my own eyes and swallowed hard, trying to control the wave of nausea rolling through my stomach.

As Judson spoke to the 911 operator, I turned away from Marcie's body and walked slowly toward the front steps where Linnea waited, her face drawn with concern. I'd almost reached her, but I still didn't know what to say, how to tell her that Marcie was dead.

"Come in out of the rain," Linnea said. "You're drenched."

I was about to tell her that the rain didn't matter, not when something so terrible had happened, but another scream cut through the air.

"What on earth?" Linnea came down two steps so she could get a better look along the walkway.

Karidee had appeared from somewhere and now stood over Marcie's body, wailing hysterically. I put an arm around Linnea's shoulders and turned her toward the door.

"Is someone hurt?" she asked. "It looks like there's someone lying on the ground."

The front door flew open and Gemma rushed out onto the steps, Connie right behind her.

"Is that someone crying?" Gemma asked. "Has something happened?"

There was no escaping it; I had to break the news.

"It's Marcie," I said, addressing everyone but keeping my eyes on Linnea's. "We think she must have fallen from an upstairs window. I'm afraid she's dead."

All color drained from Linnea's face. "No. No, she can't be."

She rushed past me and ran along the walkway toward Marcie. Judson stood with an arm around Karidee. The young woman had stopped wailing, but it looked as though she was still crying, just more quietly. Gemma and Connie hurried after Linnea.

I nearly followed, but a question formed in my mind, holding me in place.

How had this happened?

Stepping out from beneath the cover of the overhang, I counted the windows from the corner of the building to the one that stood open on the third floor. Maybe there were witnesses upstairs who could shed light on what had happened. It struck me as a slim chance, but I decided to investigate anyway. Linnea would need answers once the worst of the shock had worn off. Connie had an arm around her and was comforting her, so I returned inside and headed for the elegant curving staircase.

I slipped on the marble floor on my way across the lobby, grabbing hold of the edge of the reception desk to save myself from falling at the last second. When I'd regained my balance, I continued more carefully, picking up my pace once I had a hand on the stairway's smooth banister.

On the second floor I had to head a few feet down the spacious hallway to reach the next flight of stairs. Everything was quiet when I arrived on the third floor. So much for finding witnesses. If someone had seen Marcie fall or heard her scream, surely it wouldn't have been so peaceful.

Counting the doors from the end of the hall, I guessed which room the open window might belong to and knocked on the door. When I received no response, I tried to open the door. It was locked. I realized that I was dripping water onto the carpet runner that ran the length of the hallway, but I couldn't bring myself to care in the circumstances.

I decided to knock on the next door down. If I didn't get a response there either, I'd go back downstairs and do my best to comfort Linnea.

I'd only moved a few paces along the hall when I heard rushed footsteps. Gemma appeared at the top of the stairway a second later.

"Do you know how this happened?" She appeared flustered and almost distraught.

"No. I was hoping to get a look in Marcie's room to see if I can figure that out."

"This isn't Marcie's room. She and Linnea both have rooms on the second floor." Gemma produced a master key card and unlocked the door. "This room's unoccupied because the window latch—" She choked back a sob. "The window latch is broken."

I pushed open the door and stepped into the spacious guest

room. Across from where I stood, the large French windows provided a sweeping view of the front lawn and gardens, although at the moment everything had a gray cast from the rain and heavy clouds. The windows creaked and swung slightly in the breeze, and I detected the faint sound of approaching sirens.

In a matter of seconds, I took in the rest of the room. Two nightstands flanked a four-poster, queen-size bed, and a chest of drawers sat against another wall, its wood matching that of the bed's frame. There was also an armchair in one corner and a small desk. A door to my left stood ajar, leading to a bathroom. The carpet was thick underfoot and the room was decorated in shades of white and pale gray. What I noticed the most, however, were the torn curtain, the toppled desk chair, and the twisted bedspread that hung off the side of the mattress.

"Brad was planning to fix the window latch," Gemma said from behind my left shoulder. She stifled another sob. "But he hadn't had a chance. We were leaving this room unoccupied until it was fixed, but we never imagined someone would fall out the window."

A heavy weight settled in my chest. "Maybe she didn't."

"What?" Gemma stepped forward, as if to move around me so she could go farther into the room.

I grabbed her arm to stop her. "We need to get downstairs."

The sirens had grown louder and I caught sight of flashing lights through the window as emergency vehicles turned into the driveway.

Gemma noticed the lights too. "Yes, of course. We'll have to talk to the police."

That wasn't the reason I wanted both of us to get out of the room, but I didn't correct her. I was about to follow her out into the hallway when something caught my eye. An earring lay on the carpet, half under the bed. It was gold with deep red stones. I swept my gaze across the room, but didn't spot its twin.

Outside, the sirens cut off. I quickly left the room and shut the door behind me.

"Will it lock automatically?" I asked Gemma.

"Yes, all the guest room doors do." She was already on her way down the hallway.

As I hurried after her, I shivered, and only partly because of my wet hair and clothes.

After seeing the state of the room we'd just left, I had a terrible feeling that Marcie's fall wasn't an accident.

The police requested that no one leave the manor while they conducted a preliminary investigation. I sat in the dining room, along with Linnea and the other manor guests, as well as the Honeywells and their staff. Linnea hadn't said more than a few words since I'd returned from the third floor. Her eyes were red, but she'd only shed a couple of tears that I'd seen. I suspected more would come later once the shock wore off.

After we'd all gathered in the dining room, Judson had disappeared for a moment and returned with a blanket for me and others for Linnea and Karidee. I was grateful to have the soft blanket around my shoulders. I'd become all too aware of my cold, damp dress.

Linnea and I sat alone at our table and Karidee sat at the neighboring one by herself. She had her blanket pulled tightly around her and she kept her eyes downcast, except for now and then when she shot a furtive glance Linnea's way. I wanted to ask her why she'd returned to the manor after Marcie had sent her away, but it wasn't any of my business and I didn't want to distress her further. She looked as though she could burst out crying again at any moment.

Trying to keep my mind off what had happened to Marcie, I studied the people around me. Like Karidee, the blond woman I'd seen at lunchtime sat at a table by herself. She'd removed her sunglasses and alternated between tapping her painted fingernails against the table and staring at her cell phone. Connie sat at a table across the room, twisting the ring on her left hand around and around. Another woman I didn't recognize wore the same housekeeping uniform as Connie and sat next to her, staring off into space. Judson shared their table, though he'd turned his chair away and had his forearms resting on his knees, his head bowed.

Brad and Gemma huddled together in a corner of the room. Brad was whispering into his wife's ear, urgently I thought. Gemma sat stiffly, hardly responding to whatever her husband was saying.

Other guests and staff members were scattered around the room. A couple of kitchen workers set about serving tea to everyone. When a young man set a steaming cup of tea in front of me, I thanked him quietly and wrapped my hands around it. I jerked them away when the heat stung my skin. I took a careful sip of the tea. It was a bit too hot, but I drank it anyway, desperate for the warmth it offered.

Linnea didn't bother to touch her tea. I wanted to say something to comfort her, but I couldn't find any words. She was already grief stricken by Marcie's death. How would she cope when she found out that someone had intentionally pushed Marcie through the window?

I didn't yet know for sure that Marcie had been murdered, but I had a terrible suspicion that she'd struggled with someone before falling to her death.

But who would want to hurt Marcie? What was she doing in the third floor room? And how did she get in there if the door was locked?

All those questions circled around in my head, almost making me dizzy.

When I'd finished my tea, I wasn't quite so cold, but I wasn't any less unsettled.

Finally, after what felt like hours, the chief of Shady Creek's police force and Officer Eldon Howes entered the dining room. I'd met Chief Walters briefly back in the fall and I'd spoken to Officer Howes during a murder investigation I got tangled up in before Christmas. I hoped he didn't remember how I'd thoroughly embarrassed myself during our last conversation.

As soon as the Honeywells noticed the police officers, they got to their feet.

Brad rushed forward. "Have you finished your investigation? Are our guests free to go?"

"Our investigation is still ongoing," Chief Walters said, loud enough for the entire room to hear. "I'm afraid I need you all to remain here a little longer. One of my officers will speak to each of you. Once you've given your statement, you may go."

Gemma clutched at the string of pearls around her neck. "I don't feel well," she said, her voice faint.

Brad quickly put an arm around her. "My wife needs to lie down," he said to Walters.

The chief gave a brisk nod of assent and accompanied the Honeywells out of the room.

Since Judson and I had been first on the scene, the police questioned us before anyone else. Officer Howes talked to me while an officer I didn't recognize appeared and moved to a quiet corner with Judson. I told Officer Howes that I'd heard Marcie's scream while I was in the lobby and had run outside at the same time as Judson had come around the corner of the building. After detailing what had happened in the next minute or two, I explained that I'd gone upstairs, looking for witnesses or any clue as to how Marcie had fallen.

"When I saw the state of the room, I thought . . ." I lowered my voice so I wouldn't be overheard. "I thought maybe Marcie hadn't fallen accidentally. As soon as I realized that, we left the room."

"We?"

"Gemma Honeywell was there with me," I explained. "She unlocked the door with her master key."

"How far into the room did you go?" Howes asked.

"Three or four steps." I remembered what I'd seen as I was leaving. "There was an earring on the floor, partly under the bed. I don't know if that's important or not. Mrs. Honeywell said that no one's staying in that room. She had to unlock the door, so I don't know how Marcie got in there."

Officer Howes wrote something in his notebook, but didn't offer up any theories.

I lowered my voice further. "Do you think she was murdered?"

He continued to write for another second or two before responding. "We're treating her death as suspicious."

The chill that the hot tea had banished swiftly returned. Officer Howes had confirmed my fear.

Someone had pushed Marcie out that window.

Chapter 6

When I was allowed to leave the manor, I stopped to talk to Linnea on my way out of the dining room. She sat staring at her untouched tea, only raising her eyes when I stopped next to her.

"Is there anything I can do for you?" I asked. "Anything I can get you?"

"No, thank you, dear." She took my hand and gave it a squeeze. "I appreciate your kindness."

"Please don't hesitate to get in touch if you need anything."

She thanked me again and I left her there as Officer Howes approached her. I swallowed a lump in my throat as I walked away. I was still shaken by Marcie's death and I felt terrible for Linnea.

On my way across the lobby, I heard a murmur of voices and slowed my steps. I should have kept going, but when I recognized Chief Walters's voice, I strained to hear what he was saying.

"Where were you when Ms. Kent fell?" Walters asked.

His voice was coming from the office behind the reception desk. The door had been left open a crack.

"There's a storage room down one of the back hallways," I heard Gemma reply. "It's where we keep all the linens. I was there with Connie Archer, one of the housekeepers."

"Did you hear a scream?"

"No, I didn't. Connie did, though. I was talking on my cell phone, and when I hung up, Connie asked if I'd heard a scream a moment earlier. We both came to investigate. It wasn't until we got outside that we realized something terrible had happened." Gemma's voice nearly broke on those last words.

Footsteps sounded somewhere nearby, reminding me that I didn't want to get caught eavesdropping. I scurried across the lobby and out the front door before anyone saw me.

The rain still poured down from dark clouds. Marcie's body was gone, as was the ambulance, leaving two police cars parked in front of the manor. I couldn't wait to get home, so I didn't linger on the front steps. Not caring about the rain soaking my hair and dress, I followed the walkway to the parking lot and set off for home.

When I reached the Inkwell, I bypassed the front door, knowing I probably looked half drowned. I entered through the back way and stood in the hallway for a moment, taking comfort from the low hum of conversation coming from the pub and the delicious smells wafting out from the kitchen.

I'd returned much later than expected, so I wanted to check in with Mel before going upstairs to change. I headed straight into the kitchen, not wanting the customers to see me in my current state.

Booker stood at the stove, his shoulder-length braids tied back and an Inkwell apron over his jeans and black T-shirt. I was of average height, but at six-foot-three, Booker towered over me. He'd played college football before going to culinary school and he was also a musician. When I entered the kitchen,

he was humming to himself as he flipped a couple of burgers.
He cut off mid-note when he saw me.

"What happened to you?" he asked. "You look like you fell
in the creek."

"I wish I could say that was all that had happened."

"Uh-oh. What *did* happen?"

Fortunately, Mel came into the kitchen then, so I didn't have
to explain twice. They were both shocked by the news of Marcie's death, and Mel assured me that it was fine for me to take
some more time away from the pub.

"Take the rest of the day off, if you need to," she said.

"I think I'll want to keep busy, at least once I'm warm and
dry." I didn't like the idea of sitting around, replaying Marcie's
scream in my head.

"What you need is a cup of tea," Booker said, reaching for
the stout blue kettle he always used to brew his own tea.

I didn't mention that I'd already had some tea at the manor.
Its effects had long worn off and I appreciated Booker's ges-
ture. Once the tea was brewed, he poured it into one of the
beautiful cups he'd inherited from his grandmother. This one
was decorated with red poppies.

The first time I'd seen the former football player drinking tea
out of a fine china cup, I'd done a double take, but now it was a
normal sight at the Inkwell. He'd told me that some of his best
childhood memories were of drinking tea with his grandmother, a woman who'd played a significant role in his up-
bringing.

I thanked Booker for the hot drink and carried it upstairs
with me. It smelled of oranges and spices and when I took a sip,
both the warmth and the flavor brought me some immediate
comfort. Somehow he'd known exactly the type of tea I needed.

I was happy to find my white-haired, blue-eyed cat, Wimsey,
at home. Sometimes he used the cat doors to head outside to

watch birds, prowl around at the edge of the forest, or sit outside the pub's front door, watching people come and go from his kingdom. At the moment, however, he was curled up on the back of the couch.

When I shut the apartment door, he got up and stretched before hopping down to greet me.

I set my tea on the kitchen table. "Hey, buddy. I hope your day's been better than mine."

I gave him a pat on the head, receiving a brief purr as a reward. He padded across the kitchen and stopped by his food dish, sending a pointed stare my way with his blue eyes. Dutifully, I fetched his bag of treats and shook a few into his dish. With His Lordship satisfied, I finished my tea before shedding my damp clothes and getting in the shower. Like the tea, the hot water helped to warm me up, but even the shower couldn't wash away the memory of what had happened to Marcie.

After drying my hair and getting dressed, I decided it was about time to head down to the pub. I was swiping mascara onto my eyelashes when someone knocked on my apartment door. I thought it might be Mel, wanting to talk to me about some pub-related issue, but I opened the door to find my aunt Gilda on the landing.

Instead of standing back to let her in, I threw my arms around her.

"Oh, honey." She patted my back. "Mel told me what happened."

I blinked back tears, determined not to cry. "It's terrible." I stepped out of her hug and moved aside so she could come into my apartment.

"You didn't see her fall, did you?" my aunt asked, concern evident in her brown eyes.

"No."

"That's one small mercy."

That was true. I'd have even more fodder for nightmares if I'd seen Marcie fall to her death. It was bad enough that I'd seen the aftermath.

"And the police think someone pushed her?"

"I think so too." I told her about what I'd seen in the third-floor guest room, details I hadn't shared with Mel and Booker.

Aunt Gilda pulled a bobby pin from her updo and tucked a stray strand of her auburn hair back into place. Everything about her was so familiar and comforting. When she took a seat on the couch, I joined her there.

"I can't imagine why anyone would want to hurt her," she said. "No one in Shady Creek even knew her, did they?"

"I don't think so. As far as I know, the only person who knew her for more than a day is Linnea, and she definitely didn't push Marcie. She was with me when it happened."

Gilda patted my hand. "The police will figure it out."

I knew from her tone that she was telling me to leave the investigating to the professionals. I'd already found myself in a couple of dicey situations after getting involved in murder cases.

"I hope you're right. Linnea will need answers and so will Marcie's family." I decided I'd had enough of talking about the events at the manor. "Is Betty here with you?"

Betty was Gilda's friend and a coworker at her salon. The two women often came to the Inkwell together for a drink and a meal.

"Not today. I came by to talk to you."

"About something important?" I asked.

"Nothing that can't wait. It's getting busy downstairs. A big group of tourists came in right behind me."

She stood up, and I did too. After another hug, we headed downstairs and I welcomed the distraction of a pub full of hungry and thirsty customers.

*　*　*

By early evening everyone in town knew there'd been a suspicious death at Shady Creek Manor. I didn't let on that I'd been present when Marcie fell, but somehow that information got out and spread from customer to customer. Several times throughout the evening I confirmed that I'd heard Marcie scream but didn't see her fall. I didn't provide any further details, not that I had many, and I told everyone that I had no idea what had happened. That was pretty much the truth. Other than sharing the police's suspicion that Marcie's death wasn't an accident, I didn't know anything.

I tried to keep my composure through all the questions, but as the hours passed, I grew more and more tired. I was glad Damien was working the evening shift with me. He'd been a bartender at the pub even before I bought it, and I'd relied on his expertise more than once while I was getting used to being a business owner. It was nice to know I could rely on him to pick up any slack caused by my growing exhaustion.

Tonight, he wore his typical outfit of jeans and a short-sleeved T-shirt that showed off his tattoos and his biceps. He wasn't overly bulky, but he was muscular enough to be a reassuring presence during the evening shifts. Although we rarely had any real trouble from the Inkwell's patrons, it was still nice to have some muscle around, just in case.

As we worked, I tried to mask how I was feeling, but it must have still shown on my face.

Damien cast me a sidelong glance as he filled a pint glass with beer. "You look like you could use some kip," he said.

I smiled at his use of British slang. He was originally from England and still had an accent.

"You're not wrong," I told him. "I am pretty tired."

"Why don't you call it a night?" he suggested. "I can close on my own."

It was a tempting idea. I was about to take him up on it when

I spotted a familiar face. My neighbor Grayson Blake was threading his way through the tables toward me. I was glad to see him, and I realized in that moment how relieved I was that our initial animosity was now a thing of the past.

"I might head upstairs in a bit," I said, wanting a chance to talk to Grayson.

As Damien carried a tray of pints across the pub to waiting customers, I summoned up what was probably a tired smile, but it was genuine nonetheless.

"How are you doing?" Grayson asked as soon as he reached the bar.

I could tell by the concern in his blue eyes and from the way he asked the question that he'd already heard the news.

"It's been a rough day," I admitted. "But I'm glad to see you."

That last bit slipped out before it occurred to me to hold my tongue. I thought it might have surprised him, too.

"How about you?" I asked, hoping to cover up the awkwardness that was stealing over me. "You've been busy lately, from what I've heard."

He sat down on one of the bar stools. "I spent some time at beer competitions in Europe."

"I saw in the *Tribune* that you did really well at the competitions," I said. "Congrats."

The *Shady Creek Tribune* was the local paper.

"Thanks. I'm happy with how we did. It's nice to get recognition for the work we've been doing at the brewery."

"I bet. And it's well deserved." I realized I hadn't taken his order yet. "What can I get you?"

"I'll go with The Malt in Our Stars."

"Anything to eat?"

"Not tonight, thanks."

I set about mixing his cocktail, which featured scotch, ginger ale, and lemon.

After setting his drink in front of him, I served another customer before returning to talk with him.

"I hear the *Craft Nation* crew is in town," I said.

Grayson set down his drink. "Filming started yesterday."

"How's that going?"

He grimaced. "It's off to a bumpy start."

"How come?" I asked with concern.

I knew how important this opportunity was to him. Having the Spirit Hill Brewery featured on an episode of the show would be great exposure for Grayson's business and for the whole town.

"The crew had their van's windshield smashed yesterday," he said, "and this morning the director's phone disappeared. She freaked out over that. It had all her contacts and the filming schedule on it. Things should be okay on that front, though. She bought a new phone and her coworkers have copies of a lot of the information she lost."

"That's good," I said. "Any idea who smashed their windshield?"

"Nobody knows. Probably a teenager with nothing better to do." He paused to take a drink. "I wanted to talk to you about the *Craft Nation* episode. Olivia Lo, the director, is interested in getting a few shots of the Inkwell, inside and out, since you sell my beers here and the pub is one of the town's highlights."

"Really?" For the first time since Marcie's death, my spirits perked up.

"You're okay with it?"

"Okay? I think it's fantastic." The publicity would be great for the Inkwell and it would be exciting to see my pub on a television show, even if only for a few seconds.

"Good. I'll let Olivia know. She'll probably drop by to talk to you sometime tomorrow."

"Sounds good."

I took a moment to survey the pub, checking to see if I was needed anywhere. Everything seemed to be under control. The crowd had thinned out over the past hour and only about half of the tables remained occupied. It was time for the kitchen to shut down for the night, so there were only drinks left to serve. Damien was across the room, chatting with a couple of customers. No one seemed in need of my attention, so I turned it back to Grayson.

"Are you going to the masquerade?" I wanted to kick myself as soon as the words slipped out of my mouth. I didn't want him to think I was fishing for a date.

"Unfortunately, no. I've got some meetings in Boston around that time, so I won't be in town."

"That's too bad," I said, hoping the extent of my disappointment wasn't obvious. "I hear it's a fun event."

"I've heard that too."

"You've never been?"

Grayson had lived in Shady Creek for several years now and usually took part in community events, so it surprised me that he'd never been to one of the masquerades.

"No, but maybe I'll have to change that sometime." The way he held my gaze made my stomach give a giddy flip. "Are you going?"

"I've already got my ticket." I hesitated and my tongue got tied up.

Did he want to know if I had a date for the dance? I couldn't think of any subtle way to let him know that I didn't. If he didn't care one way or the other, I'd end up embarrassing myself by telling him straight out that I was going on my own. I wanted him to care, though, and realizing that left me flustered.

Fortunately, Damien came behind the bar at that moment and greeted Grayson, his presence dissipating the awkward tension that had infused the air around me. Damien was still busy behind the bar when Grayson finished his drink and got up to leave, so I didn't have any further alone time with him. That was both a relief and a disappointment.

After Grayson was gone, I took Damien up on his earlier offer and left the Inkwell in his hands so I could go to bed early. I hoped the next day would be far better than the one now drawing to a close.

Chapter 7

I didn't sleep well that night and I woke up earlier than usual, my mind too wired to allow me to fall back asleep. Wimsey was pleased that he got an early breakfast, which was clear from all his purring, but I wasn't quite so thrilled to be up an hour before I needed to be. I decided to make the most of the extra time by reading the first few chapters of *Midnight's Shadow* while enjoying a leisurely breakfast of oatmeal with chocolate chips melted on top. The book was a real page-turner. As usual, Linnea had crafted a suspenseful story full of atmosphere and intrigue. The book kept me entertained and brightened my mood, but after I'd set it down my thoughts drifted to the events of the previous day.

My heart ached terribly for Linnea and for Marcie's family. I wanted to do something to help Linnea, but I doubted anything would ease her suffering. Maybe I could take her some flowers, though, so she'd know that she and Marcie were in my thoughts.

I hung around the Inkwell for a while, since the pub was receiving some deliveries that morning, but I knew I'd have time to spare later in the morning. Once the delivery trucks had come and gone and everything was where it was meant to be, I set off for the flower shop, crossing the village green on foot. The signs of spring were just as abundant as they'd been the day before, with birdsong and the scent of flowers in the air. Somehow I appreciated the beauty around me even more than usual, probably because Marcie's death had reminded me how quickly and unexpectedly life could be snatched away.

When I reached Hillview Road on the south side of the green, I decided to make a brief stop on my way to the florist. My best friend, Shontelle, owned a gift shop on Hillview Road and I wanted to see if she was available for a brief chat. The store was open, but when I peeked through the large display window, I couldn't spot any customers.

The bell above the door jingled cheerily as I stepped inside. Classical music played softly and tiny rainbows danced on the floor, cast there by the morning light that was shining through some crystal vases by the window. Aside from the soft music, the store was still and silent, but not for long. By the time I'd taken a few steps deeper into the shop, Shontelle had appeared from the back room. She had a bright smile on her face, but when she saw me her expression changed to one of concern.

She hurried over and pulled me into a hug. "I heard the news."

I blinked back tears as I returned the hug, not wanting to cry. "It was terrible," I said as I stepped back. "Her scream was blood-chilling and then . . ."

"You were *there*? I didn't know that!" She hugged me again, giving me a squeeze before letting go. "I'm so sorry, Sadie. How awful! Do you want to stay for a bit? I could make you a cup of tea or coffee."

"Thanks," I said with a sad smile, "but I'd better get going. I want to buy some flowers for Linnea and drive them over to the manor before the Inkwell opens."

"I'm sure she'll appreciate that. I'll get in touch with all the other members of the romance book club. Maybe they'll want to go in together on a nice bouquet, or maybe a gift basket."

I had to fight back fresh tears. "I know she'll appreciate that too."

"We should do something fun," Shontelle said. "Get your mind off of Marcie's death for a while."

"You're working," I reminded her.

"I was thinking tomorrow," she clarified. "I could ask my mom to watch the store for a while and we could go shopping for our masquerade dresses."

"That does sound like fun."

"So we're on?"

"Definitely," I said, already looking forward to the outing.

After another hug from Shontelle and a promise to meet up the next day, I left the store and followed Sycamore Street to Briar Road. Like the Treasure Chest, the flower shop was quiet and empty of customers when I arrived. That wasn't surprising since it was midweek and not during any of Shady Creek's many festivals and events. Once the weekend hit, the tour buses would arrive and all of the businesses in town would see an increase in customers. As much as I loved and appreciated my regular customers at the pub, the Inkwell—like most other businesses in town—relied on tourists to stay afloat.

I greeted Yolanda, the shop's owner, and told her what I was looking for.

"Feel free to look around at the bouquets already made up," she said, "but I can always put something together for you too."

"Thank you," I said. "I think I'll browse a bit first."

A display of beautiful bouquets had drawn my eye, so I headed that way. The shop smelled so good, and all the beautiful flowers perked up my mood, despite the sad reason for my trip to the store.

As I was browsing, the shop's door opened. I didn't turn around to see who'd arrived until I heard a woman's voice.

"Morning, Yolanda. Mind if I put one of these up in the window?"

"Of course not. Go right ahead," Yolanda said.

Jan Finch, the plumber I'd seen out at the manor, taped a sheet of paper to the inside of one of the front windows, careful not to block the view of the flowers on display.

As soon as she had the paper secured to the glass, Jan called out her thanks and disappeared out the door.

"Is she advertising her plumbing business?" I asked.

"The cat shelter," Yolanda replied. "She and her mom run it out at their farm. Jan's plumbing jobs pay the bills, but helping out cats in need is her true passion."

"That's great that she and her mom do that," I said as I selected a pretty bouquet of white roses, lavender stock, and purple waxflower. I carried my selection over to the counter.

"I think so too." Yolanda rang up my purchase. "I've got three cats at home. Two of them came from Jan's shelter."

I slid my credit card out of my wallet. "I've just got one, but I love him to bits. I'd be lonely all on my own."

"I know what you mean. After my divorce, I thought I might go crazy living in my house all alone. My sister gave me a kitten and after that I was so much happier. I'm sure there are some people who think I'm a crazy cat lady, but my little fur babies have added so much good to my life."

"Wimsey's done the same for me."

After I'd finished paying for the bouquet, I thanked Yolanda and headed back across the village green to the pub's small parking lot, where I kept my car. My mood had improved since I'd first set out that morning, but as I turned my car in the direction of Shady Creek Manor, I became more subdued again.

I wondered if the police would still be at the hotel. I also wondered if they had any idea who had killed Marcie and why.

One of my questions got answered as soon as I pulled into the driveway. The yellow police tape that had cordoned off the scene of Marcie's death when I left the manor the day before was now gone, but a single police car was parked near the front steps.

I drove past the hotel and parked in the lot behind the screen of trees. At least it wasn't raining today, so the bouquet wouldn't get damaged on my way inside. With the flowers in hand, I climbed out of my car, smoothed down my hair, and then made my way around to the front door, averting my eyes from the spot where Marcie had died. If there were still bloodstains on the pavement, I didn't want to see them. My memories from the day before were already far too vivid. Even without looking that way, I had to squash down a rising sense of panic as I climbed the stairs to the front door.

Pausing before entering the hotel, I took in a deep breath and let it out slowly. The upsetting events of the day before were getting the better of me and I wanted to regain control of my emotions before going inside. My plan was to leave the flowers at the front desk for Linnea, but I didn't want to be shaking like a leaf when I entered the lobby.

After another deep breath of fresh air, I steadied my nerves and pulled open the door.

Gemma Honeywell was seated behind the reception desk, so I headed straight toward her. When she glanced up from the computer and saw me approaching, she stood up with a smile.

"Morning, Sadie," she said. "How are you doing today?"

"I'm all right, considering," I replied. "How are you and your husband holding up?"

Her smile faltered. "It's difficult, of course, but we're doing the best we can in the circumstances."

"Any word from the police on their investigation?" I asked, unable to keep my curiosity at bay.

"Not a word," she said, and I sensed she was a bit miffed by that. "Several of our guests checked out early because of what happened. I suppose I can't blame them, but I do wish the police would give us some reassuring news."

I wondered if she was only concerned about the killer getting caught for the sake of her business. I couldn't tell, so I decided to give her the benefit of the doubt.

I gestured to the flowers. "I brought these for Linnea. How's she doing?"

Gemma lowered her voice. "She's devastated, naturally. We're trying to make sure she's as comfortable as possible, but . . ." She trailed off as her attention drifted toward something over my shoulder.

When I turned around, Linnea was coming along the hallway that led from the dining room. Several wispy strands of hair had come loose from her updo and there were dark circles under her eyes. She looked as though she'd aged ten years overnight. My heart ached for her and I wished there were something I could do to ease her grief.

A fleeting, ghost of a smile touched Linnea's face when she noticed me, but it was a sad one, and it made my heart ache even more.

"Sadie, it's good to see you again," she said.

"I stopped by to bring these to you." I held up the flowers and she took them with another hint of a smile.

"That's so kind of you."

"How are you holding up?" I asked.

"Hanging in there," she said, clutching the flowers. She turned her attention to the bouquet. "These are beautiful. Thank you."

"I'll fetch you a vase," Gemma said, slipping out from behind the reception desk and disappearing down a corridor.

"Will you join me for a cup of tea in my suite?" Linnea asked.

"I don't want to bother you," I said quickly. "I just wanted you to know that I'm thinking about you."

"That's very sweet of you and it's no bother. Actually, I'd appreciate the company. I've been spending too much time alone with my thoughts."

"In that case, I'd love to."

Gemma returned with a pretty purple-tinted glass vase. I carried it for Linnea as we headed up the curving stairway. When Linnea led the way into her room, I followed for a few steps before stopping and staring at my surroundings. Linnea had a suite rather than a single room, and we'd entered a beautiful sitting room with antique furnishings, plush carpet underfoot, and French doors that led out onto a balcony with sweeping views of the hotel's lush green grounds.

"It's beautiful, isn't it?" Linnea said. She must have noticed my wide eyes. "Gemma and Brad have done a lovely job with the place."

I had to agree as Linnea took the vase from me and headed around a corner. I heard running water a second later and she soon reappeared with the flowers arranged nicely in the vase. She set the bouquet on an antique side table that sat next to a beautiful settee upholstered in blue damask fabric.

Linnea disappeared around the corner again, and when I took a few steps farther into the room, I realized there was a small alcove with a quartz countertop and a sink. A kettle, a coffeepot, and a basket of tea bags sat on the counter along with two cream-colored mugs. Linnea offered me my choice of tea or coffee, and I decided to go with tea, remembering how much Booker's orange spice blend had soothed me the day before. Linnea didn't have that particular flavor, but we were both happy with orange pekoe. Once we both had steaming mugs full of tea with cream and sugar added to it, we settled on the gorgeous settee. I silently warned myself to be careful. I'd be horrified if I spilled tea on the beautiful upholstery.

"I don't suppose you've heard anything about the police investigation?" Linnea asked.

"No, I haven't. Are they keeping you in the loop?"

"If they are, they haven't had much to report. They told me yesterday that they believed Marcie was pushed out the window after some sort of struggle." Tears pooled in Linnea's eyes. She produced a tissue from her pocket and dabbed at the tears before continuing. "They had so many questions about Marcie and who might have wanted to harm her. I had no answer to that question. Marcie didn't suffer fools gladly and sometimes she could come across as a bit of a smart aleck, but that's no reason to hurt her."

She paused, taking a moment to steady her emotions. "The police contacted Marcie's family. I spoke to her parents too. It was terribly difficult, but I felt it was something I had to do. I considered Marcie a dear friend as well as my assistant. Her poor parents have already been through so much. Her father was very ill last year and now they've lost their only child." Fresh tears welled in Linnea's eyes and this time a couple escaped down her cheeks before she could wipe them away. "I just don't understand why this happened."

"I don't either. Did she give any indication that something was wrong yesterday?"

"No. She had a headache coming on, but other than that she seemed fine." Linnea's forehead creased. "That's another thing that doesn't make any sense. Marcie said she was going to lie down because of her migraine, so what was she doing up on the third floor? She was staying in the room right next to this one."

"I wish I had answers for you," I said, truly meaning it. The confusion seemed to be adding to Linnea's grief. "Hopefully the police will solve the case quickly."

"I hope so too." Linnea sighed before taking a sip of her tea.

"Are you still planning to stay in Shady Creek for a while?"

I wouldn't have blamed her if she wanted to head home as soon as possible.

"I'm going to stay for at least a few more days, in case the police need any more information about Marcie. I'm the only person in Shady Creek who knew her."

That was true, so why had someone killed her?

Chapter 8

As much as I would have liked to ask Linnea more questions about Marcie, to see if I could uncover any possible reason why she was killed, I didn't have the heart to do it. I didn't want to add to her distress. Now that Linnea's assistant had been murdered, I was more curious than ever about Eleanor Grimes's claim that Marcie had a shady past. I didn't consider Eleanor a particularly trustworthy source of information, since she seemed to be motivated by spite more than anything else, but I couldn't help but wonder what it was she'd referred to. There was no way I was going to ask Linnea about that, though. Even if Marcie hadn't died, I wouldn't have followed that line of questioning. Linnea had most definitely not appreciated Eleanor's comment and I didn't want to shatter the rapport I'd established with the author.

I kept my curiosity in check as we finished our tea, sticking to the less distressing topic of our favorite books. We discovered that we both enjoyed mysteries by Louise Penny and thrillers by Ruth Ware. Linnea also shared my admiration for Mary Stewart and Agatha Christie.

By the time we'd finished our tea, Linnea seemed calmer.

When I got up to leave a few minutes later, she thanked me profusely for my visit, assuring me that it had done her a lot of
good. I was glad of that, but as I descended the front staircase,
my hand sliding along the polished banister, I couldn't help but
wish that I could do more for her.

Ever since moving to Shady Creek, I'd developed a habit of
getting wrapped up in murder investigations. My irrepressible
curiosity made it hard for me to sit back and stay focused on
my own life when people I knew and cared about were affected
by an unsolved mystery. I hadn't yet made any conscious plans
to try to solve the mystery of Marcie's murder, but when I
spotted Brad Honeywell behind the reception desk in the
lobby, my inner sleuth perked up.

Marcie had argued with Brad the day before her death. I
wished I knew *why* they'd argued. Maybe Marcie was dis-
pleased about service at the hotel.

No, that didn't strike me as right. I didn't hear much of what
they'd said to each other, but I did recall Marcie telling Brad to
stay away from her. That didn't sound like she had a problem
with the hotel. That sounded personal.

I was still making my way down the stairs when Gemma appeared in the lobby. She said something to Brad that I couldn't
hear and they both ducked into the office behind the reception
desk. I was glad I'd worn flats instead of high heels that day. It
was far easier to move quietly across the lobby's marble floor. I
crept up to the reception desk and strained to hear what was
going on in the office. I could hear muffled voices, but I couldn't
make out any words.

After glancing around to make sure I was alone in the lobby,
I slipped around the desk and moved silently right up to the office door. I knew I shouldn't be eavesdropping, and I almost
forced myself to turn my back on the office door and march
straight out of the hotel, but the words I picked up in the next
moment kept me rooted to the spot.

"I don't have an alibi," Brad said. He sounded tense, on edge.

"What does that matter?" Gemma asked with a hint of exasperation. "You shouldn't need one. It's not like you had a reason to kill poor Marcie."

"That's true," Brad said, almost too quietly for me to hear.

I couldn't see him to read his expression or body language, but I suspected by the tone of his voice that he was still worried, despite what his wife had said.

"Did Marcie say anything to you before she died?" he asked.

"About what?"

"I don't know. Me, maybe."

"No." Suspicion colored Gemma's next words. "Why would she?"

"No reason," Brad said quickly.

"*Something* made you ask me that." Gemma's voice held a definite note of irritation now. "What's going on, Brad?"

"Nothing! She ordered room service the other day and thought it should have been faster. She complained to me and I told her the meal was on the house. That's all."

I strongly suspected that wasn't what they'd argued about.

"Eavesdropping, are we?"

I spun around at the sound of the female voice, my heart leaping into my throat.

The blond woman I'd seen in the dining room the other day descended the last few steps to the marble floor. The black ballet flats she wore with her skinny jeans and white blouse allowed her to move silently.

Heat flared in my cheeks. I scooted out from behind the reception desk, terrified that Gemma and Brad might have heard her.

"I wasn't . . ." I tried to come up with an innocent explanation for my presence behind the desk, but my mind went blank.

The woman winked at me before slipping on her oversized sunglasses. "I won't tell."

With a pink designer handbag hanging from the crook in her arm, she strode out of the hotel with the haughty confidence of a runway model.

I didn't dare risk any further eavesdropping. Getting caught once was bad enough and the next time I might not get off so easily. I hurried out the front door and then slowed my steps, not wanting to catch up with the blond woman in case she brought up my eavesdropping again. She was headed around the building toward the parking lot, just as I was, so I stopped for a moment, pretending to admire the beautiful blooms on a rhododendron bush. Once the woman had climbed into a silver sedan, I hurried to my own car and headed back to the Inkwell.

A familiar voice called my name as soon as I climbed out of my car. Joey Fontana, a friend of mine who co-owned the local newspaper with his father, was walking up the road. He broke into a jog to catch up with me as I reached the footbridge that led across the creek to the pub. A breeze had picked up since earlier in the day and it ruffled Joey's dark hair as he fell into step beside me. He held a white paper bag in one hand, imprinted with the logo of Sofie's Treat, the local bakery.

"I see you've been indulging," I said with a glance at the bag.

Joey grinned. "I brought something for you too."

"That must mean you want something in return." I didn't give him a chance to confirm or deny that. "Let me guess—you have questions about Marcie Kent."

"Got it in one."

Joey wrote many of the articles for the *Shady Creek Tribune* himself, and he wasn't one to shy away from asking questions.

"You've had more contact with her than most people in this town," Joey said as I unlocked the Inkwell's red front door. "The Honeywells won't give me anything other than a two-line statement, and the author Marcie worked for is *unavailable for comment*." He hooked air quotes around the last three words.

"Of course she is." I pulled open the door and Joey followed me inside. "She's distraught. She doesn't need to be pestered by reporters."

"Would I pester anyone?" Joey asked with mock innocence.

"Seriously, Joey," I said as we made our way across the dimly lit pub.

"Hey, I hear you," he assured me. "That's why I'm here instead of hanging around the manor like a vulture."

When I reached the bar, I slipped behind it and flicked on the overhead lights. Joey took a seat on one of the stools, setting his bakery bag on the bar. He produced a chocolate-drizzled croissant and then held the bag out to me. My mouth already watering, I accepted the remaining croissant.

"Thank you." I pulled a piece off the end of the buttery treat. "But don't think I'm going to be dishing out any juicy rumors in return."

"So there are juicy rumors about the author's assistant?"

All I could do was shake my head, since my mouth was full of chocolate and croissant.

He studied me from across the bar, a little too closely for my liking. "I'm not sure I believe you, but we'll let it go for the moment."

I didn't want to share with him that Eleanor had made insinuations about Marcie's past. Even though I was just as curious as he would be to know more details, I felt protective toward Linnea. She probably wasn't likely to read the next issue of the *Tribune*, but I still didn't want to be responsible for upsetting her if what Joey reported somehow reached her. Maybe once I knew what it was about Marcie's past that Eleanor had referred to, I could reassess whether I'd share the information with Joey. Until then, I was determined to keep quiet about it.

After savoring another delicious bite of croissant, I decided to turn the tables and do a little digging for information of my own.

"I hear you've been spending a lot of time at the bakery lately," I said. "Any particular reason?"

It was hard to tell for sure, but I thought Joey's cheeks flushed slightly. I envied him the fact that his cheeks didn't turn a flaming shade of red like mine had a tendency to do.

"Sofie's a magician with flour, sugar, and butter," he replied.

"She is," I agreed.

He wouldn't meet my eyes and I decided to take pity on him and not press the matter any further. The rumor was that he'd started spending so much time at the bakery because he had a crush on Sofie. Judging by Joey's reaction to my questioning, the rumor was true.

It wasn't hard to see why he'd like the baker. She was cheerful, friendly, and pretty. She was probably in her late twenties, like Joey was, and she had a head of thick, dark curls that cascaded down her back, at least when she didn't have them tied back for work. For Joey's sake, I hoped his feelings were reciprocated. I considered Joey a good friend and I wanted him to be happy. His new crush also brought me some relief. It wasn't that long ago that he'd had an interest in me. Since I hadn't felt the same way, I'd worried about how that might affect our friendship. It seemed I didn't have to worry about that anymore.

"Anyway," Joey said, meeting my eyes again, "I came to talk about the murder, not baked goods."

I sighed in disappointment, not because of the change in topic, but because I'd just finished my last piece of croissant.

"I'm guessing you heard I was at the manor when Marcie died," I said.

"Yep." He sobered. "How are you doing? That couldn't have been nice."

"No, it definitely wasn't. But I'm doing okay."

"So you'll give me your eyewitness account?"

I didn't see how that could hurt, so I agreed. If he hadn't already talked to other people who'd been at the manor at the time, he would soon. I didn't venture beyond the basics, however, and I left out the fact that I had suspicions about Brad Honeywell. I also didn't mention that I'd done some eavesdropping at the hotel.

When I'd finished relaying my account of the tragedy to Joey, I asked if he knew anything about the police investigation. He didn't—not yet, at least—so I was left with all my unanswered questions about who'd killed Marcie and why.

Joey left the pub shortly before I opened it to the public and I kept busy throughout the afternoon, mixing cocktails and serving customers with Mel's help. After Mel's shift had ended and Damien had taken over for her, I slipped into the kitchen for a short break and a dinner of The Red Cabbage of Courage, a salad made with crispy ramen noodles, grated carrot, sunflower seeds, red cabbage, and a vinaigrette. The nacho platter Teagan had just put together for a customer made my mouth water, but I forced myself to resist temptation and choose the healthier, but still delicious, option of the salad.

"Did you buy a masquerade ticket?" I asked Teagan between forkfuls of salad.

She removed a tray of crostini from the oven. "Yep. Zoe too. We made sure to get them early in case they sell out."

Zoe was Teagan's identical twin sister. If not for the streak of red through Teagan's dark blond hair, I would have had trouble telling them apart whenever I saw them together.

"Do you have a date?" she asked as she flipped burgers on the grill.

"No date and so far no dress," I said. "You?"

"Zoe's going with her boyfriend, Cal, but I'm going solo. I do have a dress, though. You don't have much time left to get one."

"I know, but Shontelle and I are going shopping tomorrow."

"I can't wait to see what you choose."

"Same here," I said with a smile before scooping the last of my salad onto my fork.

When I left the kitchen moments later with a full stomach, Olivia Lo was taking a seat at the bar. Not a single strand of her jet-black hair was out of place, despite the fact that she'd just come in out of the stiff breeze that was causing tree branches to wave and dance outside the windows. She wore the same black leather jacket as I'd seen her in before, and when I drew closer I noticed that her fingernails were painted a dark shade of red.

"Sadie, right?" she asked me as I approached.

"That's right. And you're Olivia?"

She confirmed that with a brisk nod. "Grayson spoke to you about getting some shots of the pub for the episode?"

"He did. Can I get you anything to eat or drink before we talk? It's on the house."

"A glass of Merlot, please." Her gaze dropped to her phone and she tapped at the screen, pausing our conversation for the moment.

I had hoped she'd want to try one of the literary-themed cocktails from the menu so she could get a taste of what made the Inkwell unique, and hopefully decide to showcase that on the episode, but I didn't dare attempt to steer her that way. Her manner was cool and she seemed a bit tense. I didn't want to annoy her and have her change her mind about including the Inkwell in the *Craft Nation* episode.

When she had her glass of wine, we moved to a small table in a quiet corner to chat. It didn't take long for Olivia to fill me in on her plans for filming at the pub. She got straight down to business, not bothering with any small talk, only pausing now and then to take generous sips of her wine.

"You open at noon tomorrow, right?" she asked.

"That's right."

"We'll get some exterior shots of the pub around nine in the morning, if the weather's right. Can you get a dozen or so people to come in and eat or drink while we get a few interior shots? We don't want to do it during your regular business hours. No telling how many people would rush the doors, hoping for a chance to get their face on TV."

"A dozen or so shouldn't be a problem," I said, already thinking about whom I should text that evening. Aunt Gilda topped the list, followed by Shontelle.

"Good." Olivia tapped at her phone while she talked. "Get them here by ten. I don't want this to put us behind schedule."

She tipped her glass to drain the last of her wine and then she pushed back her chair and grabbed her handbag.

"Nice talking to you," she said, although the words sounded automatic rather than sincere. "See you tomorrow."

"See you." I barely got the words out before she was striding across the pub and out the door in her high-heeled boots.

Despite the director's somewhat prickly personality, the meeting left me with a smile on my face. After what had happened the day before, it was nice to have something exciting to look forward to.

Chapter 9

I woke up the next morning with a flurry of excitement in my stomach. The film crew would be arriving in a couple of hours and I was thrilled to have the chance to show off the Inkwell to the *Craft Nation* audience. I knew full well that any footage shot at the pub could end up on the cutting room floor, or the pub might get only a few seconds of screen time, but I was choosing to stay positive and holding on to the belief that the Inkwell would get enough coverage to capture the interest of at least some viewers.

Since I was so eager to get on with the day, Wimsey didn't have to employ any of his usual tactics to get me out of bed. I threw back the covers without any assistance from him and almost beat him out of the bedroom. Once he was fed and satisfied, I got myself ready, taking a bit of extra time to make sure I was looking my best. Olivia hadn't said that I'd be in any of the shots filmed at the Inkwell, and I didn't mind if I wasn't, but I wanted to be camera ready just in case.

I was too antsy to cook a bowl of oatmeal or even to make some toast, so I decided to walk over to the Village Bean to pick up one of Nettie Jo's delicious carrot muffins and some coffee. Wimsey followed me out the front door, but had no intention of going any farther. He hopped up onto one of the two whiskey barrels that flanked the door and set to work washing his face.

"Stick around and you might end up on TV," I said, giving him a pat.

He shook his head to dislodge my hand from his fur and got back to his grooming. He certainly didn't seem interested in a few seconds of fame.

Leaving Wimsey on his barrel, I set off across the footbridge. I hadn't yet made it to the other side when I stopped in my tracks. A police cruiser was parked up the street, outside of the Creekside Inn. I hoped nothing bad had happened to Cordelia or her grandmother, Grace.

I temporarily abandoned my plan to visit the Village Bean and hurried off in the opposite direction. When I reached the beautiful Queen Anne that housed the Creekside Inn, I started along the paved pathway to the front steps. As I drew closer to the house, I heard voices coming from nearby. Instead of heading up to the porch, I followed the narrow path that led around to the side of the property. A gravel driveway gently curved from the road to a small parking lot surrounded by maple trees with green leaves waving gently in the hint of a morning breeze.

When a head of crinkly red hair came into view, I picked up my pace. Cordelia stood at the edge of the parking lot, wringing her hands and looking on as Olivia Lo, Alex Nevarez, and a young man I didn't recognize spoke with Officer Eldon Howes of the Shady Creek Police Department.

When Cordelia saw me coming, she left the others to their conversation and met me on the pathway. By the time she approached, I'd noticed that a black van parked in the small lot was sitting at a tipsy angle, one of its rear tires completely flat.

"What's going on?" I asked Cordelia. "Are you all right?"

"I am, but . . ." She cast a glance over her shoulder, her red hair practically glowing in the sunlight. When she turned back my way, her blue eyes were filled with worry. "Somebody smashed the windshield of the film crew's van and slashed one of its tires last night. Right here in the inn's parking lot! Olivia's terribly upset. Before the police got here, she was yelling at me, asking why we don't have security cameras." Cordelia's voice rose in pitch. "This is Shady Creek! We never needed security cameras before!"

"But nobody's hurt?" I checked.

"No, thank goodness. Do you think Olivia will sue us?"

"I doubt it," I said, hoping to ease Cordelia's concerns. I didn't actually know if Olivia would or wouldn't, or even if she had grounds to sue the inn's owners, but I hated that Cordelia was so distraught over what had happened.

Fortunately, my words seemed to have the desired effect. Cordelia at least stopped squeezing the life out of her fingers.

"I'm going to move Gran's station wagon out of the garage so the crew can park their vehicle inside at night. Hopefully that will satisfy Olivia. It would be awful if they all decided to move elsewhere for the rest of their stay. The host of the show just checked in last night."

Officer Howes passed by us on his way back to his cruiser. "Ladies," he said as he tipped his hat.

I would have liked to ask him questions about the vehicle damage and the murder investigation, but his stride was quick and purposeful, and I suspected he had more pressing business to attend to than my curiosity.

Over in the parking lot, Olivia threw her hands in the air. "I can't deal with this! We're supposed to be filming in less than an hour!"

"I'll change the tire and call the garage about the windshield," Alex said calmly, his cell phone already out.

"I'd better go clean up the broken glass," Cordelia said as we watched their exchange.

"I'll help you," I offered.

"Really? You're the best, Sadie. Thank you."

She hurried inside to fetch brooms and dust pans. Seconds later, Olivia stormed into the inn through a side door while Alex paced slowly back and forth, talking into his phone. The crew had already had their windshield smashed when they first arrived in Shady Creek. As far as I knew, there hadn't been any other recent acts of vandalism around town, so did someone have it out for the *Craft Nation* crew?

By the time Cordelia and I had cleaned up the last of the broken glass, Alex had changed the tire and had driven away, heading for the local auto body shop. Fortunately, he was able to make the short drive, despite not having a windshield. I left the inn soon after we'd finished the cleanup job so Cordelia could get on her way. She'd promised to go pick up Alex to give him a ride back to the inn. That was a good thing, since Olivia was still fuming when she arrived at the Inkwell. I could tell she was about to share her frustration and complaints with me, but when Grace King's ancient station wagon drove up the street toward the Creekside Inn, with Cordelia at the wheel and Alex in the passenger seat, she calmed down. Slightly.

I decided to forgo my trip to the Village Bean and tried my best to ignore my rumbling stomach as Alex carried some gear out of the inn and along the road to the pub. He set everything on one of the two picnic tables on the lawn before hefting his camera up onto his shoulder. Without wasting any more time, he started filming the Inkwell under Olivia's direction.

I could have slipped inside between shots to grab something to eat, but everyone I'd invited to come by the pub for the interior shots would start arriving soon and I wanted to be there to greet them. I was afraid to leave them completely in Olivia's hands. She was calmer now, and focused on the job at hand, but her words had a sharpness to them that made me suspect she'd be quick to anger.

After getting a few shots of the old gristmill from the vantage point of the village green, Alex and Olivia crossed the footbridge to film from another angle, one that would encompass the front door. Wimsey was still on the whiskey barrel, settled down now with his front paws tucked beneath him, and I was pleased when Olivia told Alex to make sure he got a close-up of the cat.

As Alex continued to film, Olivia checked her phone.

"Jules and Evan better get over here pronto," she muttered. "Like we need any other problems to deal with."

Alex lowered his camera. "They'll be here. Jules is probably just getting himself ready. You know what he's like."

"Every hair has to be in place," Olivia said with an exasperated sigh. She glanced up the street and her frown eased slightly. "Here they come."

Sure enough, the host of *Craft Nation* was walking down the street toward us, dressed in dark jeans and a turquoise and gray plaid shirt with the sleeves rolled up to his elbows. The young man I'd seen in the parking lot earlier struggled to keep pace at his side. He was laden down with equipment that Jules made no move to help him with.

I expected Olivia to grouse at Jules and his companion, but to my surprise her expression changed like a switch had been flicked.

She smiled at Jules. "Ready?"

The show's host rubbed his hands together. "Let's make some magic!"

I hung back, wondering if Olivia would introduce me to Jules, but she made no move to do so. It didn't matter in the end, because Jules stepped forward and offered his hand to me anyway.

"Jules Beamer," he said as I shook his hand.

"Sadie Coleman," I returned.

"You own this place?" He nodded at the gristmill.

"I do."

He surveyed the building. "Nice," he said with appreciation.

I smiled, ridiculously pleased that he approved. It felt a bit surreal to be meeting him in person after having seen him on TV. He was even better looking in person than on screen, but the friendly smile he gave me didn't stir up any butterflies in my chest. These days, my butterflies only seemed to flutter for one man, a certain craft brewer with blue eyes and dark hair.

While Jules chatted with Olivia, Alex and the other man busied themselves with the equipment that they'd carried over from the inn. The young man didn't introduce himself like Jules had, but I gathered he was the Evan Olivia had mentioned moments ago.

When Jules had finished talking with Olivia, Evan clipped a microphone to the host's shirt, making sure it was hidden from view. Then Evan attached a reflector to a stand and adjusted it when Jules took up his position in front of the pub.

After a few more minutes, Alex readied his camera again and filmed several takes of Jules giving a short spiel about the Inkwell, the town, and Grayson's beers. Olivia had just declared the most recent take to be the last, when people started arriving for the interior shots. Cordelia walked over from the inn and came over to stand next to me, keeping a wary eye on Olivia. Fortunately, the director was wrapped up in her work now, the slashed tire and broken windshield forgotten, at least for the moment.

Aunt Gilda and her friend Betty arrived next. They'd both cleared their schedules at the salon so they could help me fill the pub for the show. Mel and Damien showed up a moment later, with Joey arriving on their heels. Then Booker and his girlfriend arrived, followed soon after by Teagan, her twin sister, and a few members of the Inkwell's book clubs. I barely had a chance to thank everyone for coming when Olivia ushered us inside and directed each person to where she wanted them. I thought she'd want me sitting at a table or on one of the bar stools like everyone else, until she told me otherwise.

"You go behind the bar, Sadie," she said.

It sounded far more like an order than a request, but I didn't mind. I was willing to accommodate her bossiness to get my pub on her show.

She turned to Alex. "I want a shot of her pulling a pint."

"Of me?" To my embarrassment, the words came out with a squeak.

"You own the place, right?" Olivia didn't give me a chance to respond. "Isn't pulling pints part of what you do?"

"Of course," I said.

She returned her attention to Alex, giving him some more direction.

I tried to gather my wits about me so I wouldn't appear flustered. I'd figured I'd be in the background like everyone else, if I showed up at all. I hadn't expected to be the focus of any of the shots.

Damien got up from the table where Olivia had told him to sit with Mel. He leaned over the bar and spoke to me quietly. "Just relax, Sadie. You'll do great."

"Relax. Right."

He returned to the table and I tried to take his advice. Olivia was right—I poured pints for customers every day. There was no reason to be nervous. Except, I'd never been filmed while doing my job before.

I told myself to ignore the camera, but that wasn't so easy. During the first take, my hands shook and I silently berated myself. With each subsequent take, I relaxed more and more, and after half a dozen tries, Olivia was finally satisfied.

The pints didn't go to waste. They were passed around so all of the pretend customers would have a drink in front of them. I watched from behind the bar as the crew filmed my friends as they chatted quietly and enjoyed their beers. Within an hour,

Olivia declared the job done and she and her crew starting packing up.

Cordelia hurried over to me. "Isn't Jules Beamer dreamy?" she whispered. "I had a chance to talk to him last night when he arrived at the inn. He's so charming."

Her cheeks were pink and her eyes bright. I was glad she'd cheered up since earlier in the day. She had to get back to the inn, so she scurried off a moment later and Aunt Gilda pulled me aside.

"That seemed to go well," she said.

"It did," I agreed as I watched the crew get the last of their gear together. "I hope they'll use at least some of the footage."

"I'm sure they will. This place is so full of character. How could they not feature it?"

I hoped she was right.

"Can we meet up for an early lunch tomorrow?" she asked.

"I'm going dress shopping with Shontelle tomorrow morning." We'd rescheduled by text message after I found out about the filming plans. "Maybe the next day?"

Aunt Gilda squeezed my hand. "It's a date. I've got to run, but we'll have a good chat over lunch."

"I'm looking forward to it," I assured her as she turned to go.

It was time to open the Inkwell to the public, so I followed the film crew out the door and flipped the CLOSED sign to OPEN. That done, I stood outside for a moment, enjoying the feel of the warm sun on my face. As I turned to go back inside, I noticed someone over on the green. I recognized the woman a second later as the blonde from Shady Creek Manor. She wore the same oversized sunglasses and she quickly strode off toward the eastern end of the green when I spotted her, but I could have sworn she'd been watching me.

Chapter 10

The *Craft Nation* episode currently in production was already proving to be good for Shady Creek. Instead of conversations centering around Marcie's murder—a topic that might have scared the tourists away—the pub was buzzing with talk about the show. Those who hadn't been present for the filming at the Inkwell wondered if they'd have a chance to get on camera, and everyone was hopeful that the episode would increase tourism. Even those who were in Shady Creek for a vacation were excited about the production. From what I heard, the tourists were most enthusiastic about the fact that Jules Beamer was in town.

"Is it true that he's even better looking in person?" a middle-aged woman asked me as I set Happily Ever After and Yellow Brick Road cocktails in front of her and her three female companions.

"It's true," I confirmed.

All four women twittered with excitement.

"We *have* to meet him," one of the women declared, and her friends all agreed.

I left them to their drinks and returned to the bar. Two men seated on stools at the end of the bar ordered nachos and pints of beer. After I'd served them, I noticed Sofie Talbot heading for the Christie room with her friend Gina DiMarco. Sofie and Gina had both joined the Inkwell's science fiction and fantasy book club.

I wondered if Joey knew that Sofie was in the club. Maybe if I told him he'd want to join the group too. For a second I considered fishing for information from Sofie, to see if she had any feelings of a romantic nature for Joey, but then I decided I should mind my own business, even if that wasn't an easy thing for me to do.

Following Sofie and Gina into the Christie room, I asked if I could get them anything and left my questions at that. Sofie ordered a Huckleberry Gin and Gina requested a glass of white wine. I mixed the cocktail and poured the wine at the bar and then carried the drinks into the other room, setting them on the small table that sat between the armchairs the two women had claimed. So far, they were still the only club members to have arrived.

"Did you enjoy this month's book?" I asked them.

"For sure!" Gina said before taking a sip of her wine.

Sofie pulled her copy of *Darkness Shifting* by Sarah L. Blair out of her tote bag. "Have you read it?"

"No," I replied, "but maybe I should."

"You definitely should," Gina said. "It's a really clever, urban fantasy twist on the King Arthur legend."

"I'll check it out." I made a mental note to add the book to my to-be-read list. "What's the book for next month?"

"*Empyrean* by Nicole L. Bates," Sofie said. "I've already started reading it. The world building is fantastic!"

At that moment, another member of the club arrived. Matt Yanders was in his late forties and owned the Harvest Grill, one of Shady Creek's restaurants.

"Evening, ladies," he said, shrugging out of his black leather jacket. As he hung the jacket over the back of a chair, he addressed Gina. "Things must be crazy at the manor these days."

Gina set down her wineglass. "You're not kidding."

"You work at the manor?" I asked her.

"Yep."

"She's the pastry chef," Sofie added.

"You mean you made that heavenly chocolate mousse cake I ate the other day?" I asked.

Gina smiled. "That was me. So you liked it?"

"I loved it," I said.

Gina's smile brightened. "I'm so glad. I love my job."

"Even now, when you have to work where there's been a murder?" Matt asked as he pulled up his chair and sat down.

Sofie shuddered. "Maybe Gina doesn't want to talk about that."

"I don't mind," Gina said. "It's unsettling, for sure, and all of us who work in the kitchen make sure nobody goes out to their car alone after dark now, but I'm hoping the police will nab the killer soon so we'll all be safe again."

"Have you heard anything about the investigation?" I asked, hoping I'd found a new source of information. "Are the police making any progress?"

"I have no idea. Nobody really knows what's going on."

"I heard the victim didn't know anyone in town," Sofie said. "So why would anyone want to kill her?"

"I wondered the same thing." I didn't mention how much time I'd spent thinking about that and related questions.

"A murderer doesn't have to know the victim to kill them," Matt said. "Maybe it was a spur-of-the-moment thing."

"Maybe," Gina said with a shrug.

"It's all odd, though, isn't it?" I said. "Marcie fell from a vacant guest room. How did she get in there in the first place?"

"I figure she must have stolen a key card for some reason," Gina said. "If she did, it was probably a master key or a maid's key."

"It couldn't have been a guest key?" Matt asked. "Maybe one kept at the front desk?"

"Unlikely," Gina said. "I'm no expert, but my understanding is that the keys get recoded each time a new guest checks into a room, so it would be easier to use a staff key."

"How many people have master keys?" I asked.

"I'm not sure," Gina replied. "Gemma and Brad Honeywell, for starters. And the housekeeping staff has a lot of access. I think the master keys and maid keys have different codes."

That caught my attention. "So it would be possible to find out which type of key was used?"

"If you had access to the hotel computer system, sure."

"So the cops probably already know if she used a master key or a maid's key," Matt said. "They would have checked the system."

"If they even needed to," I said. "Maybe Marcie had a key on her when she died."

"She didn't," Gina said. "That's what I've heard, anyway."

Matt got more comfortable in his chair. "The cops are probably way ahead of us."

"I sure hope so." Gina frowned. "I don't like having to look over my shoulder all the time. I'll feel so much better when the killer's caught."

"Maybe the murderer is one of your coworkers," Matt suggested.

Gina paled. "I hope not. It definitely wasn't anyone who was working in the kitchen that day. We were all together when the woman fell."

So I could cross the kitchen staff off my suspect list. Not that I'd added them to my list. Heck, my list didn't even exist yet, except in my head.

"Plus, Mrs. Honeywell and one of the housekeepers were

together at the time," Gina continued, and I knew she meant Connie. "I overheard someone saying that. Rosalie—she's another housekeeper—was also working that day, but she's no killer. She's a five-foot-nothing grandmother and just about the sweetest lady you'll ever meet."

Three more members of the book club bustled into the room and I knew I couldn't grill Gina for information any longer. I took some drink orders and then left the club to their discussion of *Darkness Shifting*, still as puzzled as ever by Marcie's death.

The next morning I allowed Wimsey to roust me out of bed fairly early so I could get to the grocery store as soon as it opened. My fridge and cupboards were woefully empty and, if I didn't stock up on supplies before going dress shopping with Shontelle, I wouldn't have anything to eat for breakfast tomorrow.

I considered the trip to the store a bit of a chore, but my mood improved as I entered the produce section with a grocery basket in hand. Grayson was in the midst of selecting an avocado.

"Morning," I greeted cheerily.

"Morning, Sadie." The way he smiled at me made my heart speed up. "How did the filming go yesterday?"

"Really well, I think." I put a bunch of bananas in my basket before moving toward the bin of limes. "Hopefully the Inkwell won't end up on the cutting room floor."

"I don't think that will happen. I know Olivia loves the character of the place."

That was good to know. "Have you seen her since the filming at the pub?"

"I saw her yesterday afternoon. She and the guys were getting some shots of the brewing process."

"Was she in a good mood?" I was hoping she was pleased with how things had gone at the Inkwell.

Grayson hesitated a second. "Not exactly. But," he added quickly, "I don't think that had anything to do with filming at the pub. I've never seen her particularly happy. Right from the start she seemed stressed. The stolen phone and vandalism haven't helped matters. I think she's under a lot of pressure."

"I'm glad I don't have her job." Keeping the pub running was enough pressure for me. I didn't think I was cut out for directing a television show. "And I guess I can't blame her for getting upset about the vandalism. Did you hear that the crew's windshield got smashed again?"

Grayson added some oranges to a reusable produce bag. "I did. And a slashed tire this time."

"Someone seems to have it in for the production crew." I followed Grayson over to the bell peppers, my own shopping list now forgotten. "Any idea why anyone would want to mess with them?"

"Not yet."

"Then I guess we've got another mystery on our hands," I said.

He raised an eyebrow. "We?"

"I bet if we put our heads together, we could figure out who's responsible."

"You might be right about that. How about I stop by the pub later so we can talk it over?"

I was pleased by how readily he'd agreed to work together. "It's a date." I realized what I'd said. "I mean, not a *date* date. Just . . ." Heat rushed to my cheeks. They were probably bright enough to be seen from the space station.

Grayson laughed and then stepped closer as an elderly man navigated his cart past us. When my arm brushed against Grayson's, my heart decided it was a good time to dance the jitterbug.

"I'll see you later," he said with a grin, his blue eyes looking right into mine for a long moment before he left.

With my cheeks still hot and my heart cavorting about in my chest, I stood there by the bell peppers and watched as Grayson headed for the checkout counter.

I was able to get the rest of my groceries and pay for them without embarrassing myself any further. That wasn't particularly surprising, though. I really only had a habit of making things awkward for myself when Grayson was around.

"I can't believe I said it was a date," I muttered to myself as I left the store.

He probably thought I was a dork. Although, the way he'd looked into my eyes made me wonder if I was wrong about that.

I was still wrapped up in my thoughts when I heard angry voices off to my right. A short distance along the residential street I was passing, a thin woman with graying hair was facing off with a balding man with a gas-powered lawnmower beside him.

"That machine keeps belching out poison!" the woman groused in a raised voice. "It's bad for my roses!"

"Get a grip, Eleanor," the man said with exasperation.

I realized it was Eleanor Grimes he was arguing with. Almost without conscious thought, I turned off my original path and headed their way.

"Don't you tell me to get a grip, Henry Blackwell! You still haven't replaced my good gardening gloves that your dog destroyed!"

"I'm done with this conversation," the man grumbled.

He yanked the cord on his lawnmower and the motor started up with a loud rumble and a cloud of black smoke. He stalked away from Eleanor, pushing his mower ahead of him.

Eleanor whipped around and her beady eyes landed on me.

The glower she sent my way was almost intense enough to make me wilt right there on the sidewalk. She stormed up her front steps and into her house, slamming the door behind her.

Henry continued pushing his mower across the grass, shaking his head as he went. I considered myself lucky to not live next door to Eleanor, but that wasn't the main thought taking up space in my head. I was far more focused on the fact that I'd seen bright red scratches on Eleanor's arms.

Chapter 11

I was still thinking about the scratches on Eleanor's arms when I put away my groceries and headed out again to meet up with Shontelle. I knew from the state of the third-floor hotel room that Marcie had struggled with her killer before her deadly fall. Was that how Eleanor had ended up with those marks on her arms?

I wrestled with the possibility as I crossed the village green toward Shontelle's shop. It didn't strike me as the most compelling theory. Eleanor was as tall as I was, which made her close to Marcie's height as well, but she was thin and bony and probably in her seventies. Could she really have had the strength to push twenty-something Marcie out the window? It seemed more likely to me that Marcie would have overpowered her easily. Although, if Eleanor had been angry enough, maybe that would have given her the strength she needed.

Still, I wasn't convinced of Eleanor's guilt. Maybe I needed to look at other aspects of the murder. Did Eleanor have a motive for killing Marcie?

Not that I could think of. She hadn't liked the fact that Marcie had pointed out a problem with her book, and that was probably why she'd dug up some dirt on Marcie, whatever that dirt was. Even so, it would have made more sense to me if Marcie had killed Eleanor to keep her from revealing whatever she'd discovered about the younger woman's past, if she'd known that Eleanor had found something.

I decided that I couldn't discount Eleanor completely. It would help to know how she'd ended up with the scratches on her arms, but I wasn't sure how I'd find that out. I'd keep her on my mental suspect list for the time being, but Brad Honeywell's name was still above hers. I needed to figure out what had happened between him and Marcie. It would also help if I could know what Eleanor had alluded to when she'd brought up Marcie's past to Linnea. That information might give me a better picture of who Marcie was and why someone might have wanted to harm her.

Digging around for clues would have to wait, however. I'd reached the Treasure Chest and could see Shontelle through the glass door. When I opened it, I also noticed that her mother was there.

"Hey, Sadie. I'll just grab my purse," Shontelle called out as she disappeared into the back of the shop.

"Hi, Yvette," I greeted Shontelle's mom. "Are you on shop duty this morning?"

"You bet," she replied with a smile.

Shontelle reappeared with her purse in hand.

"You girls have fun," Yvette called to us as we headed for the front door.

We waved to her and stepped out onto the sidewalk.

"Where to first?" Shontelle asked.

"Let's try Sassy Gal," I suggested.

Shontelle agreed with that, so we headed for Hemlock Street. There were only two choices when it came to shopping for women's clothing in Shady Creek. Anna Stassen's shop had everything from shorts and sundresses to nightgowns and a handful of formal dresses. We'd have very limited selection at that store, but I didn't want to have to rely on our second option unless we really had to. That boutique offered business wear, semi-formal, and formal clothing for women, and would be more likely to have what we were looking for. The problem with Fashionably Late was that it was owned by Vera Anderson.

Although Vera was a member of the Inkwell's romance book club, she was far from my favorite person. She could be haughty and prickly, and on an occasion or two in the past she'd taken malicious pleasure in blindsiding me with unpleasant news. As far as I knew, Vera had at least one part-time employee who helped her run the shop, but she also spent plenty of time there herself, and I didn't want to cross her path if I didn't need to.

I knew Shontelle's opinion of Vera wasn't much better than mine, which was probably why she agreed to my suggestion without hesitation. When we arrived at Sassy Gal, the owner herself greeted us. Anna was originally from Amsterdam and still had a Dutch accent. I didn't know her well, but I'd shopped at her store a couple of times and she'd been by the pub on occasion. I knew from the town gossip that she'd met Shady Creek local Ian Weathers while they were on separate ski holidays in Switzerland. After a whirlwind romance, they'd married and Anna had moved to Shady Creek with Ian.

"Is there anything I can help you with today?" Anna asked after we'd exchanged greetings.

"We're shopping for our masquerade dresses," I said.

"Do you have anything that might work?" Shontelle ran her gaze over the shop's selection.

"In the back corner." Anna pointed in that direction. "I don't carry many formal dresses, and some have already been snatched up over the past couple of days, but there's still a few there."

We thanked her and headed for the back corner, where we

found one small rack of evening dresses. About half of the gowns were far too small for us and were likely meant for teenage girls.

Shontelle pulled a knee-length red dress off the rack. "Here's one." She held it up to me.

I shook my head and stepped back. "I can't wear that color. It clashes terribly with my hair and complexion."

Shontelle held it up against herself and looked down at the dress. She quickly returned it to the rack. "Too plain. It might be okay for a regular party, but the May Day Masquerade calls for something a little more . . . elegant."

"Yes, elegant," I agreed. "That's exactly what I want."

It only took us a minute to go through the rest of the dresses on offer. I loved the emerald-green color of one, but I wasn't keen on the style, and the size wasn't right anyway. Shontelle took a cursory look at a shimmery silver dress and a sleek black one, but she rejected both in a matter of seconds.

"You know what this means, don't you?" she whispered as she hung the black dress up again.

I let out a quiet groan. "We have to check out Vera's store."

"Maybe she's not there today," Shontelle said, with what I thought was forced optimism.

I crossed my fingers. "Let's hope that's the case."

We said goodbye to Anna and then set off for Fashionably Late on Briar Road. I tried to peek into the shop through the front window, to see who was inside, but the bright sunshine made it difficult to see beyond the window display.

Shontelle was braver than I was and pulled open the door and strode inside without hesitation. I had to give myself a mental kick to follow her. To my disappointment, Vera was behind the counter, ringing up purchases for two middle-aged women. We exchanged brief greetings with the shop owner, and then wandered deeper into the store.

So far, so good. Maybe shopping there wouldn't be so bad

after all. We certainly had far more to choose from. One whole wall of the shop was dedicated to women's eveningwear. A cobalt-blue dress immediately drew my eye, but when I took it off the rack for a closer look, I quickly decided I didn't like the style. I selected a green one next.

"That color would look gorgeous on you," Shontelle said as I held the dress up against my body.

"It's a bit too revealing for me."

The neckline split into a V that plunged all the way down to the waistline.

"I'm sure it would get Grayson's attention," Shontelle said with a wink and a smile.

I hung the dress back up with a sigh. "He won't even be at the masquerade."

"That's too bad." Shontelle stopped with her hand on a dress still hanging on the rack. "Wait. How do you know that?" Her gaze sharpened with suspicion, piercing right into me. "Did you ask him to the masquerade and not tell me?"

"No, thank goodness. It would have been way too embarrassing when he turned me down. I would have thought the out-of-town excuse was just that, an excuse. And of course I would have told you. We just happened to be talking about the masquerade and he mentioned he wouldn't be in town for it."

Shontelle's expression softened. "I'm sorry, Sadie."

"Why?" I unhooked a hanger from the rack to check out a yellow gown. "It's not like we would have gone together, even if he was in town."

"You mean you wouldn't have said yes if he'd asked you?"

"He wouldn't have asked." I hesitated. "Would he?"

"He didn't give you any clues?"

"No." I held the yellow dress up to myself and looked in the full-length mirror in the corner of the store, but I barely noticed my reflection. "And I made a fool of myself in front of him again. For the umpteenth time."

"What did you do?"

"Have you heard about the problems the film crew has had since they arrived in town? The smashed windshields and other stuff?"

"I heard about one smashed windshield."

"Well, it's happened twice, and the director had her phone stolen. Grayson and I think someone might be targeting the film crew for some reason. We arranged to get together to talk about it, to see if we can figure out who might be behind it, and I stupidly called it a date." The mere memory made my cheeks warm.

Shontelle seemed far more amused than sympathetic. She even let out a small laugh as she selected a silver dress off the rack.

"It was embarrassing!" I thrust the yellow dress at her. "This color is much better for you than me."

Shontelle put the silver dress back so she could check out the yellow one. "Was *he* embarrassed?"

"Well, no," I said, thinking back. "He seemed to think it was funny."

"Funny as in 'you're ridiculous' or funny as in 'you're cute and I want to kiss you'?"

"Shontelle!"

I glanced around to make sure no one could hear us. The last thing I needed was to have rumors floating around town about me and Grayson. That would only add to my awkwardness the next time I saw him. Although, there had been rumors about us in the past and I'd survived those.

Fortunately, Vera was still chatting with the other two customers, even though they'd long since paid for their purchases.

Shontelle was studying me closely, the dresses forgotten. "Oh my gosh, Sadie. He did want to kiss you!"

"No, he didn't!" I remembered the simmering look he'd given me at the grocery store. "But . . ."

Shontelle practically pounced on my last word. "But what?"

I sorted through the dresses on the rack without really seeing them. "There might have been a bit of a spark between us. Just a tiny one," I added quickly. "Nothing to get excited about."

Despite what I'd just said, Shontelle was almost brimming over with excitement. I thought she was about to hug me when Vera's voice floated across the store toward us.

"Is there anything I can help you with, ladies?" she asked as she headed our way.

Her two other customers had left and we were now alone with her.

"We're just browsing at the moment, thanks," I said, hoping she'd get the message and leave us on our own.

Of course my luck wasn't that good.

Vera eyed the burgundy dress Shontelle had taken off the rack. "Are you shopping for dresses for the engagement party?"

"Engagement party?" I echoed with confusion. I glanced at Shontelle, but she seemed as clueless as I was.

Something unsettling glittered in Vera's eyes as she smiled. "Surely you were the first to hear about your aunt's engagement," she said to me. "How long until she and Mr. Edmonds move?"

"Move?" The word was barely audible when it came out of my mouth.

I had trouble focusing on Vera's polished smile that didn't quite hide her underlying glee. The store started to spin around me and I tightened my grip on the clothes hanger in my hands.

"To Maine," Vera said. "I know Mr. Edmonds is eager to be closer to his children and grandchildren. So I expect they'll be going soon, won't they?"

Shontelle took the hanger out of my grasp and returned the dress to the rack. She put an arm around my shoulders and steered me toward the door.

"Sorry, we need to go," she said to Vera as she propelled me across the store.

"Give Gilda my best wishes," Vera called out to us as we rushed out the door, her sugary tone lacking any sincerity.

"It can't be true," I said, the words sounding as faint as I felt. It was as if a rug had been yanked out from beneath my feet.

"Of course it's not true," Shontelle said firmly. She hooked her arm through mine and hurried me along the sidewalk, away from Vera's store. "Gilda definitely would have told you."

"You're right," I said, my voice getting stronger. I stopped in my tracks. "Except . . . there is something she's been wanting to tell me." I turned toward Shontelle, sadness washing over me. "Aunt Gilda's moving away?"

Shontelle took hold of my arm again and forced me to resume walking. "Don't assume that everything Vera said was true."

"But what if it is?"

Before I'd moved to Shady Creek, I'd gone several years living hours away from Aunt Gilda, but I'd grown used to having her back in my life on a daily basis, and I didn't like the thought of losing that. An ache was already building in my chest at the prospect.

"You go straight to the salon and talk to Gilda," Shontelle said as we turned onto Sycamore Street. "You need to get the truth right from the source before you start worrying."

It was too late for that, because my worrying was well underway, but I knew Shontelle was right—I needed to talk to Aunt Gilda as soon as possible.

"But what about our masquerade dresses?" I asked. "I don't want to set foot in Vera's shop again if I can help it."

"I didn't really like anything she had, anyway," Shontelle said. "How about we drive to Manchester on Monday? I know some great shops we can check out."

"That sounds good." The only reason my voice lacked any

enthusiasm was because I was still focused on the bombshell Vera had dropped on me.

We'd reached the corner of Hillview Road and Sycamore Street. I drew to a stop, but Shontelle gave me a nudge.

"Go straight to the salon, okay?" she said. "Everything will be fine."

I assured her I was heading right over to see Gilda. Most likely Shontelle was right and everything would be fine. Besides, if Aunt Gilda wanted to marry Louie and move to Maine, I should be happy for her. And I would be. I just didn't know if I could be happy for myself in those circumstances.

When I reached the salon, I didn't allow myself to hesitate. I pulled open the door and walked inside, the scents of shampoo and styling products greeting me.

"Morning, Sadie," Betty said with a smile as she hung up the phone at the counter. "Did you and Shontelle have a successful shopping trip?"

"No . . ."

Aunt Gilda was in the midst of sweeping up hair clippings. She smiled but then got a good look at my face as I trailed off. Her expression immediately sobered and she stopped sweeping.

"Oh no," she said with regret. "You heard, didn't you?"

Chapter 12

Betty's next client arrived before Aunt Gilda had a chance to say anything more, so she quickly finished up her sweeping and ushered me upstairs to her apartment, where we'd have some privacy.

"I'm so sorry, sweetie," she said as I dropped down onto her couch. "I didn't want you to hear about it from anyone but me." She sank into an armchair. "I should have known better. It's impossible to keep things under wraps in this town, but I didn't want to tell you the other day right after Marcie was killed."

"I understand," I assured her. And I did. I just wished Vera hadn't been the one to break the news to me. I summoned up a smile. "Congratulations. When's the big day?"

Momentary confusion registered on Aunt Gilda's face. "There's no wedding date because I haven't accepted Louie's proposal yet."

"You haven't?" A mixture of relief and surprise rushed through me. "Vera made it sound like you two were getting married and moving away in a heartbeat."

"You heard it from Vera Anderson?" She closed her eyes briefly. "I'm so sorry. That's like having salt rubbed in a wound. I bet she enjoyed springing the news on you."

"She sure did, but that's not your fault. But why did you turn Louie down?"

"I haven't. Not yet. He proposed to me over dinner at his place a few nights ago, but he didn't want an answer right away. He knows about your uncle Houston and how hard it was for me to lose him, so he didn't want to pressure me into making a decision. That was a relief, to be honest. I was so surprised that I wouldn't have been able to give him an answer right then."

I understood that. Aunt Gilda had married Houston when she was nineteen years old, and he'd died of a heart attack thirty-three years later. They'd been madly in love right up to the end, and his death had been a devastating shock to the whole family, but of course no more so than to Gilda. It had taken her years to find true happiness again. That didn't happen until she started her new life here in Shady Creek and opened her own salon.

"I understand about needing time. It's a big decision, especially since it would mean moving away from Shady Creek. Unless Vera got that part wrong too." I hoped she had.

"No, that part is true. Louie's been talking about moving to Maine for some time now. He's got a second grandchild on the way and he wants to be closer to his family so he can be more involved in their lives and see the grandkids grow up. I completely understand that."

"And he wants you to go with him."

"He does."

"And now that you've had some time to think about it?" I asked. "Have you made a decision?"

"No." Aunt Gilda folded her hands in her lap, twisting the ruby ring she wore on her right hand. "I can't leave Louie hanging much longer, but I need to be completely at peace with my decision, and I'm not there yet."

My heart ached for her. "If you need someone to talk to about it, you know where to find me."

She gave me a grateful smile. "I do. Thank you, honey."

I knew she had a client arriving any minute, so I got to my feet. She followed suit and pulled me into a hug.

"I want you to know that I'm not eager to move away from you. It's been such a treat having you so close again."

I returned her hug. "I don't want you to move away, but I do want you to be happy."

"Thank you, sweetheart." She kissed my cheek and then we headed downstairs so she could get back to work.

I didn't hang around the salon any longer. I had such a muddle of emotions swirling around inside of me. I truly did want Aunt Gilda to do whatever would make her the happiest, but I would miss her so much if she left. And it still irked me that Vera had taken such pleasure in blindsiding me with the news, even if it hadn't been completely accurate.

Unsure of what to do next, I plunked myself down on a bench on the village green. It was a gorgeous spring day, with plenty of sunshine and singing birds. The beauty that surrounded me helped to perk up my mood, although I still wouldn't have described myself as cheerful. I decided to try my best not to worry about Aunt Gilda leaving Shady Creek, especially since I didn't know if it would really happen.

Instead, I focused my thoughts on Marcie's murder. That didn't get me anywhere, though. I still had all the same questions and no answers to match. I used my phone to do a quick search for information about Marcie online, but I didn't find much beyond a few social media profiles, and those didn't give me any insight into her past, beyond where she'd attended school. I needed to talk to Eleanor. That wasn't a task I relished, but I didn't see how else to find out what she knew about Marcie's past.

Thoughts of Eleanor rushed out of my head when I noticed Grayson crossing the street toward me. Judging by the two takeout cups in his hand, I figured he'd just been to the Village Bean. I sat up straighter when I realized he was headed my way.

When he reached the bench, he offered me one of the cups. "Can I tempt you?"

"Always," I said, accepting the cup.

My cheeks seemed to realize what I'd said before the rest of me did. They were already warm when I gave myself a mental kick.

"Why do I always do that?" I hadn't meant to say the words out loud, but that was the way my day was going. I let out a deep sigh. "I'm forever embarrassing myself." At the last moment, I stopped myself from adding, "in front of you."

Grayson chuckled and the warm sound tickled over my skin and eased my humiliation.

"Relax," he said. "You really don't need to be embarrassed."

When I glanced his way I knew I wasn't imagining the heat in his gaze, but there was something else there too. Affection?

I took a gulp of my drink to cover up the fact that I was flustered anew. My eyes widened with surprise. I'd expected coffee, maybe with some cream or sugar in it, but instead there was a delicious explosion of mocha on my tongue.

"How did you know this is my favorite?" I asked with surprise.

Grayson grinned. "I have my sources."

I rolled my eyes. It wasn't the first time he'd fed me that vague response.

"You asked Nettie Jo, didn't you?" I guessed.

"You've got me all figured out."

"No," I countered. "Not yet."

When our eyes locked I had to clear my throat and look away. The strength of the attraction I was feeling between us was overwhelming and even a tad scary. After dealing with lies and betrayal from my ex-boyfriend, I'd told myself I wanted a good long break from dating. Grayson was making me have second thoughts about that plan. At the same time, my past experiences shouted at me to go slow.

My head was listening. My heart, not so much.

I took a long drink of my mocha latte.

"What had you looking so pensive when I first got here?" Grayson asked after taking a sip of his own coffee.

"Partly Marcie's murder."

"You haven't cracked the case yet?"

"I wish," I said.

"And the other part?"

I sighed. "Have you heard that Louie Edmonds asked Aunt Gilda to marry him?"

"No."

"Then you're probably the last person in Shady Creek to hear about it. And I was the second last. Well, I guess I tied with Shontelle."

"Gilda didn't tell you?" He sounded surprised.

"She was planning to."

Over the next couple of minutes, I spilled the entire story to him, right down to Vera Anderson dropping the bombshell on me and my selfish worry that Aunt Gilda would move away.

When I finished, I closed my eyes and tightened my grip on my takeout cup. "Sorry. You were probably looking for the CliffsNotes version, not the whole drama line by line."

"I don't want to be a CliffsNotes kind of guy when it comes to you, Sadie."

It took me a full three seconds to process his words. Then, when I looked into his blue eyes, I forgot what he'd said, but not what he'd meant. I could feel my heart beating right out to my fingertips. He rested a hand on my knee, the heat from his palm warming my skin through my jeans. Without thinking about it, I put a hand to his jaw, a day's worth of stubble rasping against my fingertips. He leaned closer and my heartbeat sped up while time seemed to slow around us. His lips brushed mine and my eyes closed.

A shriek cut through the air. My eyes flew open as I nearly jumped out of my skin.

A little girl dressed in bright pink from head to toe ran past our bench, letting out another ear-piercing squeal of happiness.

"Lily, come back here!" a woman shouted as she chased after the child.

With our moment shattered, I was suddenly all too aware of how close Grayson and I were and how visible we were to everyone and anyone who might look out over the village green. Not sure what to do now that awkwardness was spreading through me, I jumped up from the bench and checked my phone.

"Good Gandalf!" I couldn't believe how much time had passed since my chat with Aunt Gilda. "I'm supposed to open the Inkwell in five minutes."

I shoved my phone back into my purse and hooked the strap up over my shoulder. Grayson got up from the bench and stood facing me, close enough that my heart decided to go into overdrive again.

"Sadie . . ."

"I'd better go," I said in a rush. "Thanks for the latte!"

Like a terrified mouse, I scurried off across the green, over the footbridge, and into the Inkwell. As soon as I stopped to catch my breath, I regretted my actions. I shouldn't have run off like a coward. It was silly of me, and unfair to Grayson. I'd probably sent him completely the wrong message.

I dropped my purse on the nearest table and hurried back outside to look out over the green. Grayson was no longer in sight and three potential customers were on their way across the footbridge, coming my way.

With disappointment slowing my racing heartbeat, I flipped the sign on the Inkwell's front door and greeted my customers with a smile.

It wasn't until I'd been serving drinks and food for over an hour that I realized Grayson and I had never talked about the sabotage. If I hadn't hightailed it away from him, maybe we would have arranged another time to do so, but because of my cowardice I'd left us both hanging.

Maybe he'd still come by to talk about it this afternoon, as we'd originally planned, but I wasn't going to hold my breath. If he thought I hadn't enjoyed our kiss—or was it an almost-kiss?—would he ever want to see me again?

"Everything all right, Sadie?" Mel's voice startled me out of my thoughts.

"Yes, fine," I assured her.

She cast a dubious glance at the cocktail I was mixing. "Really? Because I think you just added four times the usual vodka to that Evil Stepmother."

I glanced down at what I was doing and realized I hadn't been paying any attention to how much of anything I was putting in the cocktail shaker.

"Shoot. You're right." I discarded the vodka-heavy drink and started fresh.

"What's going on?" Mel asked as she filled a pint glass with beer.

Beer that was brewed by Grayson. The man whose lips had touched mine far too briefly.

I could feel my cheeks getting warm and I was tempted to take a big gulp of the cocktail I'd just finished mixing.

"I've got a lot on my mind right now," I said.

That was an understatement. There was the murder, the vandalism, Aunt Gilda, Grayson . . .

"But I'm fine," I added. "I'll keep my mind on the job from now on."

I wasn't sure if I'd entirely convinced Mel, but she let the matter drop. I really needed to get it together, but my thoughts kept hopping around like a rabbit hyped up on espresso. Maybe I needed to talk things out with Shontelle. I realized I needed to get in touch with her anyway. There was a good chance that someone had seen me on the bench with Grayson, and if Shontelle didn't hear about it from me before somebody else spilled the beans, she'd probably never forgive me.

As soon as I had a minute to spare, I sent her a quick text message, telling her we needed to talk ASAP. After that, I did my best to focus on my work. I was successful enough that I didn't make any other errors.

By the time midafternoon rolled around, Shontelle still hadn't replied to my text. Most likely she had her hands full at the Treasure Chest. We'd had a busy lunch rush at the pub, but now things had settled down. I knew business would pick up again later, but that didn't help me right at the moment. Not having so much work to do had given my mind a chance to go back to overthinking Shady Creek's two current mysteries and what had happened between me and Grayson. Mostly the latter.

"I'm going to pop out for a bit," I told Mel, deciding I needed to take some action. "I'll try not to be more than an hour, but text me if you need me back here sooner."

"Take your time," she said. "We've probably got a couple of hours before we get busy again."

I was out the door a minute later, walking briskly as I cut across the green and made my way to the Shady Creek Museum. I'd never actually been inside the museum, but I thought I'd read somewhere that it was open for a few hours a day, several times a week. Eleanor had been at home earlier, but maybe by now she was at her beloved museum. That's what I was hoping, anyway.

When I arrived at the brick building that housed the museum in one half and the seniors' center in the other, I discovered that I was in luck. There was an OPEN sign on the door to the museum, so I went straight in.

I had to pause on the threshold while my eyes adjusted to the dimly lit interior. It was a stark contrast to the bright sunshine outside. Slowly, a rack of brochures took shape to my left and a counter to my right. I'd barely had a chance to realize someone was standing behind the counter when Eleanor spoke to me.

"Can I help you?" Her chilly tone was far from welcoming.

After I blinked a couple of times, I could see her well enough to observe that her expression wasn't any warmer than her words. She glared at me over the reading glasses perched on the end of her narrow nose, and her lips were pursed like she'd tasted something sour.

I smiled, hoping I could defrost her icy mood. "I was hoping to talk to you about Marcie Kent."

She stared at me for two seconds before responding. "Why would you want to talk to me about her?"

Apparently my friendly smile hadn't done the trick. She was as frosty as ever.

"Because you knew something about her, something about her past," I said. "And now that she's been murdered—"

"No!" The sharp word took me by surprise. "I'm not a suspect! Don't you even imply that I am!" Eleanor rushed out from behind the counter and pushed me toward the door.

"What are you doing?" I asked, completely stunned.

She shoved open the door and propelled me out onto the sidewalk with a hard push.

I stumbled and nearly lost my balance. "What in the world of Oz is wrong with you?"

"I won't have you tarnishing my reputation!" she fumed at me.

Before I had a chance to say anything more, she flipped the sign to CLOSED and slammed the door.

Clearly, I wouldn't be getting any information out of Eleanor Grimes.

Chapter 13

Returning to the Inkwell brought me another disappointment. Business had picked up and I saw several friendly faces among the small crowd, but as soon as I got behind the bar, Mel informed me that Grayson had come by in my absence. I wanted to kick myself for missing him. I should have stayed at the pub. Either he was hoping to meet up about the sabotage, as we'd originally planned, or he wanted to talk about . . . us. Whichever it was, I'd missed out. I hoped he wasn't annoyed with me.

I thought about texting him, but couldn't quite work up the nerve. So far most of our phone calls and occasional text messages had been primarily business related. I could always keep the message simple, saying, "Sorry I missed you," or something similar. I'd almost decided to go ahead and do that when a group of half a dozen tourists came into the pub, with a few locals on their heels. The influx of customers did away with any time I had for sending personal text messages and I happily got into the swing of mixing cocktails, pulling pints, and taking food orders.

It was well into the evening when I allowed myself to stop

for a moment and think about anything other than work. Shontelle came into the Inkwell and made a beeline for me as soon as she spotted me over by the bar.

"Sorry I didn't see your message for a few hours. The shop kept me busy all afternoon."

"No worries," I said. "Business has been brisk here for the past few hours too."

"Does that mean you're too busy to tell me why we need to talk? Is it about Gilda?"

"Only in part." I glanced around the pub. "Hmmm."

"You can't keep me in suspense, Sadie. Five minutes?"

"We might need more than five," I said.

"Okay, now you're killing me."

A bell dinged in the kitchen. Damien was busy taking care of a large drink order, so I knew I'd have to go fetch the meals Teagan had ready.

"Just give me a couple of minutes," I told Shontelle. "Then we can pop upstairs for a bit. I need to feed Wimsey anyway." I turned for the kitchen but then stopped. "Have you eaten? Can I get you anything?"

"I'd love a Red Cabbage of Courage."

"Coming up," I said as I pushed through the swinging door into the kitchen.

By the time I'd delivered the meals to hungry customers and had checked on a couple of other tables, Teagan had two salads ready and a side of fries for me and Shontelle to share. Damien didn't mind holding down the fort on his own for a short while, so Shontelle and I hurried upstairs to my apartment to eat our dinner and have a chat.

"No more suspense," Shontelle said as we set the food down on my kitchen table.

Wimsey meowed and rubbed up against my legs, but his dinner would have to wait another minute.

"Right." I took in a deep breath and my next words came out in a rush. "Grayson and I kind of sort of might have kissed."

"What?!" Shontelle stared at me, wide-eyed. Then she practically tackled me, throwing her arms around me and squeezing hard. "Sadie!"

Wimsey scampered out of the room.

"I can't breathe!" I gasped as my ribcage constricted.

Shontelle released me. "Sorry! But, Sadie! Oh my gosh! That's fantastic!" She paused and studied my face, worry clouding her expression. "It is fantastic, right?"

"I think so?"

"You don't sound very sure." She pulled a chair out from the table and pointed to it. "Sit and tell me everything."

I did as requested, starting with my visit with Aunt Gilda and then moving on to Grayson finding me on the bench. I managed to eat a few fries as I filled Shontelle in, but I talked far more than I ate. When I reached the part where Grayson and I had kissed—or sort of kissed—we both forgot all about the food on the table.

Shontelle was hanging on my every word, but then I wrapped up my account by telling her how I'd basically run away from Grayson.

"I'm such a coward," I said morosely, before chomping down on a French fry. "And then he came by the pub when I wasn't here. What if he regrets our kiss? Almost kiss. Sort of kiss. I don't even know what to call it!"

"Sounds like it was a near-miss kiss."

I almost cracked a smile at that.

"And I doubt he regrets it," Shontelle added. "He came by to see you. If he'd regretted it, he'd probably be avoiding you."

"What if he thinks I'm avoiding him?"

"Make sure he doesn't think that. Talk to him."

I groaned and dropped my face into my hands.

"This is a good thing, isn't it?" Shontelle asked.

I raised my head. "If I don't mess it up."

"You won't." She pointed a fry at me. "Talk. To. Him."

I promised her that I would, and then we shifted our conversation to Aunt Gilda while I fed Wimsey. By the time Shontelle left the Inkwell, I was still preoccupied by thoughts of Grayson and Gilda, but I'd come to two conclusions: I had no control over whether Aunt Gilda would stay in Shady Creek or move away, but I could take the reins and make the next move in my relationship with Grayson. Even if I didn't quite know where that move would take us.

I barely made it through a slice of toast the next morning when I sat down to breakfast. The night before, I'd sent Grayson a text message, saying I was sorry I'd missed him when he'd come by the Inkwell. He'd responded almost right away, saying he was sorry too and he hoped he'd see me soon. That had eased my concern that he might have regretted our almost-kiss. It had also given me the courage to ask if it was okay for me to stop by the brewery the next day, which was now today.

I'm looking forward to it, had been his reply.

My original plan was to walk over to the Spirit Hill Brewery around midmorning. The Inkwell didn't open until noon and Aunt Gilda had texted me to cancel our lunch date, so my schedule was clear for the next while. There was a murder to solve, of course, but at the moment I wasn't quite sure what step to take next in that regard. And now that I was awake and dressed, I decided I needed to change my plan. Nervousness swirled around inside of me, robbing me of my appetite and distracting me so much that I couldn't focus on reading *Midnight's Shadow* while I ate my toast.

It was pointless to try to concentrate on anything. I needed to get over to the brewery so I could see Grayson and, hopefully, put an end to the nervous whirling in my stomach.

I made the trip to the brewery on foot. Although Grayson

was my next-door neighbor, it took a few minutes to follow the long driveway that led up the wooded hillside. When I reached the fork in the driveway, I hesitated, wondering where I'd most likely find Grayson. His house was off to the right, while the brewery's buildings were up ahead.

In the end, I kept going straight, figuring he'd most likely been up and working at the brewery for a while already. I'd seen him out on an early morning jog with his dog, Bowie, on occasion, usually through my window while I was still in my pajamas, so I knew he tended to be up and about long before I was ready to start my day.

My guess turned out to be a good one. As I crossed the brewery's parking lot, I spotted Grayson emerging from one of the buildings, heading for the smaller structure that housed the offices. My steps faltered when he noticed me, but even from a distance I could see the grin that appeared on his face. Butterflies danced in my stomach, but they were fueled by excitement more than nervousness.

"Sadie," he said as he approached, and the warmth in his voice increased the fluttering of my butterflies.

He was about to say something more when I blurted out, "I came to apologize."

"Apologize?" He seemed genuinely surprised. "What for?"

"Running off yesterday after . . ." I couldn't bring myself to finish the sentence.

The reappearance of his grin brought me a rush of relief. "Don't worry about it. As long as we're okay." He held my gaze. "Are we?"

"Very much so," I said before I had a chance to second-guess myself.

"In that case," he said, "will you have dinner with me on Tuesday?"

"I'd love that." I could feel shyness threatening to take over me, so I quickly changed the subject. "I was wondering if you could help me with something."

"I'll try my best," he said.

I hadn't planned to ask him for help with my investigation, but I realized now that he was the perfect person to assist me. At least, I hoped he was.

"Before Marcie was killed, Eleanor Grimes insinuated that there was something shady about her past. I tried asking Eleanor about it, but she literally pushed me out of the museum and slammed the door in my face."

His forehead furrowed. "Eleanor's not known for having a friendly disposition, but that seems extreme even for her."

"Right? She really didn't want me implying that she was a suspect. Maybe because she's guilty?"

"Of murder?" Grayson didn't sound convinced. "It's hard to imagine her getting the upper hand in a struggle with someone less than half her age. Unless Marcie had some health or mobility issues?"

I remembered that he'd never met her. "Aside from suffering from migraines, she seemed healthy. She was in her late twenties, I think. Eleanor's got to be at least seventy."

"Exactly. It seems unlikely."

"It does," I agreed. "But I noticed that Eleanor has scratches on her arms."

"From a struggle?"

"Could be."

He still didn't seem convinced, but that didn't worry me.

"She's not the strongest suspect," I conceded. "But I still want to know what she found out about Marcie's past. It could be important, even if Eleanor's not the killer. And I don't want to upset Linnea by asking her. I'm not even sure she knew what Eleanor was referring to. So that's where you come in."

Grayson raised an eyebrow. "Oh?"

"Since you used to be a private investigator, I was hoping you might know how to find out about someone's past." I waited eagerly for his reply.

"Google is always a good start, but I'm guessing you already tried that." There was a hint of a teasing tone beneath his words, but I didn't mind.

"I couldn't find anything helpful. Just some social media profiles and a couple of mentions of her name in relation to Linnea."

I waited as Grayson studied me. I didn't know what he was thinking, and that brought my nerves back to the surface, making me eager to fill the silence.

"You know how to check someone out, right?" When I realized what I'd said, I slapped my hands to my face. "That came out wrong."

Grayson laughed and tugged my hands away from my face. "Yes, I do. And yes, I will."

"Really?"

He kept hold of one of my hands and took a step closer to me. "Sadie . . ."

I held my breath, wondering what he'd say next, but the sound of running footsteps interrupted us, wrenching our attention away from each other.

Annalisa, the brewery's receptionist, ran toward us from the direction of the offices.

"Mr. Blake!" She came to an abrupt stop when she reached us, pressing a hand to her chest as she gasped for breath. A few strands of blond hair had come loose from her French braid.

"What's wrong?" Grayson asked as my hand slipped out of his.

"It's Ms. Lo from the film crew," Annalisa said between breaths. "She's gone missing!"

Chapter 14

"Where and when did you last see Olivia?" Grayson asked Alex and Evan.

We'd gathered in the small reception area of the building that housed the brewery's offices. Annalisa was behind her desk, trying to reach Olivia by phone for the third time since Alex and Evan had realized that she'd gone missing.

"We were inside the main building, getting ready to film a couple of the workers doing their thing," Alex replied. "Olivia said she needed to make a phone call, so she stepped outside."

"That's the last we saw of her," Evan added.

Alex shoved his hands in the pockets of his jeans. "I went outside to see what was taking her so long, but she'd disappeared. I looked around, called her name, tried phoning her. Nothing. I called Jules too. He's at the coffee shop. He hasn't seen or heard from Olivia in more than an hour."

When Grayson glanced Annalisa's way, she shook her head, letting him know that the third call had gone straight to voice-mail, just like the previous ones.

"Did you all drive up here in the same car?" Grayson asked.

Alex nodded. "And it's still in the parking lot. I've got the keys."

Grayson pulled out his cell phone. "I'm going to call my head of security. He can check the surveillance footage and see where Olivia went once she got outside."

Grayson moved into a corner of the room as he spoke into his phone.

"This totally isn't like her," Alex said. "She's such a stickler for being on schedule, and now we're half an hour late getting started on today's filming."

"Maybe she cracked," Evan said.

Alex shot him a dirty look.

Evan shrugged. "She's been freaking out about everything that's been happening, and you know she's worried about getting the ax."

"She didn't crack," Alex said, steadfast in his opinion.

"She's worried about losing her job?" I asked. "Why?"

"This is her first episode as director," Alex explained. "The last director got fired, so Olivia's worried that if things don't go smoothly, she'll look bad and get fired too."

"Even though the vandalism isn't her fault?" I said.

Alex ran a hand through his dark hair. "She shouldn't be so worried. We've almost got all the footage we need and, like you said, the smashed windshields and stuff aren't her fault. Besides, even though she's been stressed out about the problems we've had, Olivia's got it way more together than our last director."

"What was wrong with the last one?" I asked, ever curious.

Evan pointed a finger to his head and made a circle.

Grayson ended his call and rejoined us in the middle of the reception area. "Jason, the brewery's head of security, is on his way over here. He'll check out the surveillance footage as soon as he gets here. In the meantime, maybe we should spread out and have a look around."

Olivia's crewmates agreed to that plan and headed out the door with Grayson. I followed after them, wanting to help out. We split up so we could check the perimeter of all the buildings. If Olivia had gone inside one of them, Jason would likely see that on the surveillance footage and let Grayson know. For the time being, we decided to search outdoors, although Grayson let some of his workers know to be on the lookout for Olivia inside as well.

I hoped she wasn't having a breakdown like Evan had suggested, though she had seemed stressed on all the occasions I'd seen her. I wondered if she suffered from any health problems. Maybe she'd passed out somewhere.

Worried she could be in need of medical assistance, I picked up my pace as I walked around the outside of one of the buildings. As I kept my eyes peeled for any sign of Olivia, I realized I didn't know what was inside the structure I was circling. I'd lived next door to the brewery for more than half a year now, but I'd never taken a tour of the facility, even though they were available for visitors most days of the week. I'd have to remedy that sometime soon, I decided. Even though I owned a pub, I'd never seen the inner workings of a brewery before.

As I completed my circuit of the building, I found Grayson standing outside a large door, currently shut.

"No luck?" I guessed.

"No." He nodded at the door. "This is where she came out. I don't know where she would have gone, if not to the car. Annalisa already checked the women's washroom and the staff washrooms, but they were all empty."

I was about to ask how long it would take for Jason to get a look at the security footage when I froze. "Did you hear that?" I asked.

"Hear what?"

I kept still, straining to hear anything other than the birds in the trees at the edge of the property. I'd almost concluded that

I'd imagined the distant thudding when I heard it again. Grayson's gaze snapped to his right, and I knew he'd heard it too. A second later, a muffled, desperate voice joined the thudding.

"Is it coming from that shed?" I pointed to a small building near the tree line, with a tractor mower parked in front of its door.

Grayson broke into a jog, heading for the shed. I followed hot on his heels. As we got closer, and I could hear the voice better through the pounding, I realized it was a woman calling for help. And she didn't sound happy.

"Olivia?" Grayson called as we reached the shed.

"Oh, thank God!" The thudding stopped. "Get me out of here!"

"Hold on," Grayson said, already releasing the brake on the tractor mower. Someone had parked it so close to the shed that the door wouldn't open.

I helped Grayson push the mower out of the way. The shed door burst open and Olivia stumbled out into the open, blinking against the daylight. Her fashionable clothes were rumpled and dirty, and her hair was messy.

"Are you all right?" Grayson asked as he reset the parking brake on the mower.

Olivia glared at the machine. "Is that what was blocking the door?" She didn't wait for confirmation. "Who's behind this?" Her voice rose in pitch. "They could have killed me!"

"How did you end up in the shed?" I asked, wondering if she was exaggerating.

"I was just walking around, talking on my phone, when someone hit me hard from behind." She put a hand to the back of her head and winced as she touched her scalp. She checked her fingers, but fortunately there was no blood on them. "I didn't lose consciousness, but I was stunned. Someone dragged me into that shed and shut me in there." She glanced around. "Where's my phone? Oh no!" She rushed over to a phone that lay on the ground a few feet away. "Seriously? I'm going to strangle whoever did this!"

The phone's screen was smashed, as if someone had stomped on it. Olivia finally stopped talking, long enough for Grayson to get a chance to say something.

"Did you see who did this to you?"

"All I saw was someone in a black hoodie." She tried to make her phone work, with no results.

"I'll call an ambulance, and the police," Grayson said.

"I don't need an ambulance, but I do want to talk to the police. This has gone far enough!"

"That's for sure," I said. The saboteur's conduct was escalating in an alarming fashion.

Olivia ran her fingers through her hair. "Where are Alex and Evan? We need to get filming."

"I think you should get checked out by a doctor first," Grayson said as he woke up his phone. "You might have a concussion."

"I don't need a doctor. I just need to get this episode finished!"

Grayson exchanged a glance with me and then got on his phone. I wouldn't have called Olivia hysterical, but she was far from calm. Alex and Evan appeared and jogged over our way as soon as they spotted Olivia. I moved a few feet away as they converged on the director and she immediately repeated her story—and her rant—to her crewmates.

When Grayson finished his phone call, he came over to join me and checked his text messages.

"Jason's over in the office," he said. "He wants us to come take a look at the footage."

"Hopefully Olivia's attacker was caught on camera."

"They must have been," Grayson said. "We've got cameras all around this place. Whether we can identify him or her might be another story."

Alex and Evan were up to speed now, so Grayson suggested we all head back over to the offices. Olivia assured us that she was fine to walk over there under her own steam. She certainly didn't seem any worse for wear, aside from her rumpled appearance and stoked temper.

Jason was waiting for us in the reception area. I'd met him on a few previous occasions so I needed no introduction. The first time we'd crossed paths, he'd escorted me off the brewery's property at Grayson's request. That was back when Grayson and I weren't exactly on the best of terms. Jason was a big and imposing man, standing well over six feet tall, with muscles that looked like they were made from steel. Nobody with any sense would mess with him.

"Are you all right, ma'am?" he asked Olivia. "I saw what happened on the surveillance video. That was a nasty hit to your head."

"I'm fine," Olivia said impatiently. "Did you see who attacked me?"

"Come take a look." Jason led the way into one of the offices.

Several screens were mounted on one wall, each one displaying a different part of the brewery. Jason headed for what looked like the control center. He tapped a few buttons and then pointed at one of the screens. It showed a static view of the area around the shed where we'd found Olivia.

"Watch this," Jason said.

He hit a button and the video played. At first no one was in sight, but then Olivia walked into view, holding her phone to her ear. She turned around, ready to pace back the way she'd come, when another figure darted into frame and whacked Olivia on the back of the head with what looked like a short piece of two-by-four. I winced as the footage showed Olivia crumple to the ground, her phone skittering out of her hand.

"But who is it?" Olivia demanded, still impatient. "It looks like a woman, but the hood is hiding her face."

"Just wait a moment," Jason advised.

Olivia let out a huff, but otherwise stayed quiet.

The hooded figure stomped on the fallen phone before grabbing Olivia's legs and dragging her through the shed's large door. A moment later, the attacker reappeared, pushing the tractor mower out into the open. After slamming the door, the figure maneuvered the mower into place to block the door. It didn't look easy, but the big machine was soon in place.

Olivia's attacker set the brake on the tractor and then spun around. The sweatshirt's hood fell back, briefly revealing the woman's face and long blond hair, before she yanked it back up over her head and sprinted away.

"I don't believe it!" Olivia said, staring at the screen.

Jason backed up the footage and froze the frame that showed the woman's face.

Alex swore as he took a step closer to the screen.

I was almost as surprised as Alex and Olivia.

"You know who that is?" Grayson asked them.

"I told you she was crazy," Evan muttered.

"Wait." I put two and two together. "You mean that's the director that got fired?"

Olivia's hands balled into fists, her gaze still fixed on the screen. "I'm going to wring her skinny little neck."

"She's the one who got fired," Alex said in answer to my question.

Olivia had completely ignored me.

"What's her name?" Grayson asked.

"Tiffany Clearwater." Alex shook his head. "I can't believe she'd do this."

"I can," Evan said.

"Where is she now?" Olivia shot the question at Jason. "Where did she go?"

"She took off down the driveway," he replied. "That was nearly half an hour ago now."

"Great!" Olivia fumed. "She'll be long gone. How will the police find her?"

"I know where they can look," I said.

All eyes turned to me.

"You've seen her before?" Grayson asked.

"A couple of times," I said. "She's staying at the Shady Creek Manor."

Chapter 15

Sirens wailed in the distance as I left the building. Olivia and her colleagues stayed inside to wait for the police, but Grayson followed me out the door. The sirens cut off and I figured the emergency vehicles were on their way up the driveway. A second later, the sound of rumbling engines confirmed that.

"Sadie," Grayson called as I hurried away, "Tiffany's dangerous. Leave it to the police to confront her."

"I will," I said over my shoulder.

A glance in that same direction gave me a glimpse of the suspicion in Grayson's eyes. I sent him a quick wave and darted across the driveway just before a police cruiser crested the hill. An ambulance wasn't far behind. I glanced back again. Grayson was still watching me, but he'd stopped to meet the two police officers who were now climbing out of the cruiser. I picked up my pace and continued down the drive.

I half walked and half jogged all the way over to my car in the Inkwell's parking lot. When I turned my car out onto the road, I had second thoughts. Grayson was right—Tiffany was dangerous. She'd proven that by attacking Olivia. I didn't have any intention of confronting her, though, so I figured I wasn't being too foolhardy. All I wanted to do was make sure that Tiffany was still at the manor. If she was, maybe the Honeywells and I could keep an eye out so we'd know if she tried to leave town. Hopefully the police would arrive before she'd get a chance to flee.

The truth was that I was glad to have an excuse to go back to the manor. Brad Honeywell still held the dubious honor of sitting at the top of my suspect list, and I wanted to see what I could find out about him. I also wondered if Tiffany belonged on the list. I didn't know why she would have wanted to kill Marcie, but she clearly had anger issues. Maybe she'd lashed out at Marcie on the spur of the moment. Her attack on Olivia proved that she was capable of violence. I figured it was at least worth looking into her as a suspect.

When I turned into the manor's long driveway, I wasn't able to enjoy the beautiful surroundings as much as I had on previous trips. I was too preoccupied to appreciate Judson's work in the gardens and I didn't bother to roll down the window to catch the scent of flowers in the air. The closer I got to the manor, the more nervous I became.

Maybe I should have waited for the police to approach the hotel first.

As I pulled my car into a free space in the parking lot, I saw that my concerns about Tiffany making a run for it were valid. Through my rearview mirror, I watched as she rolled a suitcase across the lot until she reached a silver sedan. She opened the trunk and hoisted the suitcase into it. She wore the oversized sunglasses I'd seen her in before and she'd ditched her all-black outfit for skinny jeans, a flowy blue top, and a white cardigan.

I gripped the steering wheel, wondering what I should do. I had no desire to confront Tiffany and put myself in danger of being on the receiving end of her violent temper. Maybe I could follow her car at a discreet distance so I could contact the police and let them know where she was heading. I'd almost decided on that course of action when I realized I wouldn't have to do anything.

A police cruiser turned into the manor's driveway, its lights flashing but its siren shut off. A second cruiser followed right behind it. I relaxed my grip on the steering wheel, relief washing over me. I almost got out of the car, but then I told myself it would be smarter to stay put. Who knew how Tiffany would react when she realized the police had come for her.

I continued to watch Tiffany in the rearview mirror. She slammed the trunk shut and only then did she notice the police cruisers heading her way. She froze for a split second before making a dash for the driver's-side door. She yanked it open, but then the lead cruiser switched on its siren for a few seconds. The sound made her freeze again.

The first of the two police vehicles pulled into the lot and stopped, blocking the exit. Tiffany took two steps back from her car, looking this way and that, as if searching for an escape route. By then, three officers were converging on her.

I shifted in my seat so I could look out the back windshield. Tiffany didn't resist when Officer Eldon Howes placed her in handcuffs, but she clearly wasn't happy about it. I opened the car door and climbed out, figuring it was safe to do so now that the police had Tiffany under their control.

"She stole my job!" Tiffany shrieked as Officer Howes led her over to the nearest cruiser. "She deserved everything she got! They all did!"

Officer Howes spoke calmly to her as he placed a hand on her head and guided her into the back seat of the cruiser. Tiffany was still screaming when he shut the door, muffling her tirade. An unmarked car turned into the driveway and headed our way. The driver pulled the vehicle off to the side before stopping, leaving room for the cruisers to get past if needed. Detective Marquez climbed out of the car and joined the other police officers as they conferred next to the vehicle holding Tiffany.

I'd first met Detective Marquez when she'd led the investigation into the death of my ex-boyfriend back in the fall. Even though I knew she wouldn't want me meddling in her investigation, I was tempted to ask her if she thought Tiffany could be responsible for Marcie's death. I'd almost given in to that temptation when someone spoke from nearby, startling me.

"What's going on?"

I spun around to see Judson leaning on a spade as he watched the police.

"Is that one of the guests they've got in the cruiser?" he asked.

"Yes," I replied. "Tiffany Clearwater. Do you know her?"

"I don't mix much with the guests," he said. "She's the killer?"

"I'm not sure. You know the *Craft Nation* film crew?"

"Sure. I heard they were in town."

"Tiffany assaulted the director," I explained. "Apparently *she* was the director before she got fired."

"This place is going crazy," Judson said with a shake of his head.

He left the spade sticking into the edge of a flower bed and tucked his work gloves into the back pocket of his jeans, coming over to join me by my car. We watched as Detective Marquez strode around to the front of the manor while the other officers got into their cruisers, turning the vehicles around so they could head off down the driveway.

"If she's violent, maybe she is the killer," he said as the cruisers turned out onto the road, disappearing from sight.

"Could be," I said.

Judson rubbed his wrist across his forehead before resting his hands on his hips. "Guess there's nothing more to see here. Might as well get back to work. See you later, Sadie."

"Later," I returned, already heading for the manor.

Maybe if I slipped quietly into the lobby I could overhear what Detective Marquez was saying. If she was saying anything.

It turned out I was too late. As I pulled open the front door, I came face-to-face with the detective, who was on her way out.

"Ms. Coleman," she said, a hint of suspicion evident in her voice. "What are you doing here?"

She probably thought I was there to snoop. Not that she was wrong.

I smiled, hoping I could allay her suspicions. "I came by to check on Linnea Bliss. Her book signing was at my pub the other day."

Her gaze remained sharp as she watched me pass, but she didn't object to me going into the lobby. I forced myself not to check over my shoulder until I heard the door shut. With the detective gone, I relaxed with relief, but then I quickly refocused. Although I was too late to overhear what Detective Marquez might have said to Gemma Honeywell, there was still a chance that I could do some investigating.

Gemma stood behind the reception desk, nervously fiddling with the earring in her right ear. When she saw me, she dropped her hand and smiled, but the expression didn't erase the stress that tightened her features.

"What can I help you with, Sadie?" she asked.

"I was wondering how Linnea's doing today," I said.

Gemma's forced smile faded away. "The poor woman. She went for a walk in the gardens earlier and she's resting now. It's probably best not to disturb her."

"That's fine," I assured her. "I don't want to bother her. I just wanted to see how she was holding up. Has she made any plans to head home?"

"From what I understand, her brother is coming up from Virginia the day after tomorrow. He'll stay overnight and then drive her home the next day."

"I'm glad she's got family coming." I leaned against the reception desk and lowered my voice, even though we were alone in the lobby. "I saw the police arresting Tiffany Clearwater out in the lot. Is she the one who killed Marcie?"

A pained expression crossed Gemma's face. "I can't believe all of this drama is happening here at the manor. It's terrible for business!" She closed her eyes briefly and seemed to gather herself together. "I'm sorry. That was an insensitive thing to say. Of course Ms. Kent has suffered far worse than what Brad and I are going through."

"It's understandable that you're worried about the manor," I said. "You worked hard to build it into what it is today."

She seemed relieved that I understood. "We really have."

"If the police have the killer now, things should settle down."

"But they don't have the killer," Gemma said. "They arrested Ms. Clearwater for some unrelated crime. The detective that was just here was asking if I knew Ms. Clearwater's whereabouts when Ms. Kent was killed. I thought I recalled that she'd scheduled a massage that day so I checked with our masseuse, and she confirmed that Ms. Clearwater was with her when all the commotion happened."

So there was no point in adding Tiffany to my suspect list. That avenue of investigation was a dead end, so I decided to head in a different direction.

"Did you and Mr. Honeywell know Marcie before she and Linnea came to stay at the manor?"

"No. Not at all." Her attention suddenly focused more sharply on me. "Why do you ask?"

I wasn't about to tell her that I suspected her husband of killing Marcie, so I quickly came up with a sort-of-fib. "I was curious about what Eleanor Grimes said."

Gemma sighed and rolled her eyes toward the ceiling. "That woman! She's been nothing but a pain lately. What did she say?"

"She insinuated that she knew something about Marcie's past, something not so good."

"I wouldn't put too much stock in anything Eleanor says, personally," Gemma said. "She's an unpleasant, spiteful woman, and I wouldn't put it past her to make things up."

The sound of high heels clicking against the marble floors drew our attention to the wide hallway leading toward the ballroom and dining room. A woman in a gray pencil skirt and cream silk blouse walked our way with brisk, purposeful steps, a tablet in one hand.

"Mrs. Honeywell?" she said, as she approached. "Could you join me in the ballroom? I have a few final details I'd like to go over with you."

"Of course," Gemma said. To me, she explained, "The decorator for the masquerade."

Without another word, Gemma hurried out from behind the reception desk and fell into step with the decorator, disappearing down the hallway.

I drummed my fingers on the reception desk, thinking over what Gemma had told me. I didn't know Eleanor well enough to judge if it was a real possibility that she'd lie about knowing something about Marcie's past, so I wasn't ready to give up on trying to ferret out that information. As for Brad Honeywell, he was still my number one suspect. I thought Gemma had told me the truth when she said that she and her husband hadn't known Marcie before she arrived at the hotel, but it was possible that Brad did know Marcie, and Gemma simply hadn't been aware of that. Even if he hadn't known Marcie before she arrived in Shady Creek, something had happened between them to cause the argument I'd witnessed. If only I'd heard more of what they'd said to each other that day.

Instead of leaving the manor and getting back into my car, I wandered deeper into the hotel. I'd eliminated Tiffany as a suspect in Marcie's murder, but other than that I hadn't accomplished much of anything since my arrival. I didn't want to go home without more information if it was at all possible to find some.

I walked quietly along the marble-floored hallway, not wanting to draw attention to myself. As I passed the ballroom, I took a quick peek inside. Gemma was deep in conversation with the decorator. Neither of them noticed me as I continued along the hallway.

When I reached a set of double doors at the end of the corridor, I ignored the sign that said STAFF ONLY, and quietly slipped through them. As soon as I was on the other side, I could hear voices, pots clanging, and sizzling. Delicious cooking smells wafted toward me, and I let my nose and ears guide me to the kitchen.

The double swinging doors separating the kitchen from the corridor had a round window on each side, so I was able to get a look inside without opening the doors. I hadn't planned on interrupting the kitchen staff, but someone caught sight of me peering through the window. For a split second I wondered if I was about to get in trouble for sneaking around this part of the hotel, but my worries faded in a flash when I realized it was Gina who had spotted me.

She smiled at me and then spoke to someone I couldn't see. A moment later, she hurried toward the doors. I stepped back as she emerged from the kitchen.

"Hey, Sadie." Gina was dressed in a white chef's jacket with a black collar and cuffs. A matching hat covered her head. "What are you doing here?"

She asked the question with a smile and without a hint of accusation in her voice, so I knew she wasn't about to turn me in.

"Snooping," I admitted.

Gina's smile brightened. "I've heard that you're an amateur sleuth."

"That sounds better than nosy parker," I said. A certain blue-eyed craft brewer had called me that in the past.

Gina laughed. "Hey, if it gets results . . ."

"I don't think I'm getting any results at the moment," I confessed. "I'm not even sure what I was hoping to find back here."

"Well, if you want to find out what really goes on in a hotel, who better to talk to than the staff?" She lowered her voice. "The Honeywells might own the place, but we employees tend to know the gossip."

"And what's the gossip lately?" I asked, intrigued.

She kept her voice low. "Lillian, one of the waitresses, has a thing for the gardener, Judson. She flirts *shamelessly* with him. She's ticked off because she thinks Connie from housekeeping has a thing for him too. But Connie's married, and I personally think she's just friends with Judson." Gina's smile reappeared. "But something tells me that's not the gossip you're after."

"Not exactly," I said. "Have you heard anything about Marcie Kent, the woman who died? Or maybe Mr. Honeywell?"

"Funny you should ask. I did hear something a few days ago about both of them."

That caught my attention.

"Tamara works in the kitchen with me, but she's not here today," Gina continued. "Anyway, she told me she overheard the two of them arguing."

"Do you know what the argument was about?" I was trying not to get too excited, but I was failing miserably.

"Tamara said it sounded like they'd known each other in the past, but Mr. Honeywell had forgotten. When Marcie reminded him, he was asking her not to tell anyone."

"Did Tamara get any sense of *how* they'd known each other in the past?" I asked.

"I don't think so, and once they saw her, they took the conversation outside."

That must have been when I'd arrived in the parking lot on the day I'd come to meet Linnea. Assuming Brad and Marcie hadn't had multiple arguments.

Gina lowered her voice further, whispering now. "I wondered if maybe they'd had an affair. Marcie was almost half his age, but that doesn't make it impossible."

"No, it doesn't," I agreed. I was wondering the same thing.

"Tamara didn't think that was it, though," Gina said. "She said she didn't get that vibe and plus, Mr. Honeywell didn't remember her at first. If they'd had an affair, you'd think he would have recognized her."

"Gina!" a man's voice called from the kitchen.

Her eyes widened. "Sorry. I'd better get back to work. Good luck with your snooping!"

She pushed through the kitchen doors and disappeared.

I heard footsteps approaching from the other side of the doors marked STAFF ONLY. I didn't want to get caught where I wasn't supposed to be, in case the Honeywells banned me from coming back.

Fortunately, an exit sign glowed red at the other end of the hallway. I made a dash for the door and slipped outside, making a clean getaway.

Chapter 16

I drew in a deep breath of fresh air as I stood outside the door at the back of the manor. Finally, I had a useful tidbit of information. Marcie and Brad had known each other in the past, in some capacity. Of course, I still didn't know the exact nature of their relationship, or whether it could have led to Brad pushing Marcie out the window. Maybe I hadn't made as much progress as I'd momentarily thought.

I was about to head for my car when I caught a whiff of cigarette smoke. A driveway curved around the manor and led to a service entrance where goods were likely delivered. Connie stood out on the driveway, dressed in her housekeeping uniform, smoking a cigarette. Instead of setting off for the parking lot, I walked over her way.

"Hey, Connie," I greeted. "On your break?"

"Yep." She shot a dark look at the cigarette between her fingers. "I've tried to give these things up, but I can't seem to kick the habit."

"I'm sure it's not easy." I stood back a few feet, not wanting to breathe in her secondhand smoke. "Any word on what's happening with the murder investigation?"

"Not that I've heard." Connie took a drag on her cigarette and let out a stream of smoke. "I sure hope the cops catch the killer soon. It's creepy working here knowing there could be a murderer among us. I keep looking over my shoulder, especially when I'm on my own cleaning the rooms. To be honest, the whole third floor gives me the heebie-jeebies now."

"I bet." I was glad I didn't have her job. I'd be expecting a killer to jump out from behind every piece of furniture. Of course, her job probably had some advantages, from a snooping perspective. "You must see and hear things while you're working. Any idea who the killer might be?"

"No, that's the problem. I find myself suspecting everyone. I consider some of the other staff my friends, but how well do I really know them? I've only been here a few weeks. The whole thing freaks me out." She shivered before taking another puff of her cigarette. "I'd quit but I need the money. My husband doesn't have a job at the moment."

"I'm sorry to hear that," I said.

She dropped her cigarette to the pavement and ground it under the toe of her shoe. "Thanks. We'll be all right."

"Did you notice anything unusual on the day of the murder?" I asked before she could tell me her break was over.

"Do you moonlight as a detective?" she asked with a touch of humor.

"I'm just curious," I said. "I'm really hoping the case will get solved soon."

"You and me both. But, no, I didn't notice anything strange. I didn't have much of a chance to. I was working with Mrs. Honeywell, sorting through all the linens."

"Was she there with you the whole time?"

"Hold on," Connie said with surprise. "You think Mrs. Honeywell might be the killer?"

"I think it could be almost anyone," I answered.

"Not her. She left me to do most of the work with the linens, but she was right outside the door the whole time, pacing up and down the hall, yapping away on her cell phone. Besides, I'm guessing the killer was a man."

"Why do you say that?" I asked.

Connie shrugged. "Marcie's room was on the second floor and the room she was pushed from was vacant, so what was she doing up there in the first place?"

"You think she was there to meet a man," I surmised. "But which man?"

"That's the million dollar question." Connie unwrapped a piece of gum and slipped it into her mouth. "Time to get back to work. See you around."

I barely had a chance to say goodbye before she disappeared into the manor.

Alone now, I stayed put, thinking over what Connie had said. Her theory made sense. It would explain why Marcie was in the room on the third floor when she'd told Linnea she was going to her room to rest. That could have been an excuse to cover up the fact that she was going to meet a man, one who didn't want to be seen entering or leaving Marcie's room. And if that man was Brad Honeywell, he would have had easy access to the vacant room. Marcie had been upset with Brad and had told him to stay away from her, but maybe she'd changed her tune later. If the two of them had a romantic history, it was possible.

It wouldn't be good to let that theory blind me, though. I had a hard time picturing Marcie agreeing to meet Brad alone after what I'd witnessed between them, and Tamara's impression was that they didn't have a romantic history. I couldn't discount the idea completely, but I also needed to consider other possibilities. Maybe she'd arranged to meet another man. Again, I was left with the question of whom. Someone who worked at the manor? Another guest?

I wasn't sure how to find the answer.

My stomach gave a rumble of hunger, distracting me. I checked my phone and decided I had time to squeeze in a quick trip to the dining room for a slice of Gina's heavenly chocolate mousse cake before heading home to open the pub. Some people might have considered it too early in the day to eat chocolate cake, but I didn't let that bother me. It was, as the saying went, five o'clock somewhere.

I decided to use the door Connie had disappeared through, hoping I'd be able to find my way to the dining room without getting lost in the back corridors. When I stepped inside, I found myself in a narrow hallway with closed doors on both sides. I hurried along, hoping not to get caught sneaking around, even if I wasn't snooping right at the moment.

The coast seemed clear until I rounded a corner and walked into view of someone coming down a stairway to my left. My heart skipped a beat, but it settled back into its normal rhythm when I realized it was Jan Finch, the plumber, not one of the Honeywells. She wore her typical outfit of jeans and a flannel shirt, but her usually tidy, cropped brown hair stood up in places, as if she'd run her hands through it a few times.

She seemed as startled by my presence as I'd been by hers, and she nearly lost her footing, grabbing the railing just in time.

"Hi," I said, pausing at the foot of the stairs. "It's Jan, right? I'm Sadie Coleman. I've seen you at my pub a few times."

Jan averted her eyes from mine and mumbled something I didn't catch before darting past me and hurrying toward the back door.

I watched her go, finding her behavior odd. It was as if I'd caught her when she didn't want to be seen. She was gone now, so I continued on my way to the dining room, but I couldn't help but wonder why she'd acted so shifty.

Shontelle and I had much better luck shopping for dresses in Manchester than we did in Shady Creek. There was no Vera to dampen my spirits, and we had far more dresses to choose from. Shontelle bought a gorgeous full-length dress in dark red, while I fell in love with a deep purple gown.

I tried on several dresses in green, black, and silver, but none of them felt or looked as right on me as the purple one. The pleated, A-line satin skirt reached down to the floor, and the shoulder straps and waistline were encrusted with sparkly faux diamonds. The same stones embellished the neckline and dipped down in a V to meet the gems at the waist.

As soon as I tried it on, I felt like a princess and knew I wouldn't be able to leave the store without buying it. It wasn't cheap, but fortunately it wasn't way out of my budget either.

At another store, we'd found masks to go with our dresses. Shontelle's was mostly black, with dark red accents and some sequins for sparkle. Mine was black and purple with a few feathers of the same colors. Shontelle bought a new pair of shoes to wear to the masquerade, but I managed to resist that temptation since I had a pair of heels at home that would go well with my gown.

"Just wait until Grayson sees you in that dress," Shontelle said as she drove us back toward Shady Creek after we'd eaten lunch at a Manchester restaurant.

"He won't be at the masquerade, remember?" I said. "He'll be out of town."

"He'll wish he'd been there, once he sees a picture of you."

"How would he see a picture of me?" I asked, suddenly suspicious. "I'm not going to show him one."

Shontelle smiled, her eyes on the road ahead of us. "There are always photos from the masquerade in the *Tribune* and on the newspaper's website. I'm sure Joey won't mind featuring you."

"*I* might mind," I said. I wasn't entirely sure if I wanted my picture in the paper. "Besides, I'm pretty sure the only woman Joey will want to feature in his photographs is Sofie Talbot."

"I've heard he's been spending a lot of time at the bakery."

"You heard right."

"Well, picture or no picture," Shontelle said, "at least you've got your dinner date with Grayson tomorrow. I'll need all the details, by the way."

"I'll fill you in," I promised.

"Maybe you should have bought another dress for your date. Do you have something to wear?"

"I have plenty of things to wear, but I'm not sure what to choose." This was something I'd thought about repeatedly, in between musings about Marcie's murder. "I don't know where we're going for dinner. Maybe I should ask. I don't want to be overdressed, but I also don't want to be underdressed."

Shontelle sent me a cheeky smile before returning her eyes to the road. "I don't think Grayson will mind if you're under-dressed."

"Shontelle! You know what I meant."

She laughed. "I do. Go with something that will work for Lumière, the manor, and the Harvest Grill. I doubt Grayson's going to take you to the pizza joint for your first date."

"You never know, but I think you're right. I've got that blue wrap dress."

"Perfect. It looks great on you. He'll love it."

"I hope so."

Shontelle glanced my way as we reached the outskirts of Shady Creek. "You're not nervous, are you?"

"Maybe just a little," I confessed. "I haven't been on a date in a while, and we both know how things turned out with my last relationship."

"Grayson isn't Eric."

"He isn't," I agreed. "And I'd like to think I'm a little wiser now."

"You are." Shontelle pulled up to the curb in front of the Inkwell. "And you can relax. Grayson's really into you already."

"You think so?" I asked, hoping she was right.

Shontelle rolled her eyes. "Of course! Those sparks between you have been flying both ways for months. I'm pretty sure he would have asked you out weeks ago if he didn't know what you'd been through in the past year."

Maybe that was true. After all, he did know that my ex had been murdered in October. We'd found Eric's body together, with the help of Grayson's dog, Bowie.

"But he also knows that I broke up with Eric long before the murder," I reminded her.

"Sure, and he knows Eric lied to you repeatedly, stole from you, and made you afraid to trust a man again," she added.

I thought she was getting carried away. "I'm not sure he knows all those details."

"Honey, we live in Shady Creek. The whole town knows."

I rested my head against the back of the seat. "Oh, great."

"Welcome to small town living."

"I might not even have to fill you in on the details," I grumbled. "You'll probably know everything before I do."

Shontelle laughed. "I still want to hear it all from you."

With another promise that she would, I gathered up my purchases and crossed the footbridge toward home, already wondering if I should change my mind about wearing the blue wrap dress.

After eating out several times in the past week—and indulging in two generous slices of chocolate mousse cake at the manor—I decided a late afternoon bike ride was in order. I retrieved my new bicycle from my equally new shed and strapped on my helmet. The shed, along with my old bike, had been destroyed by a fire back in the fall. Fortunately, my insurance had helped to cover the cost of rebuilding the small stone structure that matched the gristmill.

As soon as the snow had disappeared and spring had shown the first signs of arrival, I'd gone out and bought myself a new bicycle. I enjoyed taking peaceful bike rides around Shady Creek and I liked to make sure that I got some exercise on a somewhat regular basis. I'd managed to improve my strength and stamina over the winter, thanks to regular snowshoeing and the occasional trip to the town's outdoor ice rink, and I was hoping to continue that trend.

Shontelle and I hadn't arrived home until the middle of the afternoon, but I still had plenty of daylight left to get out and enjoy the spring weather. With any luck, the exercise would help to rid me of my pre-date nerves while also clearing my mind. My thoughts on Marcie's murder were so jumbled and muddled lately. Maybe getting some fresh air would untangle them. It was a long shot, but worth a try.

I decided to head south, so I hopped on my bike and set off around the village green. When I turned the corner onto Sycamore Street, I spotted Karidee sitting in the window of the coffee shop. I slowed down and waved. She had a laptop in front of her and was typing away furiously, so she didn't notice me. Giving up, I resumed pedaling, but slowed down again mere seconds later.

Grayson had just emerged from Aunt Gilda's salon, his hair freshly trimmed and stylishly tousled. Unlike Karidee, he noticed me right away and lifted a hand in greeting. I checked for traffic and waited for a car to pass by before hopping off my bike and walking it across the street to the sidewalk, where Grayson waited for me.

"Your hair looks great," I said when I reached him.

He ran a hand over it, tousling it even more. "Thanks to your aunt."

"She can work magic with hair," I acknowledged, "but yours always looks good."

Grayson reached out and touched the end of my braid where it rested over my shoulder. "So does yours."

My cheeks heated up a touch, not so much from the compliment but from the fact that I knew I looked far from my best with my bicycle helmet squashing my hair. Taking the helmet off would have been worse, though. That would have subjected him to the sight of a major case of helmet-hair.

"It was interesting," Grayson said, distracting me from my embarrassment.

"What was?" I asked, wondering if I'd missed something.

"Talking with your aunt."

The amusement in his eyes made me immediately suspicious. "Why? What did you talk about?" I feared I already knew.

"The brewery," he said. I relaxed until he added, "And you."

My apprehension returned in a flash. "Why were you talking about me?"

Grayson grinned. "Gilda was telling me some stories about you."

My eyes widened with alarm. "Which stories?"

"A few different ones."

He was being intentionally vague. The laughter in his blue eyes gave that away and alarmed me further.

"Which ones?" I demanded.

He took a step back, getting ready to leave. "About you when you were younger."

Oh, sweet Sherlock. That couldn't be good.

"I'll pick you up tomorrow at six," he said. "Does that work?"

The change of topic caught me off guard. "That works," I managed to say after struggling with my tongue for a moment.

"Great. I'm looking forward to it."

"Me too."

He treated me to a grin that stirred up butterflies in my stomach, and then he set off along the sidewalk, heading in the direction of the brewery.

"Which stories?" I called after him, realizing he'd successfully distracted me.

He didn't turn back to respond, but I heard his laughter as he walked away.

I tried not to worry too much about what Aunt Gilda had

told him, but it wasn't easy. There were far too many embarrassing stories she could have shared with him. There was that time I'd fallen into the river at Volunteer Landing, for starters. That was something my brothers had never let me live down. There was also that incident when I was eight and got my tongue stuck to the freezer when I licked at a frozen dribble of ice cream. Aunt Gilda had been the one to save me by pouring warm water over my tongue until it was free.

I cringed as more embarrassing events from my past replayed in my head while I cycled along a quiet country road. I was thinking of canceling my date with Grayson and moving to Antarctica when I noticed a sign by the entrance to a driveway up ahead.

HAPPY PAWS CAT SHELTER, the sign read.

I slowed to a stop and read the smaller print beneath the shelter's name. Sure enough, the sign confirmed that the property was home to the cat shelter run by Jan Finch.

I continued on my way a moment later, but the tone of my thoughts had changed. Now, instead of worrying about what Aunt Gilda had told Grayson, I was back to wondering why Jan had acted so shifty when I'd last seen her at the manor, and whether she had something to hide.

Chapter 17

I woke up the next morning with Aunt Gilda on my mind. No matter how hard I tried, I couldn't squelch the unsettled feeling that arose in my stomach every time I thought of her moving away. I worried that she might be feeling even more unsettled than I was, considering that the decision wasn't an easy one for her.

Maybe she'd made up her mind since I'd last spoken with her. I considered texting her to ask, but decided it was a question I'd rather put to her in person. I read a couple of chapters of *Midnight's Shadow* while I ate a bowl of oatmeal, so absorbed in the story that I was surprised when I tried to spoon up more oatmeal and realized my bowl was empty. After I tore myself away from the book, I brushed my teeth and decided to swing by the salon to see if Aunt Gilda had a few minutes to chat.

Wimsey followed me downstairs, streaking past me when I opened the back door. He slowed his pace once he was out on the grass, and sat down to gaze out over his kingdom, listening to the birds in the nearby trees. I left him to his feline pursuits and strolled across the footbridge, not in any hurry, enjoying the beautiful spring morning.

After crossing Creekside Road, I paused at the edge of the village green. A maypole had been set up and a group of school-kids was practicing a dance with the ribbons, under the watchful eye of their teacher. I recognized Shontelle's daughter, Kiandra, among the children. She was too intent on her dancing to notice me, and a moment later I moved on. I planned to watch the full performance on May Day.

When I arrived at the salon, I didn't end up going inside. I could see through the window that both Betty and Gilda were busy with clients, and two other women sat in the waiting area. Aunt Gilda was clearly too occupied for a private chat, so I decided to try again another time. As I was about to leave, Aunt Gilda caught sight of me through the window and waved. I smiled and returned the wave, but set off for home when she refocused on the woman in her chair.

Back at the Inkwell, I perched on a stool at the bar with a notebook and pen in front of me. I was hoping to add a new cocktail or two to the pub's menu in the upcoming weeks, and that meant I needed to do some brainstorming. I wanted to make a red and white layered cocktail that I could name The Cat in the Hat, but I wasn't sure yet which flavors to go with. The layers made it all the trickier, as I had to come up with ingredients with different specific gravities so they would sit one on top of the other, and yet they still had to taste good together.

I decided to make two lists to start: one of possible red ingredients and the other of white or clear ingredients. Under the red column, I added raspberry liqueur, cranberry juice, and grenadine. I tapped my pen against the page, my mind wandering.

Had Marcie really been up on the third floor of the manor to meet a man? And could that man have been Brad Honeywell?

I refocused on my notebook, writing gin, vodka, white crème de cacao, and cream of coconut in the white/clear column. I stared at what I had on the page so far, without feeling a single spark of inspiration. Shoving the book aside, I decided it was pointless to work on creating a drink while I was so distracted.

Maybe I could make another trip to Shady Creek Manor and find out more about Brad. Then again, maybe I could find out more about him from the comfort of home.

I spent the next while looking up Brad Honeywell on the Internet. By the time my eyes started to hurt from staring at the screen of my phone for so long, I hadn't found anything particularly interesting. I'd learned that Brad had worked for a large medical equipment sales company for fifteen years before he and Gemma bought the Vallencourt estate and turned it into the Shady Creek Manor. Prior to his time at the large corporation, he worked for two smaller companies and had received a business degree from George Mason University in Virginia. I also learned that he enjoyed playing squash and golf, but since Marcie hadn't been killed with a golf club or squash racquet, I didn't think that helped my investigation at all.

I did some cleaning to give my eyes a rest, making sure the pub was ready for customers. Then I returned to my phone and did another search, this time using Marcie's name. I didn't find anything different from the last time I'd looked her up. From what I could see online, Marcie had been a much-loved young woman with a passion for books and her job as Linnea's assistant.

Reading about Marcie online and seeing so many pictures of her made my chest ache with sadness. The tributes on her social media profiles were a testament to how much she was missed by so many. I put away my phone and blinked away the tears that were threatening to spill onto my cheeks. Whatever Eleanor knew about Marcie's past, the young woman hadn't deserved to be murdered, and I wished I could do something to help put her killer behind bars.

Any further investigating would have to wait, however. It

was time to open the pub, and work kept me busy for the next several hours.

By late afternoon, I couldn't ignore the bursts of nervousness and excitement that skittered through me as the clock ticked closer to six. Damien already knew I'd be taking the evening off, and Mel had offered to come in during the evening if the pub got extra busy and he needed a hand.

I gave myself enough time to get ready for my date, but not enough time to change my mind multiple times about my outfit. I stuck to my plan to wear my blue wrap dress, remembering to use a lint roller to remove the long white cat hairs that had a way of always finding my clothes.

I called Wimsey inside and fed him his dinner. He was contentedly gobbling up his food when I headed downstairs to wait for Grayson. Instead of cutting through the pub, I left through the back door. I didn't need the town gossiping about my date already. There'd be plenty of time for that later.

Grayson pulled up to the curb in his black sports car just as I rounded the corner of the gristmill. He climbed out of the car as I crossed the footbridge, and my heart gave a giddy skip in my chest when I took in the sight of him. He wore dark jeans and a blue button-down shirt that matched the color of his eyes. When he smiled at me, my heart skipped again.

"You look beautiful," he said as he opened the passenger door for me.

"Thank you. You look great too." I ducked into the car, hoping he wouldn't notice how my cheeks had turned pink at his compliment.

He rounded the car and slid into the driver's seat. "I need to make a quick stop to pick up our food."

"Where are we taking it to?" I asked, curious.

He gave me the familiar smile that told me he wasn't going to give away all his secrets. "There's a place I like to go for quiet time. I want to show it to you."

"I'm intrigued."

He pulled the car to a stop outside of Lumière. "I'll be back in just a moment."

He left the car idling and disappeared into the restaurant. True to his word, he wasn't gone long at all. When he returned, he tucked a large paper bag of food behind the seats before fastening his seat belt.

"The food smells amazing," I said as the delicious aromas filled the car.

My stomach rumbled. Quietly, thank goodness. I glanced Grayson's way, but he didn't seem to have noticed.

He turned into the brewery's driveway a few seconds later, surprising me. I didn't know where he planned to take me, but for some reason I'd thought it would be away from his property. We drove past his house and continued on to the parking lot by the brewery's buildings.

"You come to your brewery for quiet time?" I asked, puzzled. I wouldn't have thought he'd get any peace in the middle of his business.

"You'll see in a minute," he said, his enigmatic grin making a comeback.

When he parked the car, he hurried around it to offer me a hand as I climbed out of the passenger seat. We'd parked right next to one of the buildings, and Grayson opened a large door and held it for me. I stepped inside and found myself in a cavernous room with lots of stainless steel equipment. I thought I recognized a mash tun, but I couldn't put a name to anything else.

"I've been meaning to come for one of the tours of the brewery," I said, gazing around.

"I'm happy to give you one," Grayson offered. "Maybe after dinner?"

I caught another whiff of the food he held and agreed enthusiastically.

He led me to a set of metal stairs. "Careful on the steps," he cautioned.

He waited for me to precede him, so I held onto the railing and heeded his advice, taking care to stay steady on my high heels as I made my way up. The stairway led right up to the rafters and beyond. I paused on a landing and Grayson took the lead from there, ascending a narrow set of stairs that led up into a small hut-like structure that rose up higher than the rest of the roof.

When he opened the door at the top of the stairs, daylight filled the narrow space.

Grayson held the door open and offered me a hand up the last couple of steps. I took it without hesitation, trying not to be too distracted by the way my hand seemed to fit perfectly in his.

When I first stepped out onto the roof, all I saw were the treetops of the surrounding woodland. Then Grayson put a hand to my back and guided me around the hut we'd emerged from. As soon as we moved around the corner, my breath caught in my throat.

Ahead of us was a spectacular view of Shady Creek. The brewery's position on a hill gave us an incredible vantage point. I could see the village green, the shops that lined it, and much of the rest of the town as it spread out in three directions. The sun was just starting to get low in the western sky, but there was still plenty of daylight, allowing us to enjoy the view to its fullest.

"Wow! This is amazing," I said once I'd had a chance to take in the sight of the town below us.

"I was hoping you'd like it."

"I definitely do," I assured him.

Now that my initial surprise had worn off, I became more aware of our immediate surroundings. A table and two chairs had been set up on the roof, situated so we could enjoy the view while eating. Plates, cutlery, and glasses sat on the white tablecloth.

Grayson pulled out one of the chairs for me and I sat down, noticing a cooler next to the table. When Grayson lifted the lid, I saw that he'd stocked the cooler with ice, a bottle of wine, a bottle of water, and an opaque container.

He set to work unpacking the food while I poured us each a glass of white wine. My mouth watered when I caught a glimpse of the dishes he'd ordered.

"Those are my favorite," I said when he opened a carton of crispy shrimp.

Zucchini strips with dipping sauce followed, and then Grayson opened a container of seafood linguine and another of roasted vegetables.

"These are all my favorite dishes from Lumière," I said, my stomach threatening to let out a loud rumble.

Grayson smiled. "I know."

"But how . . ." I guessed the answer before I got the rest of the question out. "Gilda told you, didn't she?"

"She was very helpful."

I couldn't withstand the temptation of the delicious smells any longer. We both doled out food onto our plates, some from each dish, and I savored the crispy deliciousness of one shrimp before my mind kicked back in.

"That must have been when you got your hair cut," I said. "Was that all she told you about me? My favorite foods?"

I hoped that was the case. Unfortunately, that hope was dashed a second later when Grayson chuckled.

"No, that was only one small part of the conversation."

I speared a piece of zucchini with my fork. "And the rest?"

Grayson twirled linguine around his fork, his grin both charming and somewhat maddening. "She told me a couple of stories about your childhood."

I set down my fork. "Oh, Jeeves, help me." I took a drink of wine.

Grayson laughed again. "Don't worry. She just told me about how you always had your nose in a book when you were a kid."

"That's true." I set down my wineglass with a hint of relief.

"And that you never liked to be outdone by your brothers."

"Also true." I enjoyed a heavenly bite of linguine, feeling more at ease now.

"And then she showed me some pictures."

I nearly choked and had to take a big sip of wine before I could speak. "What pictures?" My voice came out sounding panicked.

Grayson's grin was definitely maddening this time. "Some of you and your brothers on family vacations."

Maybe that wasn't so bad.

"And one of you and your date for your senior prom," he added.

My stomach dropped. "She didn't."

"Was that dress seafoam green?" He tried to contain his grin, but failed miserably.

"She did," I said weakly. I rallied enough to attempt to defend myself. "I had a very short-lived fascination with seafoam green at that age. Don't we all have misguided phases as teens?"

"She couldn't remember the name of your date," he continued, ignoring my question and clearly enjoying the conversation far too much.

"It wasn't worth remembering," I said, cringing inwardly at the memory.

Wesley Lambert flirted with other girls at the prom, drank from a flask hidden inside his suit jacket, and then vomited on the gym floor, narrowly missing my shoes. We'd never spoken again after that night.

I was tempted to slide out of sight underneath the table. "What was Gilda thinking?"

"Don't be mad at her," Grayson said. "She likes talking about you because she loves you. And don't be embarrassed. You looked cute in all the pictures."

"I don't think anyone could look cute in that dress." I really didn't know what I'd been thinking back then.

"You did. Trust me."

Our gazes locked for a second before I averted my eyes, focusing on my plate.

"Wesley Lambert didn't seem to notice," I said, to break the charged silence that had fallen between us.

"I thought it wasn't worth remembering his name."

"It's not," I said emphatically. "I wish I could forget."

"For what it's worth, he must have been an idiot if he didn't appreciate you."

"He was an idiot," I said. "And thank you." I was about to dig my fork into my linguine when I paused. "Are we done with the teasing?"

"For now."

This time when Grayson grinned, I smiled back, suddenly not quite so bothered by his glimpse into my past.

Chapter 18

We spent the rest of dinner talking about less embarrassing subjects, like the pub and the brewery. When we'd cleared our plates of food and Grayson produced a covered dish, I assumed he'd bought dessert from Lumière as well as dinner. I soon saw that I was wrong.

"It might not be the right season for pumpkin pie," Grayson said as he uncovered a scrumptious-looking pie with a perfect golden crust. "But I know you enjoy it, so I thought I'd make one."

"It's always the right season for your pumpkin pie," I said, unable to take my eyes off the gorgeous dessert.

Grayson cut generous slices and topped them with whipped cream he'd stored in the cooler. We lapsed into comfortable silence as we started in on our desserts, and I savored every bite, enjoying the way the pumpkin filling and the whipped cream blended together perfectly. This was the third time I'd had a chance to sample Grayson's award-winning pumpkin pie, and I still couldn't get over how delicious it was. I didn't bother to ask him his secret this time. I knew from past experience that he wouldn't share his recipe with anyone. I didn't mind so much now, since he'd baked one for me twice.

We were halfway through our slices when Grayson spoke. "I looked into Marcie Kent's background last night."

I couldn't believe I'd temporarily forgotten about my request, but it only took a split second for my curiosity to re-awaken. "Did you find anything interesting?"

"Not really. It seemed she was an upstanding citizen, save for one incident."

"What kind of incident?"

"She was charged and convicted of trespassing six years ago. She'd broken up with her boyfriend and went back to his place to retrieve some belongings. They got into an argument and he called the police."

"That's all there was to it?"

"From what I can tell."

"Not exactly a dark, criminal past."

"No," Grayson agreed. "But it could be what Eleanor was hinting at."

"I can picture her blowing it out of proportion," I said. "But how can we be sure it wasn't something else?"

"We could ask Eleanor."

I set down my fork with a sigh, my plate now empty. "I doubt she'll talk to me. I think she believes I'm an undesirable addition to the town because I run a pub and she'd reinstate Prohibition if she could."

Grayson had finished his pie now as well. "She might talk to me."

"You brew beer," I pointed out. "Why would she like you any more than me?"

His easy smile sped up my heart rate. "I think I can win her over."

I reached for my nearly empty wineglass. "This I've got to see."

*   *   *

We stayed up on the roof long enough to watch streaks of orange and pink color the sky as the sun disappeared below the horizon. Grayson assured me that he'd clean everything up later, so we left our dishes behind and strolled down his driveway and into town. We'd decided to leave the brewery tour for another time so we could seek out Eleanor instead. Although the museum would have closed hours earlier, Grayson said that Eleanor was known for spending the vast majority of her time either in her garden or at the museum. Since dusk was falling over the town, she wasn't likely to be in her garden, but we decided to walk past her house to see if the lights were on. If they weren't, we'd swing by the museum to see if she was there.

Eleanor's front garden was as immaculately tidy as the last time I'd been past her house, but there was no sign of the woman herself and no lights shone through the front windows. We continued on toward the museum, talking about my other suspects.

"I'm sure Brad and Marcie had met before she and Linnea arrived at the manor," I said, after telling Grayson about the argument I'd overheard. "But I don't know how they knew each other."

"I could look into Brad's background, if you'd like," Grayson offered.

"Really? That would be great. I looked him up online, but all I really found was a bit about his education and employment history." An idea struck me. "Maybe you could teach me how to do your fancy background checks."

"Share all my secrets?" Grayson asked with a smile. "Then you wouldn't need me anymore."

I held my breath for a second, worried I might say something embarrassing like, "I'll always need you."

I was a little concerned that the thought had run through my head. It was far too early for any declarations of that sort, even if voiced only in my mind.

Well on my way to getting flustered, I switched my focus to my other suspect. "Do you know Jan Finch?"

"The plumber? She fixed a problem with my furnace last winter, but I haven't exchanged more than half a dozen words with her at any other time."

We stopped at a corner to wait for a car to drive past before we stepped into the intersection.

"Why?" Grayson asked. "Is she connected to Marcie somehow?"

"Not that I know of, but there's something odd about her." I told him how she'd seemed spooked when I saw her at the manor the other day. "And she was there the day Marcie died."

Grayson didn't give me his opinion on Jan as a potential suspect because we'd arrived at the museum. As we'd hoped, a light was on, although no one was visible through the front window.

I knocked on the door, without any real hope that Eleanor would tell us anything useful. I could admit—to myself, at least—that Grayson could be charming, but I wasn't sure Eleanor would be susceptible to anyone's charm.

Nobody responded to my knock. Maybe he wouldn't even get a chance to try to work his magic on her.

Grayson rapped on the door this time, announcing our presence more loudly. Several seconds passed, and I was about to give up when I spotted movement at the window. Eleanor peered out at us, her typical sour expression firmly in place. I smiled back at her, but her expression only grew more dour. She disappeared from sight, and for a moment I thought she'd leave us standing there on the doorstep, but then a lock clicked and the door opened a crack.

"The museum's closed," Eleanor said, glaring at us through the narrow opening.

"We were hoping to speak with you for a moment," I said before she could slam the door shut. "If it's not too much trouble."

"It is too much trouble," she grumbled. "I have boxes of documents to get sorted."

Grayson spoke up for the first time. "Mrs. Grimes, I'm Grayson Blake."

"I know who you are," she said before he could add anything further. "You run the brewery on Spirit Hill." She said the word "brewery" like it tasted bitter. "Feeding the depraved appetites of Shady Creek's morally feeble citizens."

I fought the bubble of laughter that tried to work its way out of me. Eleanor was so over-the-top with her disapproval that it verged on comical. Still, I knew that laughing at her would only get the door slammed in our faces.

"I hear you've written a book about Shady Creek," Grayson continued, unfazed by what Eleanor had said. "I know it's after museum hours, but I'm heading out of town tomorrow and I was really hoping to have a copy to read on my trip."

To my surprise, Eleanor's churlish expression eased slightly. "You're interested in the town's history?" Surprise laced her words.

"Absolutely," Grayson said, sounding completely sincere.

For all I knew, maybe he was being honest.

"You're not even from here." It sounded like an accusation.

Grayson wasn't the least bit bothered. "That's true. I wish I had a chance to grow up in this town, but I'm glad I've been able to make a life here as an adult. I know Shady Creek has a rich history, and I'd like to learn more about it."

I really couldn't tell if he was feeding her a load of donkey dust. He sounded so sincere. That ignited a flicker of worry inside of me. If he was lying to Eleanor so convincingly, how would I ever know if he was lying to me?

To my surprise, Eleanor stepped back and opened the door farther so we could enter the museum. I shoved my worries aside, realizing that Grayson was waiting for me to precede him through the door.

THE MALT IN OUR STARS   157

Eleanor crossed the creaking hardwood floors to a wire rack that held a selection of brochures and several copies of her book. She picked up one of the paperbacks and held it out to Grayson.

"Thirty dollars," she told him.

I raised my eyebrows at the price.

Eleanor must have noticed because she glared at me. "All profits go to the museum." It sounded like she was daring me to object.

"A very worthy cause." Grayson already had his wallet out.

When he handed over thirty dollars, she relinquished the copy of her book.

"There's information in there about Edwin Vallencourt and the history of Shady Creek Manor, right?" I asked.

"Chapter nine." Her response was grudging and I sensed she was about to dismiss us.

Pure curiosity spurred my next question. "Does it include anything about the hidden treasure?"

"Hidden treasure?" Grayson echoed.

"Some say Edwin hid valuables in the manor," I explained.

Eleanor scoffed. "Fanciful stories! My book is based on historical facts."

I couldn't help but wonder if she had a narrow view of what the facts were, but that wasn't my concern at the moment. "You were at the manor when Marcie Kent died, weren't you?" I hoped the question sounded casual rather than accusatory.

"You're bringing up that dreadful business again?" Eleanor sniffed. "I was not. I'm glad I left before it happened."

"You left? I thought maybe you'd hung around after talking to Linnea Bliss."

"What on earth for? Mrs. Honeywell treated me with utter disrespect. I didn't stay one minute longer. Besides, I had to get back to the thrift shop. I volunteer there every Wednesday. I am *not* a suspect, and I don't appreciate you insinuating otherwise. Now, if you'll excuse me . . ."

I wasn't ready to give up on my questioning. "The other day, Marcie suggested there was some incorrect information about Vallencourt in your book."

I nearly withered in the face of the icy glare she directed at me.

"What would she know about Shady Creek's history?" Eleanor asked. "This is *my* town. She was just a city girl."

The vitriol behind her response took me aback.

Grayson stepped into the conversation again. "And she didn't have the best reputation. So I heard, anyway."

"Darn right," Eleanor said. "She had a criminal past!"

"She had one conviction for trespassing," I said.

She whirled on me. "Isn't that enough?"

"I just don't think that made her a bad person."

"That doesn't surprise me," Eleanor grumbled. "You young people don't have any sense."

I was about to protest when Grayson jumped in.

"I'm sure you've done a great job of recounting the town's history." He held up the book. "I'm looking forward to reading this."

Eleanor harrumphed and I suddenly longed to be out in the fresh evening air, away from her bitterness.

"We won't trouble you any longer," Grayson said.

As eager as I was to leave, I had one more issue to address. Eleanor wore a short-sleeved blouse and the scratches I'd noticed on her arms the other day were still an angry shade of red.

"Those scratches look painful," I said. "What happened?"

She glanced at the scrapes. "I was cleaning up my rose garden. I usually wear long leather gloves to protect my arms from the thorns, but my neighbor's darn dog stole them. If that man doesn't replace them soon, I'm taking my complaint to the police."

She ushered us toward the door as she spoke and by the time she finished, we were out on the sidewalk.

"Don't bother me after hours again," she ordered.

The door slammed with a resounding thud.

I shook my head. "It must be terrible being so grumpy all the time."

"I'm glad you're my neighbor and not her," Grayson said.

"You and me both."

We started walking along the street, back the way we'd come.

"You were very convincing," I said, with a sidelong glance his way. Now that I wasn't in the midst of trying to get information out of Eleanor, the worry that had taken shape back in the museum loomed large in my mind.

"About my interest in Shady Creek's history?"

I nodded.

"That's because I really am interested. I can't say I like spending time with Eleanor, but I do plan to read her book."

Relief loosened the tension that had spread through my muscles. That made me realize how much I wanted to be able to trust him.

"What do you think about Eleanor as a suspect?" I asked.

"I think there must be stronger ones."

"Same. She's so concerned about morality and character that her mind would have to be incredibly twisted to believe she was living up to her own standard when murdering someone. And even though Marcie ticked Eleanor off by pointing out a possible error in her book, killing her couldn't have undone that accusation. I guess if Eleanor wanted pure revenge, she could have done it, but I still have trouble picturing her overpowering Marcie in a fight."

"It's not impossible, but unlikely," Grayson agreed.

"Plus, I believe what she said about the scratches on her arms."

"I think she was telling the truth about that too."

"Still," I said, "I won't take her name off the suspect list until I've checked her alibi. I have a friend who works at the thrift shop. She might be able to confirm if Eleanor was there when Marcie died."

"That would be good information to have," Grayson said.

We'd nearly arrived at the Inkwell. As we reached the footbridge, we slowed our pace.

"So you're heading out of town tomorrow?" I asked.

As if by some unspoken agreement, we both came to a stop in the middle of the bridge.

"First thing in the morning. I've got a lunch meeting in Boston. The first of several." Grayson leaned against the bridge railing.

The creek babbled below us and in the distance crickets chirped.

"Have a good trip," I said. "And thank you for dinner. I really enjoyed it."

"So did I." Grayson touched a hand to mine and moved closer.

My pulse quickened.

"Sadie, I want you to promise me something."

"What's that?" I asked, relieved that I didn't sound as breathless as I felt.

"That you'll be careful. You've tangled with killers twice now, and I don't even want to think about anything bad happening to you."

His concern for me warmed me on the inside.

"I don't plan to go looking for danger," I assured him.

"Sometimes it finds you anyway." He touched my cheek. "Promise me?"

It took a second for me to focus on what he'd said. I was too distracted by his touch.

"I promise," I said, the words coming out as a whisper.

Grayson leaned in and I closed my eyes, my heart skipping a beat in anticipation.

A burst of loud laughter sent my eyes flying open again.

Grayson pulled back, his gaze on something over my shoulder. I glanced that way and saw a group of four customers exiting the pub and coming our way. I scooted off the bridge so they could go past, Grayson following me.

"Have a good night," I called to the customers as they crossed the bridge.

They waved and continued on their way, their voices gradually growing quieter as they disappeared down the street.

For a second I thought Grayson and I might be able to recapture our interrupted moment, but then the pub's door opened again and two more patrons came out into the night.

Grayson took my hand and gave me a regretful smile. "Maybe we can have dinner again once I'm back in town."

"I'd like that."

The pub patrons passed us with smiles and wishes for us to have a good evening.

Once they were on their way across the bridge, Grayson gave my hand a squeeze. "See you soon then."

"Thanks again for dinner," I said.

He met my gaze. "It was my pleasure."

He gave me one last smile, this one not quite so regretful, before he set off down the darkened road.

Chapter 19

I phoned my friend Alma Potts soon after I got up in the morning. She'd worked the same shift as Eleanor at the charity shop on the previous Wednesday and confirmed that the other woman had indeed been present at the shop during the critical time frame. I tried not to let on that I was attempting to confirm an alibi, but I got the sense that Alma suspected what I was up to.

After overseeing a delivery of beer from Grayson's brewery, I had one more item on my morning's to-do list.

I cut across the northeastern corner of the green, determined to pass right by the Village Bean. After all my indulgences over the past week or so, the last thing I needed was a mocha latte, no matter how much I wanted one. I was even wondering if I should have had the cup of coffee I'd enjoyed with my breakfast. Nervousness already tickled at my stomach and my fingers drummed against my leg, driven by anxious energy that needed a release. I hoped Aunt Gilda would have time to chat. I hadn't been able to rid myself of a lingering sense of unease and uncertainty since we'd last spoken.

When I arrived at the salon, Betty and Gilda were both busy with clients, but Gilda waved to me as she picked up a hairdryer.

"Morning, hon. Can you stick around for a few minutes? I'll be done here soon."

"I can wait," I said.

I waved to Betty as she snipped away at her client's long brown hair. I sank down onto the loveseat and grabbed a copy of the day's edition of the *Shady Creek Tribune*. Since the paper came out only once per week, this was the first issue since Marcie's death. Unsurprisingly, her murder had made the front page.

AUTHOR'S ASSISTANT FALLS TO HER DEATH. POLICE SUSPECT FOUL PLAY.

The headline alone sent an unpleasant quiver up my spine. Nevertheless, I read the accompanying article from start to finish, as well as a companion piece on one of the inner pages about Linnea's event at the Inkwell. Joey had done a great job with both articles, but the only thing I learned that I hadn't already known was that Marcie was originally from Wildwood, New Jersey.

With a deep sigh, I set the paper back on the table, the shadow of Marcie's death darkening my mood. I needed to keep control of my emotions. If Aunt Gilda was about to tell me she was moving away, I couldn't come apart at the seams. I wanted her to know I'd be happy for her, despite my own disappointment at losing her from my daily life.

Aunt Gilda shut off the hairdryer and her client, Mrs. Winslow, patted her new hairdo, smiling with satisfaction. Gilda slipped the cape off of Mrs. Winslow's shoulders and followed her over to the counter.

"I have tickets for the masquerade," Mrs. Winslow was saying as she dug out her wallet, "but I'm not sure about going anymore. I was talking with the ladies at the seniors' center and we're all unsure about it."

"But the masquerade is always such a fun event," Aunt Gilda said with surprise.

"Will it be the same, though?" Mrs. Winslow handed some money over to Gilda. "The thought of that poor woman dying there at the manor . . ." She gave an exaggerated shiver. "And what about the murderer? The police haven't arrested anyone yet. Would we be putting ourselves in danger by going to the scene of the crime?"

I had to bite my tongue to keep myself from interrupting their conversation to add my two cents, but Aunt Gilda ended up saying what I was thinking anyway.

"I doubt the killer will be lurking around the ballroom, waiting to strike again. The murder was terrible, of course, but it was probably targeted. The rumor is that it was a lovers' spat that turned deadly. If that's true, there's no reason for the killer to harm any of us."

"Perhaps you're right." Mrs. Winslow tucked her wallet back into her purse. "I'll talk it over with my bridge club tonight."

With that declaration, Mrs. Winslow said her goodbyes and left the salon.

"She's the third person who's told me they're not sure if they want to go to the masquerade anymore," Aunt Gilda said to me. "I feel terrible for the Honeywells. They put so much effort into the masquerade each year. It'll be such a shame if it's a flop. I imagine it would be a financial hit for them too."

"I'm still planning to go," I said as I got up from the loveseat. "I think you're right that the murder wasn't random, so we're not likely to be at risk. Besides, I'm not letting my new dress go to waste."

"It's a gorgeous dress," Aunt Gilda said with approval. I'd texted her a picture of it the day I'd bought it. "Such a shame that Grayson won't be there to see you in it. Speaking of which . . ." She tucked her arm through mine. "Let's go up-stairs so you can tell me all about your date."

"I was hoping you'd have something to tell *me*," I said as we headed up the stairway to her apartment.

"I do." The words came out on a heavy sigh.

Since I was following her up the stairs, I couldn't see her face and couldn't figure out the source of the sadness behind her sigh. Was she sad that she'd turned down Louie, or that she was moving away from Shady Creek?

"Don't leave me in suspense any longer," I pleaded as soon as we were in her kitchen. "Have you decided what you're going to do?"

"I have."

She filled the kettle with water before saying anything further. After she shut off the faucet and set the kettle on the stove, she turned to face me. My heart nearly broke when I saw the tears in her eyes.

"I turned him down." She blinked back her tears and switched on the stove.

"Do you regret it?" I asked, trying to interpret her almost-tears while fighting back my own. I couldn't stand to see her upset.

She drew in a deep breath. "No." Her response was firm, free of uncertainty. "I know I made the right decision. I care for Louie very much, and I enjoy his company, but I'm not in love with him. I thought perhaps I was simply comparing him un-fairly to your uncle, that maybe I cared enough to marry him even if my feelings weren't anything like those I had for Hous-ton. But after taking time to think about it, I know that's not the case. I doubt what I had with Houston could ever be matched, but even so, my heart isn't in the place it would need to be to marry Louie." Tears welled in her eyes again. "I'm just sad that I had to let him down."

I wrapped my arms around her and hugged her hard. "I'm sorry, Aunt Gilda."

She returned my hug and patted my back. "Don't be. I'll be fine. And I'm relieved, really. I didn't want to leave Shady Creek, and I didn't want to leave you."

I could no longer keep my own tears at bay. "I didn't want you to leave either, but I did want you to do what would make you happy."

"The life I have here makes me happy," she assured me as she gave me a squeeze. "Very happy."

When she pulled back, we both had wet cheeks.

"Look at the two of us," she said with a shake of her head. "I've got half an hour until my next client. Let's have a cup of tea and you can tell me about your date with Grayson."

"Speaking of which," I said over the whistling of the kettle, "it seems someone showed him pictures of me when I was younger. Including that seriously embarrassing prom picture of me with Wesley Lambert."

I kept my tone light, so she'd know I wasn't really mad.

Aunt Gilda took the kettle off the stove and poured the water into the teapot. "There's nothing embarrassing about that photo."

"Aunt Gilda! That dress! And *Wesley Lambert*."

"He enjoyed seeing the pictures."

I covered my face with my hands. "So he could tease me about them."

"Because you looked adorable in every single one." Gilda patted my shoulder. "But I won't show him any more photos if you don't want me to."

I dropped my hands from my face. "Thank you."

She poured us each a cup of tea and we moved into the living room. Once we'd settled on the couch, I told her about my date, including the brief sleuthing excursion and our almost-kiss. I didn't mind sharing those things with Gilda. She'd always been my favorite aunt, someone I could confide in. She warned me not to take my investigating too far, and I assured her that I'd be careful.

By the time we'd finished our tea, the unsettled feeling that had plagued me the last few days had disappeared and a sense of calm had moved in to replace it. Everything in my life was going well, except perhaps for my investigation into Marcie's murder.

Joey's articles in the newspaper hadn't suggested that the police knew anything more than I did, but I hoped they were nevertheless having better luck with their investigation. In case they weren't, however, I fully intended to forge ahead with my own.

Even though I was cutting it a bit short, I decided to make a quick trip to Shady Creek Manor before opening the Inkwell for the day. I sent a quick text message to Mel, letting her know that I was going out and asking her to open the pub if I didn't make it back in time.

I really wasn't sure how to get more information about Brad on my own. Maybe waiting to find out what Grayson uncovered was the best idea, but I still wanted to poke around for clues at the manor. There was a chance I could find out why Jan Finch had been sneaking around the hotel the other day. It could have been that she simply had a jumpy disposition and wasn't anywhere she shouldn't have been, but if that was the case, I wanted to know. At the moment, she and Brad Honeywell were the only people on my suspect list. If I could cross her name off it, Brad's position as the most likely culprit would solidify.

As I drove to the manor, I recalled that I'd seen Marcie talking with Judson out in the gardens. Flirting with him, I suspected. I probably should have asked him more questions before, but hopefully I could make up for that this morning.

He'd been out on the grounds the day Marcie died. There was a chance he could have seen something or someone out of the ordinary, whether or not it struck him as unusual or suspicious at the time.

Hunting for clues wasn't my first priority, however. I knew Linnea's brother was taking her home. I was hoping they hadn't left yet so I could have a chance to say goodbye. When I climbed out of my car in the parking lot, I noticed Judson out behind the hotel, riding a tractor mower over the grass. I waved to him and he waved back before steering the mower around a flower bed.

I made my way around to the front of the manor, once again averting my eyes from the spot where Marcie had died. Despite my refusal to look at the scene of her death, Marcie's scream replayed in my head. I yanked open the door and hurried inside, as if I could escape the memory of the terrible sound.

A blond-haired woman, shorter and slimmer than Gemma Honeywell, stood behind the reception desk, facing away from me. She whipped around at the sound of my arrival.

"Karidee?" Surprise colored my voice. "What are you doing?"

Her cheeks turned pink and her eyes were wide. "My . . . my pen," she stammered. She ducked out of sight for a second and then reappeared, slipping something into her purse, or pretending to, at least. "I dropped it and it rolled back here."

She scooted out from behind the desk and darted past me to the door. "Bye!" she called before disappearing from sight.

Our exchange had only lasted a few seconds, but in that time my surprise had morphed into suspicion. I peeked behind the reception desk, but couldn't see anything amiss. The desk drawers were shut tight and the few pieces of mail tucked into the numbered boxes on the wall were tidy.

Maybe I'd disturbed Karidee before she had a chance to search for whatever she was looking for, because I was certain she hadn't gone back there to retrieve a pen. Her lie had been as transparent as the windows flanking the front door.

It wasn't the first time Karidee had been found sneaking around the manor. Marcie had chased her off the day I'd come to have tea with Linnea. Had Marcie found Karidee up on the third floor, trying to find Linnea's room, leading to a squabble and a physical fight?

I didn't know the answer to that question, but I did know that I now had another suspect to consider.

Chapter 20

Gemma appeared shortly after Karidee's departure and I told her about finding the young woman behind the reception desk.

"What in the world was she doing back here?" Gemma asked with a frown, surveying the area behind the desk.

"I'm really not sure," I said.

"Nothing appears to be missing or moved." Gemma released a heavy sigh. "That girl is obsessed with Linnea Bliss. On the upside, with Ms. Bliss leaving today, Karidee shouldn't have a reason to sneak around here any longer."

"So Linnea's still here?" I asked. "I was hoping to see her before she goes."

"She and her brother had a late breakfast and now she's upstairs in her room, packing." Gemma lifted the receiver from the phone. "I'll let her know you're here."

I thanked Gemma and took a seat on the lobby's settee. A moment later, Gemma informed me that Linnea would be down shortly.

"I've seen Jan Finch here a lot lately," I said. I figured I might as well try to get some information while I waited. "Have you been having a lot of plumbing troubles?"

"Not a lot, no," Gemma said. "There was a leaky faucet in one of the guest bathrooms that Jan fixed with no problem, but there's an issue down in the laundry room that's been taking more time. Jan had to order in a new part for one of the washing machines, and then when it arrived, it wasn't the right one. So she's been back and forth a lot."

"I guess the leaky faucet was just the other day," I said.

"No, that was last week. She's only been working down in the basement lately."

Or so Gemma thought. No wonder Jan had seemed shifty when I'd spotted her coming down the stairs the other day. As I'd suspected, she didn't have a legitimate reason to be in that part of the hotel.

But *why* was she sneaking around the manor?

I didn't have time to puzzle over that question right then. Linnea descended the stairway to the lobby and smiled at me. I jumped up from the settee to greet her.

"How are you doing?" I asked.

"Better than the last time we spoke," Linnea said. "It's helped my spirits to have my brother here, and I'm looking forward to getting home."

"I hope the trip goes smoothly. I wanted to make sure I had a chance to say goodbye and to thank you again for visiting the Inkwell. I'm so sorry your time in Shady Creek took such a terrible turn."

Linnea clasped one of my hands in both of hers. "I enjoyed the event at your pub and I truly appreciate all the kindness you've shown me. Despite what happened to Marcie, it was a pleasure to meet you."

"The pleasure has been all mine," I assured her.

She squeezed my hand before letting it go and addressing Gemma. "My brother's taking the luggage out the back way to the car. I'd like to check out now, if that's convenient."

"Of course," Gemma said.

I bid goodbye to Linnea and slipped out the front door.

When I reached the back of the hotel, I searched for Judson, but he'd finished mowing the lawn. The expanse of green grass was neatly trimmed and the grounds were quiet, the rumble of the lawn tractor's motor now absent. I thought I might have to give up on my plan of talking to Judson, until I spotted a shed near the back of the parking lot, tucked between some tall trees which almost hid it from sight.

The shed's double doors stood open and I could see someone moving about inside. Figuring it was most likely the gardener, I struck off across the grass, noting that Jan's van was once again parked in the lot. I couldn't help but wonder if the plumbing issue in the laundry room was really as troublesome as Jan had led Gemma to believe. Maybe Jan had fabricated more issues than really existed, giving her an excuse to keep coming back to the manor to do . . . whatever it was she was doing when she was creeping around the upper floors of the hotel.

As I got closer to the shed, I saw that I was right in thinking it was Judson moving around inside the structure. He'd parked the lawn tractor in the middle of the shed and was sorting through some tools on a workbench.

He either heard or saw me coming, because he stepped out of the shed's shadowy interior to meet me. "Hey, Sadie. What brings you out this way?"

"I wanted to say goodbye to Linnea before she left, and I thought I'd ask a few questions while I'm here."

"I've heard you're Shady Creek's own Nancy Drew," Judson said with a grin.

"I wouldn't go that far," I said, although I found the comparison flattering. I'd been a Nancy Drew fan for almost as long as I could remember. "But I am trying to find out whatever I can about Marcie's murder."

Judson sobered. "I still can't believe that really happened, and at the same time I can't shake the memory of her lying there . . ." He trailed off, his eyes haunted.

"I know," I said with understanding. "I've been having the same problem."

Judson ran the back of his hand across his forehead. "So, have you found out anything?"

"Not a lot," I admitted. "I was wondering if you'd seen or heard anything the day Marcie died."

"I heard her awful scream. That's what sent me running around the front of the manor."

"That's what brought me running too. But what about earlier in the day? Did you notice anything out of the ordinary?"

"The cops asked me that too, but I haven't been able to think of anything." He stared out over the grounds for a moment, as if searching through his memory. "I was working on these flowerbeds until the rain settled in." He pointed at the garden behind the hotel. "I don't remember seeing anyone except a few people who work here coming and going through the back doors. Once it started pouring, I was over here in the shed cleaning off my tools. The rain didn't look like it was going to let up anytime soon, so I was going to pack up and head home. That's when I heard the scream."

I knew neither of us wanted to dwell on what we'd found after hearing Marcie's scream, so I quickly steered the conversation in a slightly different direction.

"How well did you get to know Marcie before she died?"

He seemed puzzled by the question. "I didn't."

"The only reason I ask is because I noticed her talking to you one day, and I thought it looked like she might be flirting with you."

The confusion cleared from Judson's face. "Sure, she did come over and talk to me one day while I was working. And I guess you wouldn't be wrong to say she was flirting. I was polite, but I didn't encourage her. I love my job here and I don't want to jeopardize it by getting too friendly with any of the guests. I don't think the Honeywells would approve of that."

I thought he was probably right.

"Besides," he added, "Marcie was a bit young for me and not really my type."

"So you didn't learn anything about her?"

"Other than the fact that she liked red roses and chrysanthemums, no. That's the only conversation we ever had."

"Did you see her have conversations with any other staff members?"

"No, but I'm outside most of the time. Unless the guests come out here, I don't see much of them."

That made sense, but it was disappointing. Judson seemed to be a dead end as far as finding any clues.

"How about the police investigation?" Judson asked before I could take my leave. "Any word on how that's going?"

"No, but I hope it's going better than my investigation."

I thanked Judson for his time and said goodbye before heading back toward the manor. When I was halfway across the lawn, I glanced back over my shoulder and noticed Judson watching me from near the shed. Hopefully he didn't think I was a terrible snoop for asking so many questions, but I didn't think he'd minded.

Judson turned back to his tools and I continued on my way. I was about to cut across the parking lot to my car when I spotted Brad Honeywell at the back of the manor, speaking with a man by a delivery truck parked outside the hotel's service entrance. I slowed my pace and watched as the deliveryman hopped into his truck and backed up the vehicle before following the driveway around the building.

When Brad turned toward the door, I broke into a jog.

"Mr. Honeywell!" I hailed him.

He stopped and squinted in my direction. "Oh, Ms. Coleman, right?" he said as I drew closer. "What can I do for you?"

I slowed to a stop, glad to find I wasn't too out of breath from my brief sprint. "I'm curious to know how you knew Marcie Kent."

His expression shuttered. "She was a guest here. That's how I knew her."

"Before that," I said.

His eyes looked like they'd turned to stone and his mouth twisted into a cross between a grimace and a frown. "There was no *before*."

"But there was," I pressed, knowing he wouldn't give me any information without prodding. "You were overheard arguing with her. You didn't want her telling anyone that you had a history."

His cheeks flushed with anger. "Who overheard us?"

The sharp and demanding edge to his question triggered warning bells in my head. I wished I hadn't approached him alone and I wondered if we were within Judson's sight. Would he hear if I yelled for help?

"More than one person, including me," I said. I didn't want to get Gina's friend Tamara in trouble by bringing up her name.

"You must be mistaken." Brad yanked open the door and disappeared into the manor.

I glanced around, wondering if I should follow him inside. I decided that it would likely be safe to do so, since other staff members would probably be around.

Grabbing the door before it shut completely, I dashed into the corridor that I'd followed three days ago, after speaking with Connie. I had to hurry to catch up with Brad.

"If you had an affair with Marcie, the police will find out."

I'd spoken to his back, but he drew to a sudden stop and whirled around.

"I didn't have an affair with her!" He checked himself, as if realizing he might be overheard. He lowered his voice to a harsh whisper. "It was nothing like that!"

"Then what was it like?"

While keeping most of my attention on Brad, I listened for any sign that someone else might be nearby, but didn't hear any. I took a step back, trying to look casual about it, not liking the way Brad towered over me.

He glared at me, breathing heavily through his nose, his face still flushed. He reminded me of an angry bull and I hoped he wasn't about to charge at me. After another tense second or two, he let out an exasperated breath.

"She was a server at a corporate event I attended years ago. I had a bit of a drinking problem back then. I'd had a few too many that evening and . . . I guess you could say I hit on her. She threw a drink in my face and that was that. I didn't even recognize her at first when she showed up here. When she jogged my memory, I asked her not to broadcast what had happened. Gemma doesn't know about that incident. It wasn't anything she *needs* to know about."

"That's all it was?" I asked.

"That's all." His face darkened. "And now that you know, you can keep it to yourself. Don't go bothering Gemma with this."

He didn't add a threat, but an unspoken one hung in the air between us.

"Brad, what are you doing?" Gemma's voice startled us both.

Her husband whipped around. "Nothing," he said quickly. "Just telling Ms. Coleman a bit about the manor's history." He shot a piercing glance my way. "Isn't that right, Ms. Coleman?"

"Sure," I said without much conviction. I didn't know if I should play along with his lie or not. All I wanted was to get away from him. Even if he hadn't killed Marcie, I didn't want to find myself alone with him again.

I didn't miss the suspicion in Gemma's eyes when I looked her way. I doubted she was buying her husband's lie.

"I'd better be on my way now," I said, eager to escape.

I slipped past Brad and Gemma and hurried toward the lobby. Behind me, I heard angry whispers from both Honeywells, but I didn't hang around to attempt to eavesdrop. Brad's intimidating demeanor had rattled me, and my plan was to get out of the hotel, hop in my car, and get back to the Inkwell. But when I was halfway across the lobby, an earsplitting shriek froze me to the spot.

My heart sank as a chill ran through my veins.

Not again, was my immediate thought.

Another shriek rang out, closer this time.

A fifty-something woman dressed in a pale pink suit appeared at the top of the curving stairway.

"Help!" she screamed. "Somebody help!"

"What's the matter?" I asked, already climbing the stairs toward her.

She stopped halfway down the stairs, gripping the banister. Her next words confirmed my worst fear. "There's been another murder!"

Chapter 21

"Where? Who?" I shot the questions at the distraught woman. She pointed up the stairs. "Second floor hallway."

Running footsteps announced the arrival of the Honeywells.

"Call 911!" I yelled down to them as I ran the rest of the way up to the second floor.

When I reached the corridor, I stopped, suddenly scared to go any farther. What if the murderer was still around?

Then I spotted the body, halfway down the hall to my left. No one else was in sight, but I could hear someone running up the stairs behind me. When I glanced back, I saw that it was Gemma. I pushed my fears aside and hurried toward the victim.

As I dashed down the corridor, I realized that I recognized the person lying on the carpet runner. Jan Finch was facedown on the floor, her toolbox on its side and what looked like a roll of papers sitting inches from one of her limp hands. The hair at the back of her head was matted with blood.

I dropped to my knees at her side. "Jan?" I said, not expecting a response.

She didn't stir.

Gemma gasped as she hurried toward me. "Is she really . . . ?"

I pressed my fingers to the side of Jan's neck. To my surprise, I felt a pulse.

"She's alive!" I could hardly believe it. "We need an ambulance!"

Gemma repeated my words to someone else, and I heard shouting from downstairs, followed by more running footsteps.

"Jean-Luc has first-aid training," Gemma said as a middle-aged man with blond hair rushed down the corridor toward us. He wore a chef's uniform and carried a first-aid kit.

I backed away from Jan, wanting to make room for Jean-Luc. I tripped over the toolbox, catching myself against the wall before I fell. I shoved the toolbox aside with my foot and grabbed the roll of papers so neither would get in Jean-Luc's way.

"What happened?" Gemma asked, her eyes wide and her face pale.

I joined her a few feet down the corridor while Jean-Luc assessed Jan's condition.

"It looks like she took a hit to the back of her head," I said.

Gemma let out a strangled sound of distress. "How can this be happening?" Her face had lost a startling amount of color.

Alarmed, I took hold of her arm. "I think you should sit down."

Gemma nodded and pointed toward an alcove down the corridor. When we got there, I saw that there was a couch and two side tables facing the elevator. Gemma sank down onto the couch as soon as she reached it.

"Maybe you should put your head down," I suggested, still concerned by her pallor. "Or maybe I should get you some water."

Gemma waved off my concerns. "I'll be all right. I just need to rest a moment."

Minutes later, I detected the sound of sirens drawing closer to the manor. "Help's almost here." I spoke more to myself than to Gemma.

I was concerned for Jan. Although it was such a relief to know she was alive, she hadn't shown any signs of regaining consciousness, and the wound on the back of her head looked like a nasty one. I wanted her in the care of the paramedics as soon as possible. I was also eager for the police to arrive. Whoever had attacked Jan could still be on the premises.

I was certain she *had* been attacked, because how else would she have ended up with that head wound? There wasn't anything but the walls and her toolbox to hit her head on if she'd simply fallen, and I hadn't noticed any smears of blood to suggest that had happened.

The siren grew even louder before cutting off abruptly. In the distance, I heard another siren approaching. I peeked around the corner. A young woman, also in a chef's uniform, was with Jean-Luc now and they were both huddled over Jan.

In an attempt to distract myself from my worries, I unrolled the large papers I still held in my hand. They were slightly yellowed with age and the top sheet was torn along one edge.

"What are these?" I noticed several lines on the papers. As I unrolled them further, I realized that the lines were part of a drawing of a building's layout.

"They look like the blueprints for the manor," Gemma said. "Where did you get those?"

"I found them next to Jan."

"Why on earth would Jan have blueprints for the manor? And what in the world was she doing up here on the second floor? She was supposed to be working down in the laundry room."

I didn't have any answers for her.

The elevator doors parted and two paramedics rolled a stretcher out into the alcove, Brad right behind them. Gemma pointed the paramedics in the right direction and then got up to follow them.

"Are you sure you should be on your feet?" I asked with concern.

"I'll be all right. I'm feeling much better now."

Her face had regained some color and she'd already disappeared around the corner, so I didn't protest any further.

Voices murmured in the distance and the second siren grew louder. I studied the blueprints for another moment before coming to a decision. I picked up a vase of artificial flowers that was sitting on one of the end tables and spread out the top sheet of paper. It curled up again, so I set the vase on one corner and fetched its twin from the other side table. I dug through my purse and grabbed my wallet and a pack of gum to hold down the other corners.

Using my phone, I snapped a couple of pictures of the blueprint before doing the same with the three other sheets. Then I returned my makeshift paperweights to where they belonged and rolled up the papers. By that time, the sirens had ceased wailing and footsteps clattered on the stairs. I'd just tucked the roll of papers under my arm when Officers Eldon Howes and Pamela Rogers passed by the alcove, heading for Jan and the paramedics. I didn't know all of Shady Creek's police officers by name, but I'd had dealings with a few of them in the past.

After the officers had gone by, I stepped out into the corridor but didn't follow in their footsteps. The paramedics were in the midst of loading Jan onto the stretcher while Rogers spoke with Gemma. I considered heading downstairs to the lobby, until Rogers turned my way.

"Sadie, I'd like to speak with you for a moment," she said as she approached.

We retreated toward the staircase as the paramedics wheeled the stretcher into the alcove and waited for the elevator. Jan's eyes were closed and she didn't move a muscle. I hoped she would regain consciousness soon.

"I understand you were first on the scene," Rogers said as we paused at the top of the stairs.

"Second after one of the hotel guests," I corrected. "I was in the lobby when she came down the stairs, screaming that there'd been another murder."

"Do you know the guest's name?"

"No, but she was wearing a pink suit." I peered over the banister and pointed to the woman, who was speaking animatedly to a few other guests down in the lobby. "That's her."

Rogers asked me to detail my movements from the moment I'd heard the woman scream, and she took notes as I did so. Once I'd told her everything I could remember, I showed her the blueprints.

"These were on the floor next to Jan. I moved them to make room for the paramedics. I'm sorry if I contaminated a crime scene. I was only thinking of Jan at the time."

Fortunately, Rogers didn't seem too upset. "Thank you for turning them in," she said as she accepted the blueprints.

"Mrs. Honeywell didn't know how or why Jan had the blueprints," I said. "And Jan wasn't even supposed to be up here."

"Mrs. Honeywell mentioned that."

"What she might not know is that I ran into Jan here the other day as she was coming down a back stairway. Apparently, she was only supposed to be working in the laundry room that day too, so I don't know what she's been up to."

"I appreciate you letting me know," Rogers said.

I wasn't able to read much from her expression, so I didn't know how interesting she found the information.

Rogers didn't have any more questions for me. She met up with Officer Howes by the alcove and conferred quietly with him. For once I wasn't even tempted to eavesdrop. All I wanted to do was get back to the Inkwell.

This time, when I crossed the lobby, I made it out the door without interruption. I didn't look back as I hurried to my car and drove away from Shady Creek Manor.

After parking my car by the Inkwell, I made a quick trip over to Sofie's Treat. As I'd hoped, Joey was seated at one of the tables, his laptop open in front of him, a cup of coffee and a half-eaten apple fritter within easy reach. I waved to him as I got in line behind two other people. I didn't feel right about showing up at the bakery simply to talk to Joey, so I decided I'd buy some donuts for my staff.

Once I had an assortment of half a dozen donuts in a box, I slipped into the seat across from Joey.

"Fancy meeting you here," I said with a smile.

"Ha ha." He glanced Sofie's way, so briefly that I almost missed it.

I lowered my voice. "Have you asked her yet?"

"Asked who what?"

I waited, knowing full well that he knew what I meant.

He relented a second later. "Not yet."

"The masquerade is only a few days away," I reminded him.

"I'm aware of that." He grabbed his coffee and took a long drink. When he set down the cup, he regarded me over his laptop. "Is that really why you're here? To grill me about whether I've asked Sofie to the masquerade yet?"

"Only partly," I admitted.

"That's what I thought."

"Have you heard anything new about the murder investigation?" I asked.

"Have *you* heard anything?"

I'd expected him to throw the question back my way. He rarely gave away information for free.

"As a matter of fact, I just came from the manor." I lowered my voice to a whisper. "While you're sitting here working up the nerve to ask Sofie out, the news is happening without you."

I definitely had his attention now.

"An arrest?" he guessed.

"No." I checked to make sure no one else was within earshot. "Jan Finch was found unconscious on the second floor. It looks like someone hit her from behind. She was still unconscious when the paramedics took her away."

Joey closed his laptop and grabbed his coffee, gulping down what was left of it.

"Hold on," I said before he could get up. "I shared. Now it's your turn."

He could hardly sit still, clearly itching to get on his way to the manor. "Every time a key card is used, it's logged by the hotel's computer system."

"And it notes which key was used," I said, remembering what Gina had told me.

He nodded. "The thing is, nobody used a key to get into the room Marcie fell from. Not in the twenty-four hours before she died, anyway."

"But how is that possible?" I asked.

He shrugged, getting to his feet and tucking his laptop under one arm. "Your guess is as good as mine." He grabbed the remains of his apple fritter. "Let me know if you figure that one out."

Before I had a chance to say anything more, he was out the door.

Being back at the Inkwell brought me a sense of comfort and security after the latest unsettling incident at the manor. Unfortunately, the change of scene didn't calm my thoughts. I managed to mix drinks and take orders for customers without making mistakes, but there was no denying that I was preoccupied. I'd put some puzzle pieces together in my head, but I wasn't yet sure if they truly fit or if I was forcing them to form the wrong picture.

During a lull in business, I left Mel in charge of the pub while I slipped into my cubbyhole of an office beneath the stairway that led up to my apartment. On my drive back from Shady Creek Manor, I'd recalled the earring I'd seen on the floor of the third-story guest room shortly after Marcie's death. Now that I knew Jan had been in possession of blueprints of the manor and had been sneaking around the upper floors of the hotel, I had serious doubts about the theory that Marcie had been in the vacant guest room for a secret rendezvous.

My latest theory was that Jan had the blueprints because she was hoping to find the legendary Vallencourt treasure. I also theorized that someone didn't want her to find it, or at least didn't want her searching the hotel. I figured it was more likely than not that Marcie's killer and Jan's attacker were one and the same. That person either wanted to be the one to find the treasure or had some other secret they didn't want uncovered by people nosing around the manor.

Whether Marcie had been killed because she was looking for the treasure or because she'd stumbled upon something or someone that was meant to be secret, I didn't know. The earring I'd spotted on the floor might have been part of the Vallencourt treasure. It also could have been the killer's earring, dropped during the scuffle with Marcie. I didn't recall Marcie wearing earrings like the one on the floor—or any earrings, for that matter—and I hadn't noticed any other potential treasure in the room. Of course, Marcie's killer could have taken the rest of the treasure when he or she fled.

Or, maybe the treasure didn't even exist.

There was also the question of how Marcie had accessed the third-floor guest room. Had a mystery man left it propped open the day before, knowing he planned to meet Marcie there? That seemed unlikely, but I couldn't rule it out.

I scrubbed my hands down my face, wishing I had a more concrete idea of what had happened on the day of Marcie's death. A thought struck me. Maybe there was another way Marcie could have accessed the room without a key.

Tapping at my phone, I pulled up the photos I'd taken of the blueprints, but it was hard to examine them in any detail on such a small screen. After emailing them to myself, I viewed the blueprints on my computer screen. It took a few minutes of studying the drawings for me to find what I was looking for. Off of a room designated as a study was another smaller room labeled as a "secret alcove."

Near the back of the manor, on the drawing of the ground floor, a narrow stairway was also marked as "secret." I studied the blueprints for the other floors. The hidden stairway extended only from the ground floor to the second floor, not beyond. The second floor also had a secret room off what was labeled as the master bedroom. I spent several minutes studying each of the drawings, but I couldn't locate any other secret rooms, passageways, or stairways.

I sat back in my creaking desk chair with a sigh. I'd thought perhaps a secret passageway led to the guest room where Marcie had fallen from. That would have explained how she'd managed to get in the room without a key.

Maybe I was barking up the wrong tree with my new theory. Marcie's death could have had nothing to do with the legendary treasure. Somehow that idea didn't sit quite right with me, though. As for Jan, I was fairly certain she'd been searching for the treasure, whether it actually existed or not.

I wondered if the police knew about the story of the hidden treasure. If they didn't, they could be without a critical piece of information.

I decided I should give Detective Marquez a call, to tell her about the legend and my theory about why Jan had been attacked. I was in the midst of searching through my contacts for the detective's number when Mel appeared in the doorway to my tiny office.

"Sadie, Detective Marquez is here to see you," she said.

Surprised, I set down my phone. "She must be a mind reader. I was just about to call her."

A hint of concern showed in Mel's blue eyes. "Is everything all right?"

I thought I knew what had her worried. "I'm not a murder suspect," I rushed to assure her. Second thoughts leapt out at me. "At least, I don't think I am." My stomach jittered with a sudden flash of nervousness. "I couldn't be, could I?"

"I hope not," Mel said. "But maybe you should go talk to the detective and find out."

"Right." It took another second for me to actually move. "That would be a good idea."

Mel stepped to the side of the doorway so I could pass her. When I entered the pub, I spotted Marquez right away. She was seated at a small table, away from the handful of customers enjoying late lunches. I hesitated by the bar, my nerves jangling.

When Mel spoke from behind me, I nearly jumped out of my skin.

"I'll get the cup of coffee she asked for."

I thanked her and then pulled myself together. There was no reason to believe Marquez would suspect me of killing Marcie or assaulting Jan. At least, I hoped that was the case. As Mel had said, it was best to find out for sure.

Forcing myself to relax so I wouldn't broadcast my anxiety to the detective, I crossed the pub.

"Afternoon, Detective," I said when I reached her table. "I understand you wanted to speak with me."

"That's right. If you have a moment."

"We aren't too busy right now, so it's no problem." I pulled out the chair across from her and sat down.

Marquez had her dark curly hair tied back, as she had on

every other occasion I'd seen her. She regarded me with her brown eyes, and I hoped she wasn't assessing me as a potential killer. Her gaze flicked away from mine for a brief moment as she thanked Mel, who was setting a cup of coffee on the table. Then Mel returned to the bar, leaving us alone.

"What can I help you with?" I asked, anxious to know why she'd come to the pub.

"I understand you were at Shady Creek Manor both on the day Marcie Kent was killed and earlier today when Jan Finch was attacked."

I clasped my hands on my lap, stifling the urge to fidget nervously. "I was."

"I have concerns about that."

I gulped, and hoped Marquez hadn't noticed. There was little chance of that, I realized, considering how closely she was watching me.

It would have been prudent to wait and see what she'd say next, but my nerves got the best of me. Much to my chagrin, I dug my nails into the palms of my hands and blurted out, "I didn't do it!"

Chapter 22

I wanted to clap my hand over my mouth, but instead I forced myself to relax and fold my hands in my lap.

The slightest hint of a smile tugged at one corner of Marquez's mouth. At least, I thought that was what had happened. It was such a brief movement that I wasn't sure if my eyes had played a trick on me.

"You didn't do what?" the detective asked, her voice even, not giving away her thoughts.

A hint of relief trickled through me when I glanced around and saw that none of the customers were paying attention to us. Nevertheless, I lowered my voice.

"I didn't kill Marcie Kent. And I didn't attack Jan Finch."

This time I was sure her mouth twitched up in a brief flash of a smile.

"I didn't think you did."

My shoulders relaxed. "You didn't?" I winced when I heard how surprised I sounded.

"I've gone over all the witness statements. You were with Linnea Bliss when Ms. Kent was killed, and you were speaking with Mr. Honeywell when Ms. Finch was attacked."

That was good news. I knew I was innocent, of course, but it was nice to know the police knew that too. I considered what she'd said from another angle.

"I wasn't talking with Brad Honeywell for more than a few minutes. Does that mean there's a narrow window of time when Jan could have been attacked?"

"Two housekeepers were in that corridor less than ten minutes before Ms. Finch was found. They didn't see anyone."

"But that must mean Brad Honeywell wasn't the attacker. Could he have an accomplice?"

When Detective Marquez fixed a stern gaze on me, I realized I'd said that out loud.

"That's why I'm here," she said. I knew she didn't mean to discuss the accomplice theory.

"I understand you've been a frequent visitor to the manor since Ms. Kent's death."

"I guess you could say that," I admitted, trying my best not to shrink back in my seat. I hadn't missed the disapproval in her voice. I felt a little like a student getting reprimanded in the principal's office.

"I'd like to remind you what happened the last two times you got involved in murder investigations."

"You don't need to remind me," I assured her. Having two murderers turn their wrath on me wasn't something I was likely to forget anytime soon. I still had the occasional nightmare from both incidents.

"Don't I?" Marquez sounded skeptical.

Okay, maybe she had reason to be skeptical since I hadn't exactly minded my own business since Marcie was killed. Still, I didn't want to get in hot water with the detective or any of her colleagues.

"I've been to the manor several times to visit Linnea Bliss." Technically, that was true.

"And you haven't been discussing the murder?" Marquez clearly knew that wasn't the case.

"Well, sure I have, but lots of people have been."

She took a sip of her so far untouched coffee. "I hope it's been nothing more than a bit of gossip."

She might hope that, but I could tell she didn't quite believe it.

"I was hoping to speak with you," I said, deciding a shift in topic was in order. "I have some information I want to pass on, just in case you're not aware of it."

Marquez set down her mug. "Information obtained simply through regular conversations with curious townsfolk?"

I fought the urge to shift in my seat. "Partly. And from overhearing things. And from being in the right place at the right time. Or maybe the wrong place at the wrong time."

It was so subtle that I almost missed it, but I was sure the detective released a sigh, one of either resignation or exasperation. Or possibly a mix of both.

"Go ahead," she said before taking another sip of coffee.

"Okay, but first I have to ask if Jan is all right."

Marquez rested her mug on the table. "She regained consciousness shortly after arriving at the hospital. She has a concussion, but hopefully she'll make a full recovery."

"Does she know who hit her? And did she say what she was doing on the second floor of the manor?"

"She claims not to remember anything after arriving at the hotel."

"But you don't believe her," I surmised.

Detective Marquez neither confirmed nor denied that, but I was sure I'd guessed correctly.

"Does this have anything to do with what you wanted to tell me?" she asked.

"Sort of." I tried to decide where to start. "Have you lived in Shady Creek all your life?"

One of Marquez's eyebrows raised a fraction of an inch. "No. I moved here three years ago."

I knew she was wondering about the pertinence of my question, so I quickly continued. "Then do you know about the history of the manor?"

"I know it was once owned by a wealthy man by the name of Edwin Vallencourt."

"Have you heard the story about his hidden treasure?"

"I'm aware there is a story," she said, "but I don't know the details. Is this somehow relevant?"

"I think it could be. There were blueprints on the floor next to Jan, ones that show the location of secret rooms and a secret stairway. I handed them over to Officer Rogers."

Marquez nodded. "I'm aware. And you also told Officer Rogers that you'd seen Jan in parts of the hotel where perhaps she wasn't supposed to be."

"Right. So, she's been sneaking around the manor and had blueprints of the building."

"You think she was searching for treasure."

I wouldn't have blamed her if she'd sounded incredulous. To her credit, however, she kept her voice even, never one to give much away about her thoughts or feelings.

"I think it's a real possibility," I said. "I don't know if the treasure exists or not, but it doesn't really matter if certain people believe that it does."

Marquez regarded me without speaking. Seconds ticked by. I was about to give in to the urge to squirm beneath her gaze when she finally broke the silence that had settled between us.

"Is there anything else you'd like to share with me?"

I stifled a sigh of disappointment. She wasn't going to give me even a hint of whether she thought my theory had any merit. I hadn't really expected otherwise, but maybe I'd hoped, just a little.

Forcing myself to focus on her question, I thought over what else I wanted to tell her. "This might not be relevant, since he has an alibi for the attack on Jan, but Brad Honeywell had an argument with Marcie two days before she died." I went on to explain about their brief history, as admitted to by Brad.

Next, I told her about Karidee getting chased away from the manor by Marcie, and her odd behavior in the lobby the other day. Aside from that, I didn't think there were any other clues or details I needed to share.

Marquez took out a notebook and jotted a few things down, her expression still not revealing anything. When she snapped the notebook shut, she took out her wallet.

"The coffee's on the house," I said quickly.

She put a couple of bills on the table between us. "Thank you, but that's really not necessary."

Before I could protest, she pushed her chair back and stood up. "I appreciate the information you've given me, Ms. Coleman, but please remember that amateur sleuthing is a dangerous and ill-advised hobby. Leave the investigating to those of us who have the professional training and experience, all right?"

She didn't wait for a response from me, instead leaving the table and heading for the door. I remained seated, knowing I'd deserved the reprimand, but also knowing that shutting off my curiosity would be an impossible task.

I'd gleaned two pieces of information from my chat with Detective Marquez. Jan was keeping mum about what she'd been doing at the manor lately, aside from fixing plumbing problems, and Brad wasn't her attacker. As I poured some Midori liqueur into a cocktail shaker, I considered the question that had popped into my head earlier. Could Brad have an accomplice who'd assaulted Jan? If so, then he still could have killed Marcie.

The most likely candidate for Brad's accomplice was his wife, Gemma. She had an alibi for Marcie's murder, but it was possible that she'd attacked Jan. The timing would have been tight, but if she'd hurried downstairs and met up with me and Brad immediately after the assault, then it was possible.

I couldn't think of a reason to completely discount the idea of the Honeywells working together to commit the recent crimes, but at the same time I wasn't convinced it was the best theory I'd ever come up with.

Frustrated with my lack of ability to figure things out, I tried to focus solely on what I was doing. I finished mixing up a Lovecraft cocktail and delivered it to a table across the pub, along with a pint of India pale ale. After that, I popped into the kitchen to fetch several food orders. I was in the midst of serving burgers, fries, and a Red Cabbage of Courage salad to a table of three customers, when I noticed Cordelia coming into the pub.

She waved at me and headed over to the bar, where she perched on a stool.

"Things are quiet at the inn right now, so I thought I'd come by for a bite to eat," she said when I'd made my way back from serving the customers. "And some gossip. I hear you're dating Grayson." She propped an elbow on the bar and rested her chin in her hand, smiling wistfully. "He's dreamy."

"We've been on one date," I said. "It's not like we're officially an item."

Not that I was against the idea, but I didn't want to put the cart before the horse. I couldn't argue with the rest of what she'd said, though.

"And where did you hear that?" I asked, wondering just how far the gossip about me and Grayson had spread.

"From my Gran. She heard it from another lady in her class this morning."

"Class?"

"Chair yoga. At the community center."

So Shady Creek's entire senior population probably knew about my date with Grayson. I didn't want to think about what the yoga class might have said about us, beyond the fact that we'd had dinner together.

"Are you going to the masquerade with Grayson?" Cordelia asked.

"He won't be in town." I should have been over that disappointment by now, but I still wished he could go with me. "What about you? Do you have a date for the masquerade?"

"No." She sighed. "I'm going alone, as usual. Hopefully it'll still be fun."

"I'm sure it will be," I said, determined to make that the truth. "Can I get you anything?"

"Same as last time. A Milky Way Gargle Blaster mocktail and nachos, please."

"Coming right up."

Once Cordelia had her food and drink in front of her, I moved off to serve a few other customers. When I returned to the bar, I decided to run an idea by her.

"The Inkwell's book clubs have gone over well so far," I said to start.

"Mmm-hmm." Cordelia had a mouthful of nachos and cheese, but she quickly washed it down with her mocktail. "I love the mystery book club! And I've heard good things about the other clubs too."

That put a smile on my face. "Do you think anyone would be interested in a writers' group?"

"Definitely! A writers' group would be great!"

"Really?" I said, not letting myself get too wrapped up in the idea yet. "Do you know anyone in town who's a writer?"

Cordelia thought that over as she munched on another

nacho. "Marisol, a girl I went to school with, used to write a lot of poetry. I don't know if she still does. She's got a baby and another one on the way. She married her high school sweetheart." She lowered her voice. "But he's not much of a sweetheart, if you ask me." Her voice returned to its normal volume. "Other than that . . . not really, but . . ." She trailed off, suddenly hesitant.

"But what?" I prodded.

Her cheeks turned pink. "I'd love to join a writers' group." She spoke quietly, as if confessing a long-held secret.

"You're a writer? I didn't know that," I said, pleasantly surprised.

The color in her cheeks deepened. "I'm not. Not really. I just . . . dabble. But I started writing a mystery novel a few months ago."

"That's so cool!"

"It's nothing to get excited about," she said quickly. "It's probably terrible."

"Don't say that. I bet it's great."

"I don't know about that, but it would be fun to meet other people who like writing too."

"Then I'll put the word out and see if anyone else is interested," I said, warming to the idea even more. "If the Inkwell ends up hosting a group, you can be the very first member."

Cordelia beamed at me. "I'd love that."

I had to excuse myself a moment later when a bell dinged in the kitchen. I grabbed the orders Teagan had ready and delivered them to a table by the window. On my way back to the bar, I noticed a couple sitting at a table for two. They had food and drink supplied by Damien, and I hadn't taken a good look at them until that moment.

I didn't recognize the man, but he was with Connie, and I

figured there was a good chance he was her husband. I planned to say hello to Connie when I passed by their table, but as I got closer, I realized they were arguing with each other in hushed voices.

"It's too dangerous," her husband said. "I think you should quit. The sooner the better."

"Believe me, I'd like to," Connie told him.

I strongly suspected they were talking about Connie's job at the manor, but I didn't hear any more because I quickly changed course. I didn't want to interrupt and make things awkward.

I wasn't fast enough, however. Connie glanced up and noticed me. Her frown switched to a weak smile. I said a quick hello, but didn't stop, relieved that a woman at another table had just hailed me.

After Connie and her companion had finished their drinks, she stopped by the bar on her way to the washroom.

"Hi, Sadie. It's nice to see you again." All traces of her earlier frown had disappeared.

"You too." I hesitated before asking, "Is everything all right?"

It took her half a second to realize why I was asking. "You mean with my husband?" When I nodded, she sighed and said, "He thinks I should quit my job at the manor. He's worried I could get hurt with the killer still at large."

Just as I'd thought. "It's sweet of him to worry. And understandable."

"He's always looking out for me. And it *is* kind of scary to work there with a psychopath on the loose, but I can't just up and quit without another job lined up, especially since my husband's out of work at the moment."

"Hopefully the police will catch the person responsible soon and you won't have to worry anymore," I said.

"That would be nice," she said, "but I'm not holding my breath."

She disappeared into the washroom and a short while later I saw her leaving the pub with her husband. I desperately hoped that she and everyone else who worked at the manor would stay safe until the murderer was caught.

Chapter 23

When I opened my fridge the next morning, I discovered there wasn't much in it. I'd already eaten most of what I'd bought during my last trip to the grocery store. I had a craving for an omelet, instead of my usual breakfast of toast or oatmeal, but it was a bit hard to make an omelet without any eggs. The cheese drawer was empty too, and the only vegetables present were a lone carrot and a few stalks of celery.

Wimsey was more fortunate. He had plenty of food in stock, so I dished out his breakfast and set it down on the floor. He practically pounced on it, purring as he gobbled up his morning meal. I set out fresh water for him and grabbed my purse and a reusable shopping bag. Shady Creek's farmers' market was open until noon, and I hoped to make some delicious purchases there and restock my fridge before opening the Inkwell.

I enjoyed the walk over to the park, where the farmers' market took place every Thursday and Saturday morning from late April to early October. Leafy tree boughs danced in the breeze that carried with it the scent of freshly cut grass. Puffy white clouds dotted the bright blue sky, but didn't blot out the warmth of the sun. The forest was lush and green, and colorful flowers brightened window boxes outside several of the houses I passed. It was a perfect spring day.

When I reached the park, dozens of people were already browsing among the two rows of stalls set up by the merchants. The farmers' market was a popular place for townsfolk to shop for local products, and it was known for attracting tourists too. I knew at least one busload of the latter had already arrived in town that morning. I'd seen the passengers disembarking by the village green as I left the Inkwell.

I bypassed a stall selling handmade jewelry and another stocked with jams and preserves, making my first stop at the Caldwell Cheese booth. Bert Caldwell, the owner of the local cheese company, wasn't present that morning, but I purchased a wedge each of Gouda and Brie from the woman in charge of the stall. It took a good deal of effort to put the cheese in my shopping bag without opening it for a taste. Brie was my absolute favorite type of cheese, and I knew I could easily eat my way through the whole wedge in a day or two if I wasn't careful.

I moved on to a stand selling fresh produce. It was early in the season, so there wasn't as much variety as there might be in the coming weeks, but I bought some tomatoes picked earlier that morning from a local farm's greenhouses. Next to the produce stand was one displaying an array of baked goods. The woman in charge of the stall was busy chatting with two other women, but a sign on the table declared that all of her goods were home-baked and fresh.

I hadn't planned on buying baked goods when I arrived at the market, but I couldn't pass up one of the delicious-looking cinnamon buns. I picked out a wonderfully gooey one as the proprietor wrapped up her conversation, and I quickly paid for the bun. Between my most recent purchase and the two wedges of cheese in my bag, my mouth was doing some serious watering.

A sign on a stall at the end of the row advertised farm fresh eggs. Exactly what I was looking for. I was about to head in that direction when someone thrust a flyer in front of my face.

"Say no to advertising our town as a den of iniquity!" a familiar voice urged.

I pushed the paper away from my face, only to have Eleanor Grimes shove it into my hand.

"Oh, it's you," she said once the flyer was no longer blocking my face. "I'm sure *you* won't be any help."

Before I could get a word in, or figure out what she was on about, she strode off, thrusting flyers at other unsuspecting shoppers.

After moving out of the way of a group of half a dozen women—tourists, I guessed, judging by the number of photos they were taking—I got my first good look at Eleanor's flyer.

The bold letters at the top of the sheet echoed Eleanor's words: SAY NO TO ADVERTISING OUR TOWN AS A DEN OF INIQUITY.

Below that, what could only be described as a brief rant detailed Eleanor's opinion that having Shady Creek featured in an episode of *Craft Nation* would lead to the town's moral demise. She wanted the citizens of Shady Creek to band together to demand that the television network cancel the episode focused on the Spirit Hill Brewery. A meeting would take place that evening at the town hall, in an attempt to rally the troops, so to speak.

Was she serious?

Apparently so, I realized as I watched her make her way through the crowd of shoppers, shoving flyers into the hands of every person she passed.

I was tempted to crumple the flyer in my fist, but I stopped myself. It might be a good idea for me to attend the meeting at the town hall. It didn't slip my notice that Eleanor had scheduled it for a time when Grayson was out of town and unable to stand up in defense of his brewery and the show.

How Eleanor could think that the episode would ruin Shady

Creek, I didn't know. I firmly believed it would benefit the town. By giving Grayson's brewery and Shady Creek exposure across the country, the episode would most likely drive more tourists here, and that was a good thing for all us local business owners.

I hoped Eleanor wouldn't have any support for her crazy idea, but the best way to find out would be to attend the meeting. I also figured it would be a good idea to contact Grayson and let him know what was going on. He wouldn't be able to make it to the meeting himself, but he might want to send one of his staff members to represent the brewery.

Folding the flyer haphazardly, I shoved it into my shopping bag and headed for the farm fresh eggs. I hadn't taken more than a few steps when I spotted Harriet Jones standing next to a stall selling handmade soaps. Harriet was a real firecracker of a senior citizen and a member of the Inkwell's romance book club. She had one of the flyers in her hand and was shaking her head at Eleanor's retreating back.

"Eleanor is off her rocker, if you ask me," Harriet said as I approached her. She waved the flyer. "Did you get one of these?"

"I sure did," I said. "Does she really believe the *Craft Nation* episode will be a bad thing for the town?"

"I'm sure she believes it like she believes the sun will rise tomorrow." Harriet crumpled up her flyer. "She's always been an odd one." She tossed the ball of paper into a nearby recycling bin.

"You've known her a long time?"

"My whole life. We went to school together."

Somehow I couldn't picture Eleanor Grimes as a little girl, although obviously she had been at one point. I wondered if she'd always had a sour disposition.

"Getting some shopping done?" Harriet asked, changing the subject.

"My fridge was in a sorry state," I said, "but I'm remedying that."

"Have you tried the salted maple butter popcorn? I never can leave the market without at least one bag of it."

"I haven't."

"Then what are you waiting for?" Harriet hooked an arm through mine and propelled me to a nearby stand selling various types of popcorn in red and white paper bags.

Samples of different flavors sat in a row on the table. Harriet didn't bother with the samples, immediately handing over some money for a large bag of the salted maple butter popcorn. She opened it right away.

I decided to try one kernel of each flavor on offer. I started with the salted maple butter, and my eyes widened as soon as the piece of popcorn hit my tongue.

"See," Harriet said. "Can't pass that up, can you?"

"Definitely not."

I tested the other flavors, one by one. All were delicious, although I found the blue and pink cotton candy popcorn a tad too sweet for my taste. My favorite flavor was the maple butter one, followed by the white cheddar and the sour cream and chives. I purchased a small bag of the maple butter popcorn and opened it to munch on it, just as Harriet had with hers.

"If I end up addicted to this stuff, I'm holding you responsible," I warned.

Harriet let out a cackle of laughter. "I'll welcome you to the club with open arms."

She walked with me as I meandered toward the farm fresh eggs.

"So, what's your take on the recent crimes at the Shady Creek Manor?" she asked me. "And don't let me down here. You know you're our resident Nancy Drew."

I smiled at that, even though I probably was about to let her down. "I wish I knew who was responsible, but every time I dig for information, I seem to end up with more questions than answers."

I drew to a halt near the stall selling the eggs. Harriet had lived in Shady Creek all her life. I didn't know her exact age, but I figured she was at least in her mid-seventies, despite her seemingly endless energy.

"Do you know anything about Edwin Vallencourt?" I asked.

"Sure," she replied. "He was still alive when I was a kid." She sent me a sidelong glance as she dug another handful of popcorn out of her bag. "I hope you're not thinking his ghost is the killer."

"Nothing quite that crazy," I assured her. "But I am wondering if the crimes are somehow related to the stories about his hidden treasure."

Harriet made a dismissive sound. "Vallencourt's hidden treasure is probably as real as the tooth fairy."

"You don't think it exists? Why not?"

"Eddie was a real character and he loved attention. It wouldn't surprise me if he made up the story himself to create intrigue."

"It might not matter if it doesn't really exist," I said. "If some people believe it does . . ."

"Then they might think it's worth killing over?" Harriet shrugged. "If I've learned anything in this long life of mine, it's that people will do crazy things for crazy reasons." She munched on some popcorn before continuing. "You know, when I was little, I was in awe of that place."

"The manor?"

"Yep. People used to whisper about what went on there. Most of it I wasn't supposed to hear, but that never did stop me from listening in."

With my history, I couldn't fault her for that.

"I heard there used to be a lot of parties there in Vallencourt's day," I said.

"There sure were. Wild ones, from all accounts. Eddie had plenty of rich and famous friends who'd come to visit. Sometimes the parties would last days. And Eddie was a real ladies' man. A bit of a swindler too, if you believe the rumors."

"If you believe the *lies!*" Eleanor's voice startled us both. "Lies perpetuated by gossipmongers such as yourself, Harriet Jones."

Eleanor turned on her heel and marched off.

It took another second for the surprise to leave Harriet's face, but then she laughed. "I never will understand that woman."

"Why does she care what people say about Edwin Vallencourt?" I asked.

Harriet shook her head. "Beats me. I don't get it. She's usually Miss Prim and Proper. I'd have thought she'd disapprove of someone like Vallencourt, given his reputation, which, by the way, was very much deserved."

"Sometimes I think she disapproves of everyone," I said. "She's certainly not a fan of me."

"I'd wear that as a badge of honor," Harriet said with another laugh. She sobered after a brief moment. "I feel a bit sorry for her, though. If you ask me, she's full of a lot of anger, maybe even fear."

"Why?" I asked, genuinely curious.

"Who knows? But if she had any reason to kill someone, I'd say watch out."

That really got my attention. "Why do you say that?"

"She has a temper, that one. When we were teenagers, one of our classmates insinuated that Eleanor might have been conceived before her parents were married. Eleanor flew into a rage. Tore a whole handful of the other girl's hair out. Nearly got suspended from school, though it didn't come to that in the end."

"Yikes," I said.

If it hadn't been for Eleanor's alibi, I would have underlined her name on my suspect list.

"Anyway," Harriet continued, "don't worry about Eleanor not liking you. That just means you're on the same list as the rest of us in this town."

As Harriet and I parted ways a moment later, I decided to do my best to forget about Eleanor until the meeting at the town hall. First, however, I sent Grayson a text message, letting him know what Eleanor was up to and telling him that I'd be at the meeting. I didn't expect an immediate response, and I didn't get one. He was probably at one of his business meetings.

I ate another handful of delicious popcorn before forcing myself to tuck the bag away. As I headed over to buy some eggs, I wished I'd thought to bring a travel mug of coffee with me. There was regular coffee available for purchase at the farmers' market, but I decided that what I really wanted was a mocha latte.

I purchased a dozen farm fresh eggs, carefully placing the carton at the bottom of my shopping bag, and headed out of the park in the direction of the Village Bean. If I was going to get through the day—and an evening spent in Eleanor's company—I was going to need a good dose of caffeine and chocolate.

Chapter 24

When I got back to the center of town, I was so hungry that I initially bypassed the coffee shop and went straight home. I decided to have my omelet for breakfast the next day and instead scarfed down the scrumptious cinnamon roll I'd bought at the farmers' market. Wimsey tried to tell me that he was starving and hadn't eaten in days, but when I wouldn't believe him, he gave one last unimpressed meow and sauntered out of the apartment through his cat door. I knew I'd get back in his good books when I fed him dinner at the end of the day.

Maybe a cinnamon roll and a mocha latte didn't make the healthiest of breakfasts, but that didn't stop me from heading over to the Village Bean as soon as I finished eating my treat.

I was so intent on getting my drink that I didn't notice Karidee until after I had my latte in hand. She was tucked away at the back of the coffee shop this time, once again typing away on her laptop. I hesitated, remembering Detective Marquez's warning to leave the investigating to her, but the magnetic pull of my curiosity was too strong to ignore. Karidee had certainly been up to *something* at Shady Creek Manor. I wanted to know if that something was as nefarious as murder.

With a firm grip on my latte, I approached the young woman's table.

"Morning, Karidee," I said. "Mind if I join you for a minute?"

She barely had a chance to glance up from her laptop before I plunked myself down in the seat opposite her.

"Um, I'm kind of busy," she said.

"I won't keep you long," I assured her. "I just wondered how much you know about Shady Creek Manor and its history."

She wrinkled her forehead. "Why?"

"I think it's a fascinating place, and I've seen you hanging around there a few times, so I thought maybe you had an interest in it too."

Karidee's cheeks turned pink and she stared at her laptop's keypad. "I'm not really interested in the place. I was there . . . just because."

"Oh, wait," I said as if I'd suddenly remembered something. "You were there because Linnea Bliss was staying at the manor."

The pink in her cheeks brightened. "Not really," she mumbled.

I pretended I hadn't heard her. "I'm a big fan of hers too."

"You're lucky you got to meet her."

"I thought you did too," I said. "At the pub."

Karidee shut her laptop. For the first time since I sat down, she seemed to be warming up to the conversation. "Sure, but that was only for a few seconds. I didn't really get to talk to her. You probably got to hang out with her."

"I had tea with her at the manor, and lunch the next day. And I do count myself lucky. She's not just a great author; she's also a really nice person."

"I didn't get to find that out," Karidee said with a frown. "Her assistant wouldn't let me talk to her."

"You mean Marcie Kent? She was pretty protective of Linnea."

"Ridiculously so," she grumbled. "All I wanted was a few minutes of her time. All I wanted was to ask her . . ." Her cheeks flushed again.

"Ask her what?" I prompted.

"You'll think I'm dumb," she said quietly.

"I doubt that."

She put a hand on her closed laptop. "I'm . . . I'm writing a book."

"That's so cool," I said, genuinely impressed. "What genre?"

She didn't meet my gaze. "Contemporary romance."

"Is that why you wanted to talk to Linnea Bliss? You wanted some writing advice?"

"I wanted to ask if she'd read my opening pages. That's all I wanted. But her assistant kept chasing me off like I was a stalker!"

"That must have been frustrating," I said, hoping I sounded sympathetic. "What about after Marcie died? Did you try to see Linnea again? Is that why you were at the manor yesterday?"

Karidee squished her lips to one side and hesitated, as if trying to decide if she should come clean. "I thought if I could find out which room she was in, I could leave a note for her in her mailbox. I waited outside until Mrs. Honeywell left the lobby, but I didn't have a chance to leave my note."

"Because I came in and interrupted you."

She nodded.

"That must have added to your frustration," I said. "With Marcie out of the way, you probably thought you'd have your chance to contact Linnea."

"By then, Mrs. Honeywell didn't want me around, either, but I thought if I left my contact information in my note, maybe Ms. Bliss would get back to me."

I wondered how much I could push her. "It was really important to you to talk to her, wasn't it? It must have made you mad when Marcie kept trying to stop you. Did you fight with her?"

Her eyes widened. "No!" She quickly lowered her voice. "You think I killed her? I didn't! I didn't touch her!"

Even though she was whispering, she sounded on the verge of panic.

"You were there on the day she died," I pointed out. "And again yesterday when someone attacked Jan Finch."

I wouldn't have thought it possible, but her eyes got even bigger. "I didn't hurt anyone! I don't even know Jan Finch. I mean, I know who she is, but I don't *know* her."

She had a point there. I couldn't think of a reason why she'd attack Jan, unless she was lying about why she kept visiting the manor. Somehow, though, I thought she was telling the truth.

Karidee's eyes filled with tears. "I swear I didn't hurt anyone. I just wanted some help with my writing. I really want to get my book published when it's finished."

"I believe you," I said, and I did. Maybe she had me completely fooled, but I didn't think so.

She sniffled and the tears welling in her eyes subsided.

"You know how the Inkwell hosts book clubs?" I asked.

The sudden change of subject threw her off for a second. "Yes . . ."

"I was thinking of hosting a writers' group as well."

She brightened. "Really?"

"I don't know how many people would want to join, but I thought I'd put the word out and see. Would you be interested?"

"I totally would!" She smiled for the first time since I'd joined her at the table. "None of my friends are interested in writing. It would be nice to meet some people who are."

I woke up my phone and handed it over to her. "If you give me your email address, I'll let you know if it goes ahead."

She eagerly provided her contact information, and then I got up to go.

"Good luck with your writing," I said, meaning it sincerely.

By the time I was on my way out the door, she was already back to typing away furiously.

Shortly after I opened the Inkwell for the day, Aunt Gilda showed up. When I greeted her with a hug, I didn't fail to notice that her smile wasn't quite as bright as usual. She sat down at a table by one of the windows, and I pulled out a chair to join her.

"What's wrong?" I asked as I sat down. Worry shot through me. "Are you having second thoughts about your decision?"

"Not at all," she said, patting my hand. "I'm here to stay."

I smiled with relief. "I'm glad to hear it." My smile faded as I studied her face. "But something's wrong."

She sighed. "I ran into Louie at the grocery store. It was . . . difficult. I never wanted to hurt the poor man, but I did. I think it pained him to see me again."

My heart ached with sympathy for her. "I'm sorry." I took her hand and gave it a squeeze.

She returned the pressure and let out another sigh. "He's moving next month. It's probably for the best that he's going so soon. It'll make it easier for both of us to move on."

Hopefully that was true.

"Why don't I get you a drink?" I offered.

"Thank you, honey, but I can't stay." She got up from the table. "I've got another client in ten minutes. I just wanted to stop by and see your lovely face."

"I'm glad you did."

She pulled me into another hug. "See you tomorrow, all right?"

"Definitely."

Aunt Gilda was going to do my hair for the masquerade. I could hardly believe that the day of the event was almost upon us. Gilda would be going too, without a date, just like me and Shontelle. I hoped the event would provide her with a happy distraction.

When I checked my phone in the middle of the afternoon, I had a text message from Grayson, thanking me for the information about Eleanor's crusade and letting me know that someone from the brewery would attend the meeting at the town hall. He mentioned that he'd checked into Brad Honeywell's background but hadn't found anything of interest. Another dead end in the investigation.

He also added that he missed me. That put a smile on my face and also brought me some relief. It was nice to know those feelings went both ways.

I thought about filling him in on my investigation, but decided that could wait until he was back in town. Besides, what was there to tell him? I didn't feel like I'd made all that much progress since we'd last spoken. Hopefully by the time he got home the police would have Marcie's killer in custody. I figured there was a good chance Detective Marquez and her colleagues were way ahead of me in terms of tracking down the murderer.

Before putting my phone away, I sent a quick text message to Shontelle, letting her know about the meeting at the town hall. As a fellow local business owner, I thought she might want to know what was going on.

What is up with that woman? she wrote back almost right away.

A moment later, she added, I'll try to be there. And I'll spread the word.

Hopefully those of us in support of the *Craft Nation* episode would far outnumber those against it. I had trouble imagining anyone supporting Eleanor's point of view on the subject, but she'd lived in Shady Creek her whole life and it was entirely possible that she had people in her corner who would stand behind her. That thought sent a flutter of worry through my chest, but it quickly settled. Even if Eleanor had a whole army behind her, I doubted the people at the television network would even consider scrapping the *Craft Nation* episode. Nevertheless, I fully intended to be at the meeting to voice my support for the show.

Shortly before I needed to leave for the town hall, Judson came into the pub, hanging his jacket up by the door before claiming a stool at the bar. Damien served him a pint of beer while I mixed up three Yellow Brick Road cocktails for a table of local women. Made with limoncello, yellow lemonade, and lemon-lime soda, the Yellow Brick Road was a refreshing drink that had gone over well with the Inkwell's customers.

When I had a free moment, I moved down the bar to say hello to Judson.

"Do you have the day off of work?" I asked after greeting him.

"Just half the day," he said. "The Honeywells have me working extra hours lately."

"To get ready for the masquerade," I guessed.

He nodded and took a sip of his beer. "I was hoping to see you here."

"Is anything wrong?" I asked, not failing to notice that his expression had become more serious.

"No more than you already know about." He set his glass down on the bar. "But I'm worried."

"About what's been happening at the manor?"

"About you," he said, surprising me. "I know you've solved

mysteries in the past, Sadie, and I don't doubt your smarts, but I wanted to tell you . . ."

"What?" I asked, apprehension heavy in my stomach.

Judson leveled his gaze at me. "You should stay away from the manor. Otherwise, you might end up getting hurt. Or worse."

Chapter 25

The chill of Judson's warning stayed with me, even after he left the pub. Eventually, I shook it off, but I knew his concern wasn't entirely baseless. I decided not to think about that for the time being, though. I had too much else on my mind, and a meeting to attend.

When I reached the town hall, I noticed Shontelle heading my way, cutting across the green from her shop. I waited on the front steps of the old brick building, enjoying the fresh evening air and wondering how different the atmosphere would be inside. The town hall was within my sight as soon as I'd left the Inkwell and I'd yet to see anyone entering the building. I didn't know if that meant there wouldn't be many people at the meeting, or if Eleanor had shown up early with a gaggle of supporters.

"It's a beautiful evening, isn't it?" Shontelle asked as she crossed Hemlock Street to join me.

"Let's hope that doesn't change," I said as we climbed the steps to the double doors leading into the town hall.

Rows of chairs had been set up facing a podium at the far end of the building's main room. I spotted Eleanor right away. She was sitting primly in the front row, her back to us. Two women and a man also sat in the front row, and about half a dozen others were scattered among the remaining seats, most of which were empty.

"I hope the majority is on our side," Shontelle whispered as we moved farther into the room.

I held up my crossed fingers as we slipped into seats three rows back from Eleanor.

"Who are they?" I asked, also keeping my voice to a whisper as I nodded toward the three people sharing Eleanor's row.

"The younger woman is Angelica," Shontelle replied. "I've seen her at church. I don't know much about her, but her husband died a few years ago. Complications related to alcoholism."

"I guess that could explain why she's on Eleanor's side," I said, with a surge of sympathy for Angelica. I wondered if Eleanor had a similar experience in her past. She was a widow too. Maybe I shouldn't have judged her so harshly.

"The other two I'm not sure about," Shontelle said.

We didn't have the best vantage point for identifying them, since we were staring at the backs of their heads, but the other woman was closer to Eleanor in age than to Angelica, who—judging by the brief glimpse I got of her profile—couldn't have been much older than fifty. The gray-haired man with them was also of Eleanor's generation.

Shontelle glanced around the room. "Looks like just about everyone else here is a business owner, like us."

I took that as a good sign. I couldn't imagine any local businesses taking a stance against free, nation-wide publicity for our town. I recognized Bert Caldwell of the Caldwell Cheese Company, and Helen Lundquist and her daughter Katie, who ran Shady Creek's Five Owls Winery together. A couple of the other faces were familiar, but I couldn't put names to them.

A moment later, someone else walked into the room. I

turned in my seat to catch a glimpse of the new arrival. I smiled and waved when I recognized Juliana, the woman in charge of public relations at the Spirit Hill Brewery. Grayson's representative had arrived.

Juliana slipped into the vacant seat to my right. "Have I missed anything?"

"Not yet," I replied.

Eleanor stood up and smoothed down her moss-green skirt.

"Here we go," Shontelle said.

Eleanor approached the podium at the front of the room, her sharp gaze scanning over those of us present for the meeting. I wasn't entirely sure, but I thought I saw her eyes narrow when she caught sight of me.

"Good evening, fellow citizens of Shady Creek. Thank you for coming this evening. I called this meeting to impress upon you the dangers of advertising our beloved town as a haven for drunkards and criminals."

Bert let out a loud guffaw of laughter. That nearly spurred me on, but I managed to swallow the giggle that threatened to burst out of me.

"You'll have your chance to speak, Bert Caldwell," Eleanor said sharply, her expression one of annoyance and disapproval.

Bert sat back in his chair and clasped his hands over his generous stomach. "Don't let me stop you from continuing."

Eleanor sent a death glare his way before clearing her throat and addressing the room at large again. "As you all are surely aware, a television show glamorizing alcohol was recently here in Shady Creek filming an episode. Although the episode will feature the Spirit Hill Brewery"—she said the name with obvious distaste—"when it airs on television, it will also showcase our town, in what I can only describe as a negative light."

"Who are you trying to fool?" a middle-aged man called out from his seat near Bert. "The show will do nothing but good for Shady Creek. It'll bring tourists, and tourists bring money."

"Here, here!" Bert said.

Helen and her daughter applauded, and Shontelle, Juliana, and I joined in.

Eleanor scowled at us. "Some things are more important than money."

"What do you have against tourists coming to Shady Creek?" Helen called out. "The town wouldn't survive without them."

Eleanor gripped the edge of the podium. "I don't have a problem with tourists *per se*," she said, her voice tight, "but with the *type* of tourists this sort of publicity will bring."

"Ones who will visit the brewery, pub, and our winery?" Katie asked. "I don't see the problem there."

"You wouldn't, would you?" Eleanor shot the sharp words across the room.

No doubt she meant the comment as an insult, but Katie smiled, completely unfazed.

The elderly man sitting in the front row stood up and shook a finger at the rest of us. "You folks settle down and let Eleanor say her piece."

Juliana stood up and spoke politely, but firmly. "I think it's clear that the majority of us won't be swayed by Eleanor's opinion, so why don't we move things along so everybody can get on with their evening?"

The man sat down, grumbling under his breath, while the two women sitting next to him shook their heads.

Eleanor held up a sheet of paper. "I've brought this petition along. I invite all of you who understand the detrimental impact this show could have on our town to add your signature. The petition will be sent to the television network and requests that the *Craft Nation* episode featuring the Spirit Hill Brewery be canceled. I have pens available."

The two women and the man from the front row immediately got up and hurried over to the podium, where they formed an orderly line. Eleanor handed a pen to the older woman, who wasted no time adding her signature to the petition.

"That's it?" Juliana asked quietly. "It was hardly worth coming."

Shontelle and I stood up, and Juliana did the same.

"At least we know Eleanor's movement doesn't have much support," I said.

"True." Juliana already had her phone out. "I'll let Grayson know. I doubt he'll be surprised. The majority of the town's always been supportive of the brewery."

"Same with the Inkwell," I said.

We filed out of the town hall, everyone except Eleanor and her three supporters following in our wake.

We all congregated on the front steps.

"I swear, that woman gets nuttier with every year that passes," Bert said, settling a ball cap on his head. "Anyway, I'm off to the pub for a drink." He grinned and descended the steps. "See you there, Sadie."

Juliana said a quick goodbye too, and headed off across the green, texting on her phone.

I was thinking of texting Grayson too, even though he'd already be getting a report from Juliana. I wondered if he was enjoying his trip, or if his days were filled with dull meetings. At least he wasn't meeting with Eleanor Grimes.

I slipped my phone out of my purse, but I was distracted from my thoughts of Grayson when I heard Helen say, "How is Jan doing, Margaret?"

She was speaking to one of the meeting attendees I hadn't recognized, a thin woman with graying hair.

"She was released from the hospital today," Margaret replied. "She'll be laid up for a while, but she's glad to be home."

"Are you Jan's mother?" I asked.

"That's right," she said. "Margaret Finch."

I introduced myself and Shontelle. "I was at the manor when Jan was hurt," I explained. "I was worried about her, so I'm glad to hear she's out of the hospital."

"It's such a terrible thing." Margaret pulled her cardigan more tightly around her. "I can't believe somebody harmed my poor Jan."

"It's a blessing she wasn't hurt worse," Helen said. "I heard her attacker is probably the same person who pushed that poor young woman out the window."

Margaret shuddered. "I can't bear to even think about it."

Helen put a hand on her arm. "Of course not."

"I know it was a bit of a mystery why Jan was on the second floor of the manor when she was attacked," I said. "Has she shed any light on that?"

Something changed in Margaret's face, like shutters had slammed shut across her eyes. "She doesn't remember, but I'm sure she had a perfectly legitimate reason for being there."

"Of course," I said quickly, not wanting to upset her. "I hope Jan recovers quickly."

"Thank you," Margaret said, as she started down the steps.

Helen and her daughter stayed at her side. "Katie and I will walk you to your car."

We exchanged goodbyes and Shontelle and I slowly descended the town hall steps.

"Will you be going to the masquerade?" I heard Katie ask Margaret as they walked along Hemlock Street.

"Definitely not," Jan's mother replied. "I don't want to go near that place."

"I don't think we need to worry about Eleanor's petition," Shontelle said as we paused at the base of the steps.

"No, it doesn't seem so," I agreed. "That's a relief."

I glanced at my phone. Shontelle didn't fail to notice.

She smiled. "Thinking of calling Grayson?"

"No," I said quickly.

She raised an eyebrow.

"I was thinking of *texting* him."

"Same difference," she said with a triumphant smile. "Do you miss him?"

"He's only been gone a couple of days."

Her smile changed from triumphant to knowing. "Mm-hmm."

"Okay, maybe a little," I admitted. "But I don't want to get ahead of myself. It's far too early to let my heart get carried away."

"Sometimes hearts like to get carried away, no matter what," Shontelle said.

I almost said "That's what I'm worried about," but I was distracted by someone calling my name.

Cordelia ran along Hemlock Street from the direction of the Creekside Inn, her crinkly red hair streaming out behind her.

"Am I too late?" she asked as she reached us, out of breath. "Did I miss the meeting?"

"The meeting, yes," Shontelle said. "But anything of importance? No."

"Oh." Cordelia's breathing settled. "Gran wanted me to come so I could let her know what happened. She doesn't want the *Craft Nation* episode getting canceled. The inn depends on tourists coming to town."

"Neither of you need to worry," I assured her. "It looks like Eleanor's petition will end up with only three signatures aside from her own."

She let out a whoosh of breath. "That's a relief. Still, Gran won't be pleased that I missed the meeting. I was reading a book and lost track of time."

"Been there, done that," I said.

Her face brightened. "I'm starving. You ladies want to go grab some pizza?"

"I can't," Shontelle said. "I have to get home. But I'll talk to you both soon."

"I'll join you," I told Cordelia, my stomach giving a rumble of hunger. "But I can't stay long. I need to get back to the pub."

"I should get back to the inn before long too," Cordelia said.

We walked with Shontelle until we reached Hillview Road. Then she turned toward home while Cordelia and I continued on to Spice and Slice, the local pizza parlor. As we walked, I told her about what had taken place at the meeting.

"I don't understand Eleanor," Cordelia said with a shake of her head once I'd filled her in. "If she doesn't want to drink alcohol, that's perfectly fine, but why try to make the whole town teetotalers? And it's not like the pub, winery, and brewery attract drunkards."

"No, we don't."

The Inkwell rarely had trouble with patrons who'd had too much to drink. What passed for the rowdy crowd in Shady Creek tended to hang out at the local pool hall. Even there, incidents of note were few and far between.

"The town should have a viewing party," Cordelia said. "You know, when the episode airs."

"That's a great idea!" The wheels in my head immediately started turning. "I could host one at the Inkwell." I reconsidered. "Unless Grayson would rather have one at the brewery."

The setup was probably more suitable at the pub, though. The brewery had a tasting room, but no seating available. Still, I didn't want to step on any toes.

"Maybe the Inkwell and the brewery could cohost," Cordelia suggested.

"Another great idea."

I was tempted to text Grayson with the idea right away, but it could wait. Besides, we'd reached Spice and Slice, and the rumbles of hunger coming from my stomach were growing louder.

Inside the pizza parlor, the delicious smell of cheese and other toppings greeted us. "Jailhouse Rock" played on the old-style jukebox and a waitress with dark hair tapped her foot to the beat as she took orders from a group of four teenagers. The floor featured a black-and-white checkerboard pattern, and the tables and vinyl booths were all bright red. Neon signs and vintage posters decorated the walls. The place had a fun, upbeat vibe, but I knew from past visits that it also offered mouth-watering pizza. I'd heard that the spicy chicken wings were delicious too, but I'd always opted for the pizza.

The dinner rush had already passed by the time we arrived, so there were several tables available. We claimed one at the back of the restaurant, near a window that looked out over the parking lot. We ordered soft drinks and a single slice of pizza each. Then we sat back in our booth to wait for our food.

Cordelia was telling me about her plans to spread the word about the Inkwell's future writers' group when movement out in the parking lot caught my eye.

"Isn't that Karidee?" I asked as a blond woman headed away from the pizza parlor.

Cordelia twisted around in her seat so she could see out the window. "She works here. Her shift probably just ended." She was about to turn back to the table when she froze, probably for the same reason my eyes had gone wide.

Detective Marquez had just climbed out of an unmarked vehicle. She intercepted Karidee in the middle of the parking lot. They spoke for a moment or two, Karidee fidgeting the whole time, and then Marquez led her to the unmarked police vehicle and guided her into the back seat. Seconds later, the detective drove out of the parking lot, whisking Karidee away.

Chapter 26

When I parted my curtains on May Day, a cloudless blue sky greeted me, bringing a smile to my face. The weather was perfect for the festivities that would take place on the village green throughout the day. I planned to take in some of them myself, before the Inkwell opened at noon. I'd promised Kiandra that I'd watch her maypole dance. Several groups of schoolchildren would be performing the dance on the green, and Kiandra's class would be the first group of the day.

I was up and about earlier than usual because I wanted to make sure I had the pub all shipshape and ready to open before I headed out to the green. While waiting for a delivery of supplies, I checked the napkin dispensers and salt and pepper shakers, ensuring that they were all full. After that, I tucked myself away in my tiny office to pay a couple of bills. I wrapped that up just in time to greet the deliveryman bringing an order of fresh produce from a local farm.

I put everything away, either in the pub's commercial-size refrigerator or in the walk-in pantry. After that, I took a final look around the Inkwell. Everything seemed in order.

As I headed out the front door of the pub, I spotted Wimsey stalking through the grass near the edge of the forest.

"Don't bother bringing home any presents," I called out to him.

He ignored me.

He didn't leave dead creatures on my doorstep *too* often, so I hoped I wouldn't be met with any unpleasant surprises when I returned home.

Leaving Wimsey to whatever he was up to, I walked over to the village green, where several dozen people were already milling about. Food trucks had parked along Creekside Road and appeared to be getting ready to open for business. A bouncy castle had been set up at the western edge of the green and a local musical group, the Old-Time Fiddlers, was setting up at the bandstand.

My nose caught the scent of cotton candy and mini donuts on the air. My stomach rumbled in response, despite the fact that I'd eaten a bowl of oatmeal less than two hours ago. I decided I could be strong, for a while at least, and resist the temptation to indulge in junk food until after midmorning.

A group of children dressed all in white gathered around a woman near the maypole. I spotted Kiandra in the group and a second later saw her mom nearby.

"It's a perfect day, isn't it?" I said as I reached Shontelle's side.

"We couldn't have asked for better." She smiled as Kiandra bounced up on her toes and waved to us.

We both waved back.

"So, spill," Shontelle said when Kiandra had returned her attention to the other kids around her. "I want to hear all about your date with Grayson. I would have hounded you for details earlier, but things have been busy, and I didn't have a chance to grill you after the meeting last night."

"There's not a lot to tell." When I caught her disbelieving and unimpressed expression, I hurried to add, "But it was nice."

"Nice? That's all?"

"No," I said quickly. "It was . . . almost perfect."

Shontelle tucked her arm through mine as Kiandra and her fellow dancers took hold of the ribbons hanging from the maypole.

"As soon as this is over, I want to know everything."

Music began to play from a nearby speaker and, with an encouraging nod from their teacher, the children started to dance.

I was impressed by how well they pulled it off, the ribbons crisscrossing as the children danced and wove among each other. When it was over, Shontelle and I clapped and cheered along with the rest of the crowd that had gathered. Kiandra beamed with happiness and ran over to ask Shontelle if she could go to the bouncy castle with her friends.

Shontelle gave her permission and Kiandra ran off happily with two other girls and a boy her age. We followed slowly in their wake, Shontelle sniffing the food-scented air as we walked.

"I won't be able to resist the mini donuts much longer." She eyed the food trucks on Creekside Road.

"I'm with you there."

"But first, I need details," she said.

I obliged, telling her all about my date with Grayson. She was impressed by the roof-top dinner he'd arranged and she shared my disappointment about our interrupted moment on the footbridge.

After I'd related all the details, we continued to stroll around the village green. As we passed the bandstand, I noticed several portable office dividers that had been set up to showcase posters and photographs. When we got closer, I realized the display was about the history of May Day generally as well as the history of Shady Creek's annual celebrations.

We paused in front of a poster featuring photographs of Shady Creek's past Spring Queens. I'd heard about the town's tradition of crowning a young woman as queen each May Day. Hopeful young women had to apply in advance, and the winner got chosen based on community involvement over the past year.

I was on the verge of turning away from the display when one of the photographs I'd glanced at drew my more focused attention. Although the young woman in the picture had long, flowing hair, her resemblance to Jan Finch was uncanny. What caught my eye even more than that was the caption beneath the photo, naming the 1978 Spring Queen as Margaret Vallencourt.

Was Margaret Vallencourt now Margaret Finch? The resemblance between Jan and the woman in the photo was certainly strong enough. Did that mean Margaret was related to Edwin Vallencourt, the original owner of Shady Creek Manor?

Another question joined the others already bouncing around in my mind.

If Jan and her mother were related to Edwin Vallencourt, was that somehow relevant to the recent events at the manor?

I didn't know, but I planned to find out.

Chapter 27

After Kiandra had her fill of the bouncy castle, Shontelle and I took her over to the line of food trucks for a decidedly unhealthy snack. I bought myself a bag of cinnamon and sugar mini donuts, and Shontelle got the same for herself. Kiandra, however, preferred the pink cotton candy, though she did eat one of her mom's donuts as well.

I had to leave them a short time later to get back to the pub, and customers began arriving soon after the Inkwell opened for business. The air held an excited hum of energy that afternoon. Most of the patrons were chatting about the masquerade that was only a few hours away. It sounded like half the town would be at the event, and that made me feel better about closing the Inkwell early. Damien and Mel, having worked at the pub for several years before I purchased it, had assured me that it wouldn't be worth keeping the doors open during the masquerade.

Neither of them was going to the dance, but Teagan and Booker would be there. Booker was working the early shift, but Teagan would have the day off. In the late afternoon, I hurried across the green to Aunt Gilda's salon. Mel would close the Inkwell in an hour or so, allowing me to get my hair done for the masquerade.

When I arrived at the salon, Aunt Gilda was putting the final waves into a young woman's blond hair. I did a double take when I saw the woman's face in the mirror.

"Karidee," I said when she got up from the chair a minute later, her wavy hair cascading over her shoulders, "your hair looks great. You must be going to the masquerade."

"I am," she said with a smile. "I can't wait."

She clearly hadn't been arrested, and I noted that she didn't seem to be under any obvious stress.

Before she approached the counter to pay for her appointment, I lowered my voice and addressed her again.

"I saw you with Detective Marquez outside Spice and Slice last night."

Her eyes widened and her cheeks turned pink. "I was hoping nobody had seen that."

"Is everything all right?"

She nodded. "The detective wanted to question me about the murder and the assault," she whispered. "It was scary, but everything's fine now. I was behind the manor, talking to a friend of mine, when Linnea's assistant was killed. My friend works in the kitchen there. She vouched for me."

She smiled and turned her attention to Gilda, who was now behind the counter. Karidee paid and left the salon without saying another word to me.

"You know Karidee?" Aunt Gilda asked.

"I just met her recently. She came to Linnea's event at the pub."

"Now that you mention it, I remember seeing her there. She's a nice girl."

I could agree, now that I knew she had an alibi for the murder. Maybe she hadn't gone about things the best way when trying to get some time with Linnea, but aside from that she seemed nice enough.

"So, what are we going to do?" Aunt Gilda asked once I was seated in her styling chair. "Curls, waves, or maybe an updo?"

I'd spent a fair bit of time pondering that question ever since Shontelle and I had gone dress shopping.

"An updo, I think," I said. "Maybe with a few curly tendrils loose?"

"That'll look beautiful," Betty commented. She was in the midst of styling the hair of one of her regular customers, Delia Wilder.

"Sophisticated and stunning," Gilda agreed. "A perfect match for your dress."

"Which I've yet to see," Betty said.

"You'll see it tonight," I told her, "but I can show you a picture when we're done here."

Aunt Gilda and I chatted about my mom and brothers, and what they were all up to lately, while she got to work styling my hair. After Delia Wilder left the salon, only Gilda, Betty, and I remained. During a lull in our conversation, my mind drifted back to my suspect list. Karidee was officially in the clear now, but I couldn't say the same about the Honeywells. I still wondered if Brad and Gemma could have worked together, with Brad killing Marcie and Gemma attacking Jan. Maybe they didn't want anyone finding the treasure because they thought it should be theirs.

I wasn't even sure if I could completely eliminate Jan Finch from my suspect list. She obviously hadn't attacked herself, and it was more likely than not that Marcie's killer had hit Jan over the head, but there was still a possibility that there were two different culprits. And what about that earring I'd seen in the third-floor guest room right after Marcie's death? Was it part of the treasure, or a clue to the killer's identity? I still didn't know.

I also had yet to figure out how Marcie and her killer had accessed the guest room without using a key, especially since there was no sign of a secret entrance. I wondered if there were any more clues to be found at the manor, but it was a big place, and the police had already gone over the hotel.

I forced myself back to the present.

"Any more appointments today?" I asked Betty as she tidied up her station.

"Delia was my last one. I need time to get myself gussied up for the masquerade."

I smiled. "I'm sure you'll look amazing."

"Hopefully my Ted will think so," she said, referring to her husband.

"He will," Gilda assured her.

A few minutes later, my hair was piled on top of my head in a gorgeous updo I never could have come close to replicating on my own. Aunt Gilda fetched a curling iron to use on the tendrils she'd left loose on either side of my face.

"Do you two know Margaret Finch?" I asked.

"Sure," Gilda replied. "I cut her hair every two months."

"She runs the cat shelter on Magnolia Road with her daughter, doesn't she?" Betty asked.

"That's right." Aunt Gilda twirled a lock of my hair around the curling iron. She met my gaze in the mirror. "Are you asking because of what happened to her daughter?"

"Sort of. I was looking at pictures of past Spring Queens out on the green and noticed one from the seventies. The woman looked a lot like Jan and her name was Margaret Vallencourt."

"That's Margaret Finch," Betty said with a nod. "She was a Vallencourt before she married Roger Finch."

"Vallencourt, as in Edwin Vallencourt?" I doubted there were two lines of Vallencourts in Shady Creek, but I wanted to be sure.

"That's right," Betty confirmed. "Edwin was Margaret's uncle, if I remember correctly."

Although Betty hadn't grown up in Shady Creek, she'd lived here for decades and seemed to have a good handle on who was related to whom.

"Are there any other Vallencourts in Shady Creek?"

Aunt Gilda curled my last remaining tendril of hair. "I haven't met anyone by that name."

"No." Betty paused in the midst of setting bottles of styling products on a shelf. "I can't think of any others."

"What happened to the manor after Edwin Vallencourt died?" I asked. "Did Margaret inherit anything?"

"You're testing my memory here," Betty said.

"Sorry. I'm probably asking too many questions, as usual."

She smiled. "Of course not. It's good for me to make my rusty brain cells work." She thought for another second or two. "Edwin didn't have any children. He didn't have a wife, either, though there were plenty of girlfriends, especially in his younger years. He didn't live too long. I seem to remember hearing that he died in his fifties. A problem with his liver, I think."

"Too much partying, probably," Aunt Gilda said. "I've certainly heard *those* stories."

Betty nodded. "His parties were legendary. Anyway, he had three or four siblings, and I think everything went to them when he died. Margaret's father probably inherited a share of the estate."

"But the manor didn't stay in the family," I said. "I heard it changed hands a few times before the Honeywells bought it."

"That's true," Betty confirmed. "The story goes that none of Edwin's siblings could afford to buy out the others' shares of the property. At least a couple of them were pretty deep in debt. So they had to sell the place."

I thought over all this new information as Betty went back to tidying up.

When Aunt Gilda put away the curling iron a moment later, I turned my head from side to side, admiring my hairdo in the mirror.

"I love it. Thank you, Aunt Gilda."

She squeezed my shoulders. "My pleasure, honey."

"You'll be turning plenty of heads tonight," Betty said.

I sighed at that, and Gilda squeezed my shoulders again.

"Maybe not the one you'd like to," she said, reading my thoughts. "But there will be plenty of time ahead with Grayson."

"I hope so," I said.

"Why all the interest in the Vallencourts?" she asked as I got up from the chair.

"I'm trying to connect the dots in my head. Only, I'm not sure if all the dots are relevant. Jan Finch is Edwin Vallencourt's great-niece. She's been sneaking around what was once his mansion, and someone attacked her there, about a week after the murder."

"You think the attack on Jan, and Marcie Kent's murder could somehow be tied to Edwin?" Aunt Gilda asked.

"But he's been dead for decades," Betty pointed out.

"I know," I said, "but some people believe he hid treasure in the manor before he died."

I told them about the blueprints Jan had in her possession when she was attacked.

"I've always thought the stories about the treasure were just that, stories," Betty said.

"You're not the only one," I told her. "But I think Jan might believe the stories. Maybe Marcie did too."

Concern crept into Aunt Gilda's eyes. "Maybe we shouldn't go to the masquerade after all. What if the killer is still at the manor?"

I had no intention of missing the masquerade. I'd been looking forward to it for weeks.

"We'll be fine," I assured her. "There's no way the killer would dare to harm anyone with so many people around."

"I suppose you're right," she said.

I sure hoped I was.

Chapter 28

Rolling up to Shady Creek Manor in Aunt Gilda's car brought me mixed feelings. I couldn't shake the memories of what had happened there recently, and I wasn't sure if I'd ever be able to, but the windows glowed with a welcoming light, and I couldn't help but feel excited about the masquerade. After Aunt Gilda handed the car over to the valet, we ascended the front steps with a handful of other partygoers. Everyone was decked out in formalwear and masks that ranged from simple to bedazzling to slightly creepy.

One man's mask covered much of his face and had a hawk-like beak and sharp angles that gave him a menacing appearance. I almost shivered at the sight of it, especially since his eyes were hidden in shadows. When we stepped into the lobby, I lost sight of the man, to my relief. Everyone else around me wore far less frightening masks.

We left Aunt Gilda's coat and my wrap at the coat check set up in the front parlor. Then we followed the flow of newly arrived guests toward the ballroom. In the lobby and on a narrow table in the wide corridor, stunning bouquets of flowers provided bursts of color and heavenly scents.

Before entering the ballroom, I glanced across the corridor and into the dining room. A few round tables, draped with white cloths, dotted the room, but there weren't as many as I'd seen on previous occasions. Each table featured a beautiful bouquet, and a handful of masked guests sat around the tables, chatting and snacking on bite-size food. Along one wall, several rectangular tables displayed an impressive array of hors d'oeuvres and desserts.

My stomach grumbled at the sight. I hadn't eaten since lunchtime, hoping to save room for what I'd been told would be an incredible spread of food. I hadn't tasted anything yet, but from looks alone, my sources had been accurate.

As we entered the ballroom, I realized the bouquets we'd already seen were a mere taste of what was to come. The ballroom had been decked out with elaborate and eye-catching flower arrangements. Each one had probably cost three figures. Up above, ceiling draperies drew my eyes. The fabric streamers, about two feet wide, were fastened near the giant chandelier and dipped down and then up again as they reached out to the edges of the ceiling. In spring colors like green, yellow, and light pink, they reminded me of maypole ribbons, and each one was lit with fairy lights. The effect was almost magical.

As Gilda and I moved farther into the ballroom, a server dressed in black and white paused before us, balancing a tray filled with flutes of champagne and sparkling water. I took a glass of champagne and Gilda opted for the sparkling water. We thanked the woman before she moved on to the next group of guests.

At the far end of the ballroom, a string quartet was on the stage, playing a Strauss waltz. The musicians were dressed like the guests, in formalwear and masks. Several couples moved around the dance floor, and all seemed to know what they were doing. I didn't doubt that the dance floor would become more crowded as the evening progressed.

It didn't take long for Aunt Gilda to spot Betty and her husband, Ted, in the growing crowd. I took the time to greet the couple before moving on. I'd noticed Shontelle and her mother, Yvette, entering the ballroom.

"This is incredible," Shontelle said, when I reached them. They had both paused inside the door to take in the sight of the room and the decorations.

"It really is," I agreed. "And you both look stunning."

Shontelle's deep red dress looked like it was custom made for her, and Yvette was elegant and sophisticated in her black gown with a simple black and gold mask to match.

"So do you," Yvette said. "Shontelle told me your dress was amazing, but it's even better than I imagined."

"You definitely made the right choice," Shontelle said.

I thanked them. I certainly felt good in my purple and silver dress. Almost like a princess.

Once we all had flutes of champagne in hand, Yvette wandered off to greet some friends while Shontelle and I made a slow circuit of the ballroom. We said hello to some acquaintances before stopping by one of the French doors that led out onto the patio. Colorful lanterns hung outside, and a handful of guests mingled out in the fresh air.

I'd already taken a few sips of champagne when I realized it would probably be best if I put some food in my stomach so the alcohol wouldn't hit me too hard. I was about to suggest to Shontelle that we head over to the dining room to check out the hors d'oeuvres on offer, when a tall, blond man in a tux and black mask approached and addressed Shontelle.

"Ms. Williams, may I have this dance?"

"Absolutely," she said. She offered him her hand and smoothly passed off her nearly empty champagne flute to me while giving me a quick wink.

I smiled and watched as she and her partner began to dance.

I hadn't recognized the man until he'd spoken, probably because of his mask and the fact that I'd never seen Officer Eldon Howes of the Shady Creek Police Department in a tux. Most of my interactions with him had occurred while he was in uniform.

Another server passed by me, and I set Shontelle's glass on his tray. Then I wandered out of the ballroom and into the corridor. I was about to head into the dining room when I caught a glimpse of a red-haired woman near the lobby. I didn't know anyone in Shady Creek who had crinkly, bright orange hair like that other than Cordelia King.

Hoping to say hello to her, I followed the corridor to the lobby. Aside from the silver-haired couple entering the manor through the front doors, there was no one else around. Where had Cordelia disappeared to?

I crossed the lobby and peered down another hallway, but it was deserted. I did, however, hear a low murmur of voices coming from nearby.

I took a few steps farther along the hallway and was about to call out Cordelia's name, when I recognized Brad Honeywell's voice coming from behind a closed door.

"I found . . . in a box in the basement," I heard him say as I paused outside the door.

I recognized Gemma's voice next.

". . . to the police," she said.

That last word really caught my attention. I glanced behind me to make sure I was still alone in the hallway and then leaned closer to the door, hoping to pick up more words.

"Do you think it's true?" Brad asked. His next words sounded like nothing more than a mumble to me.

I wished I had super hearing. Gemma's next words were also too quiet for me to hear.

"We'll do it after the guests are gone," Brad said seconds later.

His voice was closer than it had been the last time he'd spoken.

"I'll leave these here for now." A rustle of paper followed Gemma's words.

When I heard footsteps approaching the door, I spun around and quickly returned to the lobby, moving as quietly as I could in my heels. I'd just dashed out of sight of the hallway when I heard a door open and close.

Then another door did the same. I heard several voices, and a moment later Cordelia appeared in the lobby, followed by Brad and Gemma. The Honeywells smiled at me and Cordelia before heading down the corridor that led to the ballroom. Brad wore a suit and Gemma a deep blue evening gown. Both wore masks just like their guests.

"Hi, Sadie," Cordelia greeted. "Isn't the masquerade incredible?"

"It really is," I agreed. "Were you off wandering?"

"Oh, no," she said. "I'd probably get lost if I did that. I just went to use the ladies' room." She looked me up and down. "Wow! You look like a beautiful fairy princess."

I complimented her as well. She wore an emerald-green dress that went perfectly with her hair color, and a green and purple mask, decorated with fake jewels that glinted in the light from the lobby's chandelier.

"I can't wait to taste the food," she said as we headed in that direction.

"You and me both."

As we made our way into the dining room, I bumped shoulders with a woman on her way out.

"I'm so sorry," I said as I sidestepped, managing not to spill the remains of my champagne.

I wasn't sure if she even heard me. She continued on her way out of the dining room without so much as glancing at me. She wasn't anyone I recognized, and I didn't think it was just because of the mask that covered most of her face. She was a couple of inches shorter than me and had straight black hair that hung loose and reached almost down to her waist. I couldn't think of anyone I knew in town who matched that description.

Right behind the woman was the man in the creepy hawklike mask I'd seen earlier. He brushed past me and when I glanced over my shoulder, I saw him put a hand to the woman's lower back. The two of them disappeared into the ballroom.

Cordelia was already at the hors d'oeuvres table, so I quickly joined her.

"It's too hard to choose," Cordelia lamented, hovering by the table, an empty plate in her hands.

I sympathized. There had to be at least a dozen different hors d'oeuvres set out on the table, and each one looked absolutely scrumptious.

"What's the chance that I can taste one of each without getting completely stuffed?" she asked.

"I don't know." I nodded at the dessert table. "Don't forget we need to save room to taste test some of those."

"Good point," Cordelia said. "Maybe I'll try half a dozen for now. This party goes until midnight, so we have plenty of time to come back for another round."

"True."

I studied the selection. Each platter was accompanied by a small card to identify the dish. I set a cream cheese and prosciutto bite on my plate and then added a small pastry that resembled a spring roll but which, according to its card, contained Brie, mushrooms, and rosemary. I selected two other hors d'oeuvres and then sat down with Cordelia at a free table.

"Have you done any dancing yet?" I asked her.

"No," she said with a sigh. "I'm not likely to get asked."

"Don't say that. Why wouldn't someone ask you? And besides," I added before she had a chance to respond, "*you* could always do the asking."

"Oh, no. I couldn't do that. I'd be setting myself up for rejection."

"You don't know that."

"It doesn't really matter, anyways," she said before biting into one of the Brie-and-mushroom pastries. After she'd polished it off, this time with a sigh of delight, she continued. "I'd probably just trample my partner's feet."

"You should have more confidence in yourself," I said.

I didn't have a chance to continue my pep talk, because Gilda, Betty, and Ted entered the dining room and swept over to our table. We exchanged a few words and then they gravitated toward the food table, returning a few minutes later to join us with full plates.

We chatted while we ate our snacks, but my mind kept wandering away from the topic of conversation. What had Brad and Gemma been talking about earlier? I wished I'd heard more. The gaps in the conversation left me frustrated. Maybe it was none of my business, but the fact that I'd heard them mention the police had set off my curiosity.

Were they hiding something from the police, or did they have some evidence to share with them?

I recalled that Gemma had said she'd leave something in the room until after the party.

Whatever it was, I knew I should forget about it and enjoy the masquerade.

I also knew that would be impossible.

By the time I'd polished off the last hors d'oeuvre on my plate, I'd made up my mind. Before returning to the ballroom, I was going to do a bit of snooping.

Chapter 29

I told the others I needed to use the restroom. Fortunately, no one seemed suspicious and I made a clean getaway. Almost.

Out in the corridor, I headed for the lobby, but halted after only a few steps when I heard someone call out my name in a low voice. When I glanced over my shoulder, Gina waved to me. She stood with the door marked STAFF ONLY pushed open halfway. I quickly backtracked so I could talk to her.

"Is it busy in the kitchen tonight?" I asked her.

"I'll say. I've got a five-minute break, but then I need to get back to it."

"The desserts look amazing," I told her. "I can't wait to try them."

She smiled. "I hope you'll like them."

Still standing with the door half open, she shot a quick glance behind her, toward the kitchen.

"Any news on the murder investigation?" she asked.

"Not on my end," I replied.

Although there had been some developments, I didn't want to bring up Karidee's name. I figured there wasn't any point in doing that anyway, since she'd been cleared of suspicion by the police.

I decided to turn the question back on Gina. "Have you heard anything?"

She shook her head with a frown. "There's gossip flying around, of course, but mostly the same old rumors and speculation. Everyone's on edge. A couple of people have even quit because they're too scared to keep working here."

"Really?" I supposed I couldn't blame them. "Does that leave you short-staffed in the kitchen?"

"Fortunately not, otherwise tonight would be even crazier. It was two housekeepers who quit, Connie and Miranda. And I get it. After all, they wander around upstairs on their own, going in and out of rooms. Plenty of opportunity for the killer to creep up on them."

She shuddered, and I almost did the same. Then my mind caught up to what she'd said.

"Connie quit?"

"This morning," Gina confirmed. "It's left the Honeywells in a bit of a lurch. Neither housekeeper gave any notice."

"I know Connie's husband was worried about her staying on here."

Gina startled at the sound of voices coming from somewhere behind her.

"I'd better go," she said quickly. "Enjoy the party!"

Before I had the chance to say goodbye, she disappeared, the door falling shut and latching with a click.

I waited while a gaggle of masked party guests crossed from the ballroom to the dining room, and then I resumed my previous quest, passing through the lobby before creeping along the corridor where I'd eavesdropped earlier.

When I reached the door, I paused with my hand on the knob. My heart thudded in my chest and I had sudden second thoughts. I didn't exactly have the best track record when it came to snooping without getting caught. But what if Gemma and Brad were concealing a crucial piece of evidence? I had to find out.

Still, when I turned the knob, half of me hoped the door would be locked, so I'd be forced to go back to the ballroom and enjoy an evening of partying without putting myself at risk of being found where I didn't belong. I wasn't sure if my luck was good or bad when the door opened easily.

I froze with one foot across the threshold. I thought I'd heard a noise in the lobby. Footsteps, possibly, but when I strained to hear anything further, all that met my ears was the distant music and low hum of conversation coming from the party.

Not giving myself another chance to hesitate, I slipped into the room, closing the door all but a crack behind me. The shaft of light coming through the narrow opening allowed me to see that I was in an office with a large wooden desk sitting in the middle of the room and several filing cabinets along one wall. I flicked on the desk lamp instead of the overhead light, worried that too much light might show beneath the door, even though the hallway outside was lit.

Now that I had light to see by, I quietly pushed the door closed until it latched. I stood by the desk, surveying the room. Aside from a blotter and the lamp, the only things on the top of the desk were a stapler, a plastic dish of paperclips, and a canister stuffed with pens and pencils. There were two drawers on either side, plus a long, shallow one that ran the width of the desk. I tugged at that one first, but it didn't budge.

I tried another drawer, and it opened with ease. I rifled through the contents, but it didn't hold anything of interest. Just some unused file folders and a stack of plain white paper for the printer that sat on top of one of the filing cabinets across the room. Sliding that drawer shut, I moved on to the next one. Again, it held nothing of interest. I checked the remaining two with the same result.

As far as I could tell, there was nothing in those drawers that could in any possible way be related to the crimes that had recently occurred at the manor. Maybe I was way off base and the Honeywells had been talking about something completely unrelated to the murder and assault, but I had a hard time believing that.

Not wanting to linger too long in the office, I moved on to the filing cabinets, quietly sliding each drawer open in turn. I flipped quickly through the collection of files, but if the papers I'd heard rustling before had been hidden away in one of the folders, I didn't have much chance of identifying it, unless I wanted to go through each and every one. Taking that much time to search would put me at too much risk of getting caught.

Even though I knew it was pointless, I tugged at the shallow top drawer of the desk again. It still didn't budge. I scrunched up my nose in frustration, but then my gaze fell on the dish of paperclips.

I didn't know how to pick a lock, but it never seemed that difficult on TV. I figured it was worth giving it a shot, at least.

I reached for a paperclip, and then froze with my hand hovering over the dish. Footsteps approached the office. Quiet ones, but I still heard them. My heart nearly stumbled to a stop.

Turn off the light! I silently screamed at myself.

But I didn't have a chance.

Before I could even reach the lamp, the knob turned and the door swung open.

Chapter 30

My panicked brain scrambled to come up with an excuse for why I was standing in a room where I clearly shouldn't have been.

"I was looking for the washroom!" I blurted out as a masked man stepped into the room.

Eyebrows rose above the black Zorro-type mask.

Relief rushed through me, almost making my knees weak. I would have recognized the man's blue eyes anywhere.

"That's the best you could come up with?" Grayson asked, amused.

I shushed him and grabbed his arm, pulling him farther into the room while I used my free hand to push the door shut.

"How did you know I was in here?" I asked in a whisper. "And what are you doing here? You're supposed to be out of town. When did you get back and why didn't you tell me you were coming?"

I bit down on my lower lip, wondering if maybe he hadn't told me because he'd come to the masquerade with another woman.

"I saw you sneaking off, I was hoping to dance with you, I got back two hours ago, and I thought I'd surprise you," he said, answering all my questions in one go.

"Oh." I digested that information. "But I wasn't sneaking."

He raised an eyebrow.

"Okay, fine," I relented. "I was definitely sneaking." I touched a hand to my mask. "How did you recognize me?"

"The red hair sort of gives it away. And your . . . Sadie-ness." He grinned at me in a way that made my stomach do a backflip. "Plus, there's your freckles."

From the light in his eyes, I knew he was laughing silently. At me? At my freckles?

"I happen to like my freckles," I said, on the defensive.

His gaze held mine. "So do I."

Heat spread through my chest and my cheeks.

"What are you looking for?"

His question jolted me back to reality. For a second, I'd forgotten where I was and why.

As succinctly as possible, I told him about the conversation I'd partially overheard between the Honeywells.

"But I haven't found anything of interest," I said. "The top desk drawer is locked, but now that you're here, you can pick it."

I knew from past experience that he could.

"Please?" I added.

Instead of responding, Grayson put a hand on my wrist and switched off the desk lamp in one swift motion. He tugged me over to the wall next to the door, so I was standing with my back pressed up against his chest.

"What are you doing?" I asked, startled.

"Shh."

The sound came from right next to my ear, Grayson's breath tickling my skin. He looped an arm around my waist and held me close. I was so distracted by the warmth of his body tucked up against mine that I nearly missed what had alarmed him.

Slow footfalls sounded out in the corridor, getting closer. Whoever was out there was wearing high heels. Gemma Honeywell?

I held my breath as the footsteps approached the door and then paused. Grayson's arm tightened around my waist, ever so slightly. I could feel that his muscles were taut and coiled, ready for whatever might happen next.

I was starting to feel lightheaded from holding my breath. Or maybe it was from Grayson's proximity. A combination of the two, possibly.

A second later, the footsteps started up again, disappearing back the way they'd come.

I let the air rush out of my lungs as Grayson relaxed behind me.

"Probably just someone looking for the washroom," I whispered.

They would have found it if they'd kept going down the hall.

I was about to take a step forward, hoping I'd be able to find the desk lamp in the darkness, when Grayson gave me a gentle squeeze and whispered in my ear.

"You look incredible."

His words sent a pleasant shiver through me.

"You can't see me in the dark." The words popped out of my mouth before I had a chance to think.

He laughed quietly. "I got a good look before I shut off the light."

Of course he did. Sometimes I said the dumbest things.

Taking one of his hands in mine, I stepped forward, my free hand out in front of me. When my fingers touched the lamp, I switched it on.

"You look very handsome," I said, wishing I'd said that in the first place.

He stepped closer to me, his eyes on mine, and I wondered if he was going to kiss me right there in the office where we weren't supposed to be, at risk of someone discovering us at any moment. Then I heard a quiet clink and he held up a paperclip.

"I'm always happy to help," he said.

He squeezed my hand before letting it go. By the time I'd followed him around the desk, he already had the drawer unlocked. I'd hoped to pick up some tips by watching him work, but I wasn't going to complain. Maybe I'd ask him to teach me the art of lock picking another time.

He slid open the drawer and my eyes widened. I snatched up the roll of papers that sat on top of a closed laptop.

"More blueprints!" I spread them out on top of the desk as Grayson pushed the drawer shut. "These have got to be what the Honeywells were talking about."

Like the blueprints I'd found next to Jan, these ones had yellowed with age. I was sure it was a different set, and not just because the police had taken custody of the other one. The page showing the layout of the main floor of the manor wasn't torn at the top, like the one from the other set.

"What do you mean by more?" Grayson asked, standing shoulder to shoulder with me as we stared down at the drawings.

I remembered he was out of the loop. I quickly brought him up to speed.

"People really believe the story about the hidden treasure?" he said when I'd finished. "That's what this is all about?"

"I don't know for sure, but I think it could be what's motivated the killer. I bet Jan stumbled upon the other set of blueprints when she was working down in the basement. I overheard Brad say that's where he found these ones."

I zeroed in on one part of the drawing, noticing something for the first time.

"But I think this set must be a later one," I added.

I shoved aside the top sheets to look at the layout of the manor's third floor.

My pulse beat loudly in my ears as a heavy weight of understanding settled in the middle of my chest.

"Oh no," I whispered.

"What is it?" Grayson asked.

With shaking hands, I switched between papers again, double checking to make sure I wasn't mistaken.

"Sadie?"

No mistake.

I stepped back from the desk, wishing I'd been wrong.

I met Grayson's worried gaze. "I know who killed Marcie."

Chapter 31

We decided to test my theory before contacting the police, in case the blueprints weren't accurate. We returned the papers to the drawer before hurrying out of the office, hoping no one would ever know we'd been in there. I worried that Grayson would have to pick another lock, which could cause us difficulty down the line when explaining everything to the authorities. Luck was with us, however. It probably wasn't the smartest practice, but the Honeywells had left the linen closet unlocked.

"Closet" probably wasn't the best descriptor. It was more of a spacious storage room, with shelves lining two of the walls. Everything from tablecloths to pillowcases were stacked on the shelves. I wasn't interested in the thread count of Shady Creek Manor's sheets, though. All I wanted to know was whether the room had a secret door through which Connie could have accessed the third-floor guest room where Marcie had been pushed out the window.

I figured if anyone had used a secret door in the storage room to commit the murder, it had to be Connie. She'd admitted to working in there on the day of Marcie's death, and Gemma had been out in the hall when not with Connie. Surely that meant Gemma would have noticed anyone entering the room the usual way, and if Gemma had tried to use the secret door, Connie would have seen her. It would have taken guts for Connie to sneak away when there was a chance Gemma could have looked in to check on her, but she must have decided it was worth the risk.

Grayson and I started our investigation at the back wall. Aside from the wall dividing the closet from the corridor, the one at the back of the room was the only one without shelves. It made sense that the secret door would be located there, if it existed at all.

I tapped at various spots on the wall. When I knocked for the fifth time, having moved to the right each time, the sound changed, becoming hollow.

We exchanged a glance, knowing we were getting close.

Grayson ran his hands over the white paneling while I pressed my palm against the wall at various points. Grayson then did the same.

The second time he pressed against the wall, there was a quiet click and several panels drew back into a recess before sliding to the left.

For a second all I could do was stare at the newly revealed opening.

"She really did do it," I said quietly. "Connie killed Marcie."

"Let's make sure this really does lead to the third floor." Grayson's grim expression told me he fully expected it would.

He ducked through the four-foot-high opening and I followed closely behind him. The hidden room was more of a cubbyhole, really, one that gave access to a narrow stairway. There was a light switch next to the hidden door, but when I flicked it, nothing happened.

Most likely the lightbulbs had burnt out years ago.

Grayson produced his cell phone and activated a flashlight app. I was glad he had his phone on him. I'd checked mine with my wrap earlier so I wouldn't have to carry it around all evening. At the time, I hadn't anticipated that I'd be creeping through hidden passageways.

By agreement, we left the secret door open. The thought of closing it without knowing for sure that we'd be able to open it again freaked me out more than I was willing to admit.

"Careful," Grayson cautioned as he started up the narrow wooden staircase.

I gathered up the skirt of my dress in one hand, not wanting to trip on it or have it catch on the rough, unfinished wall. I used my free hand to steady myself against the wall now and then, my fingers quickly getting covered in dust and grime.

The air inside the passageway was stuffy and I couldn't see much. Most of the light emitted by Grayson's phone was blocked by his body. I was tempted to grab onto the back of his suit jacket, more to reassure myself that I wasn't alone than to keep myself steady, but I resisted and continued to rely on the wall instead.

We moved slowly and I took care not to trip or stumble in my high heels. After what felt like an hour, although it was probably mere minutes, I tried to peer around Grayson, but saw nothing other than dusty stairs disappearing into the darkness above us.

"It feels like it's going on forever," I whispered.

There probably wasn't much chance of anyone hearing us, but somehow it felt right to keep my voice low.

"We should be past the second floor by now." Grayson spoke quietly too.

According to the blueprints we'd found, the stairway could be accessed through a hidden door in the second floor corridor, but with so little light to see by, it didn't surprise me that we'd missed the other door on our way up the stairs.

I figured Marcie must have used the second floor entrance on the day she died. She probably knew about the treasure and the existence of the manor's secret passageways from her research into Edwin Vallencourt, but I wondered how she'd found the secret door without the aid of blueprints. Luck, perhaps, or maybe a previous owner of the manor had shared the information somewhere online.

I pushed those thoughts aside as we continued our slow trek upward. My nose twitched, tickled by the dust we stirred up with our steps.

"Here we go," Grayson said after another minute or so.

He stopped and shone the light from his phone down my way so I could see the last two steps that led up to the landing where he waited for me. There wasn't much room on the small landing, but the thought of tumbling down the narrow, dark stairs sent an unpleasant shiver of fear along the back of my neck, so I squeezed in close to Grayson. As I did so, I heard a click. With a squeak and a groan, another small door opened.

Grayson climbed through the opening before reaching back and offering me his hand. I took it, my skirt still gathered up in my other hand, and ducked through the door, hopefully not too awkwardly.

Grayson shone the light from his phone around us. We were standing in one of the hotel's guest rooms. From the perfectly made bed and the lack of any luggage, I guessed that the room was unoccupied. It looked like the vacant one I'd seen on the day of Marcie's death, but all the third-floor rooms could have looked similar, for all I knew. The curtains were intact, but the Honeywells could have replaced them since Marcie's death.

Still holding Grayson's hand, I led the way to the full-sized door, opening it quietly and slipping out into the hallway. I counted the number of doors between the guest room and the main stairway. I had to make an effort not to tremble when I finished.

We'd confirmed my theory.

The secret stairway led directly to the room where Marcie had faced her killer.

Chapter 32

We searched for Officer Eldon Howes in the ballroom, out on the patio, and in the dining room, but there was no sign of him. It didn't escape my notice that Shontelle was also missing. When I asked Aunt Gilda if she knew where my friend was, she said the last time she'd seen Shontelle, she was dancing with Howes, for at least the second time that evening. I tucked that information away for future consideration. When I'd met Shontelle, she'd been in a long-distance relationship with a man in Georgia, but that had ended several months ago. She hadn't dated anyone since. Maybe that would soon change.

"Relax," Grayson said when I rejoined him at the far end of the ballroom. "Everything will be fine."

I hoped he was right. He'd called Detective Marquez to fill her in on what we'd discovered and the fact that Connie had quit her job at the manor that morning. We figured she was long gone from Shady Creek. Whether she'd found the treasure or had decided that it didn't exist or that it was too risky to keep searching, I didn't know. I just hoped the police would be able to track her down.

While it was possible that someone else had killed Marcie,

using the second floor entrance to the secret passageway to access the third-floor room, I doubted that was the case. Connie's sudden departure made me all the more certain she was guilty.

Grayson and I had planned to show Officer Howes the secret passageway, but it seemed that would have to wait, since he was nowhere in sight. I tried to watch the couples who were dancing in the ballroom, but I couldn't stay focused. An antsy energy buzzed through me, making it impossible to stay still.

"Hey." Grayson took my hand and gave it a squeeze, stopping me from fidgeting with the skirt of my dress. "How about a dance?"

I agreed, hoping it would help pass the time. I didn't expect to get swept up in the dance. The quartet was playing another Strauss waltz, and it turned out that Grayson knew what he was doing on the dance floor. With each step I relaxed a little bit more, until I was able to enjoy the moment. I became more and more aware of how close we were, of the heat of his hand on my back. When I looked into his eyes, a new type of energy buzzed through me, electric rather than antsy.

When the song came to an end, I broke eye contact and stepped back, putting some space between us. I knew from the warmth in my face that my cheeks were flushed.

"How did you learn to dance like that?" I asked him as we headed off the dance floor.

"I took lessons a few years back. How about you?"

"My mom insisted that a young lady should know how to dance," I said. "She sent me to lessons for several years when I was growing up. I wasn't impressed back then, but I'm glad of it now."

As another song started up, I spotted Cordelia near one of the sets of French doors that led out to the patio. She was on her own, watching the dancers, a dreamy smile on her face.

Grayson must have followed my gaze. "Do you mind if I ask Cordelia to dance?"

I smiled at him. "Not at all. I think she'd love that."

He gave my hand a squeeze. "I'll be back in a few minutes."

I watched as he approached Cordelia and spoke to her. Her face lit up when he offered her his hand.

I spotted Aunt Gilda dancing with a man I didn't recognize, and probably not just because of his mask. A moment later, I noticed Joey heading out onto the patio, with Sofie Talbot at his side. Shontelle and Officer Howes were still missing, though. If they were together, it would be my turn to grill Shontelle for details.

As a server passed by with a tray of champagne glasses, I eyed the drinks with longing. Creeping through secret passageways was thirsty work. I figured I'd be better off with a non-alcoholic drink, though. I wanted to keep my mind sharp in case I ended up talking to the police later in the evening.

Before getting a drink, however, I needed to make a trip to the restroom. I figured I could make it back to the ballroom before Grayson and Cordelia finished their dance.

As I left the ballroom, I passed the man in the hawklike mask again. I gave him a wide berth and hurried down the hall to the lobby and then to the women's restroom. Before leaving the washroom a few minutes later, I checked my appearance in the mirror and was glad to find that my dress and hair weren't any worse for exploring the dusty passageway.

I was about to leave the restroom when the door burst open, nearly hitting me. I jumped back, teetering on my high heels. When I'd regained my footing, I found myself staring at the dark-haired woman I'd seen with Hawk Man earlier.

"Evening, Sadie," she said in a smooth voice. "Are you enjoying the party?"

I could have sworn that my blood ran cold.

Between the wig and the mask, I hadn't recognized her. But now that she'd spoken, there was no mistaking the fact that I was standing face-to-face with Connie Archer.

Chapter 33

"But you left town," I said as I took a step backward, my stunned and terrified mind not wanting to accept that Marcie's killer was right in front of me.

"I wish." Connie took a step toward me. "Unfortunately, I have a loose end to tie up before I go."

I had a terrible feeling I was that loose end.

"That's right," she said as if reading my thoughts. "I can't leave you here to figure things out. I don't want the police on my tail when I get out of this town."

"Why did you think I'd figure things out?" I asked, hoping to stall for time while my mind whirled, trying to figure a way out of my predicament.

"You ask too many questions. You're a real nosy parker."

She wasn't the first to call me that.

She took another step toward me and I backed up again. Another foot and I'd be pressed against the sinks.

"Did you find the treasure?" I asked, surprised that my voice remained steady.

She smirked. "See? You do know too much."

"Just like Jan."

Her smirk transformed into a scowl. "Exactly. She saw the author's assistant sneaking around the hotel, just like I did, and she figured out why. Then she decided to look for the treasure herself. Can you believe that? It wasn't theirs to find!"

"What makes it yours?" I bit down on my lower lip, hoping the question wouldn't send her into a rage.

She took yet another step in my direction. "It's mine because I'm Edwin Vallencourt's great-niece."

"So is Jan."

Connie made a sound of dismissal. "She's from the wrong side of the family, if you know what I mean."

I didn't, but again it was as if she read my mind.

"The side that gambled away the family's fortune," she explained. "Jan's lucky I didn't kill her. I'm glad I'll never have to see her or this town after tonight."

"Is that why you moved to Shady Creek? Because you wanted to find the treasure?"

"Why else would I move to this nowhere town? I found one of Edwin's journals in an old box in my parents' attic. He wrote about adding secret rooms and passageways when the manor was being built. After my husband lost his job, we decided to find out if the family legend about the treasure was true."

"But he wanted you to quit," I said, recalling their conversation at the Inkwell.

"Because he was losing his nerve." She let out a huff. "I've always been the strong one in our marriage."

"Did you find the treasure?" I asked again. Despite the peril I was facing, I still wanted to know.

"Finally," Connie said, the word colored with anger. "If Marcie had told me where she'd found it, I could have been out of here ages ago."

"Marcie found it first?"

"And decided to leave it hidden in the wall of the secret staircase for safe keeping. But not before taking a few items to get appraised."

"But she never had a chance," I guessed.

"Because I caught her," Connie said with a self-satisfied smirk. "I'd seen her sneaking around more than once, and I saw her coming out of the unoccupied third-floor guest room the day before. When I slipped away to do some searching myself, I ran into her right after she'd found the treasure. But she'd already hidden most of it away again."

"And when she wouldn't tell you where, you fought with her."

"You love connecting the dots, don't you?"

I ignored her question to ask another of my own, still trying to buy time to get out of my predicament. "How did you get away on the day of Marcie's death without Gemma noticing?"

"She was blabbing on the phone with her sister. I knew she'd be hours. She always is once they get gabbing. And she wasn't paying any attention to me. Marcie's scream nearly ruined things for me, though. I had to get down the secret staircase on the double so I could pretend I was in the linen closet when I heard her scream. The whole thing was a risk, but it was worth taking. Leaving you around to rat me out isn't."

Her eyes took on a hard glint and I knew I was out of time. I didn't have many options, so I decided to take the only course of action I could think of at that moment.

When Connie moved as if to grab my arm, I charged at her, crashing into her with my left shoulder and sending her flying into one of the toilet stalls. I didn't waste time checking to see if she fell. I yanked open the door and burst out into the hallway.

I automatically turned to the right, heading for the lobby, but my shoes screeched against the floor as I came to a sliding halt.

Hawk Man stood twenty feet away, blocking my escape route.

My fear rocketed skyward. He smirked, making him even more menacing, and started toward me. I spun around and ran in the other direction. The restroom door crashed open a split second after I passed it.

"Get her!" Connie yelled as footsteps pounded behind me.

"Help!" I screamed as I ran, hoping someone from the party would hear me.

The corridor dead-ended at a locked door. I rattled the knob, but it wouldn't budge.

The masked man was gaining on me. I backtracked a few feet and practically threw myself into the linen closet, slamming the door shut behind me. I lunged at the far wall and pressed my hand against it over and over, on the verge of panicking. Why had Grayson and I returned to shut the secret door?

On the fourth try, I got the right spot and the paneling slid away. I grabbed my skirt and ducked through the door. The narrow stairway rose ahead of me, into the darkness. I didn't want to break my neck, so I kicked off my shoes and hoisted up my skirt, keeping one hand on the wall as I climbed as fast as I dared.

I heard running footsteps below me. Then there was a thud and a man cursed.

He'd probably tripped over my shoes.

That didn't buy me more than a second or two. Far too soon, he was thumping up the stairs behind me.

I stubbed my toe and a sharp sliver dug into the hand I was running along the wall, but I didn't let myself slow down. I missed a step and fell, hitting my knees hard against the stairs and scraping another toe. Biting back a whimper of pain, I gathered up my dress again and kept climbing.

My lungs and legs burned, and my heart beat out a pounding rhythm in my chest. I could hear the masked man gaining on me. I tried to move faster, but my legs wouldn't cooperate.

I fell forward and crashed into a wall. It took me half a second to realize I'd made it to the landing. I pressed my hand against the wall, trying to find the trigger point that would open the door.

Nothing happened.

I tried again, and again.

I could hear the harsh breaths of the masked man, far too close and drawing closer.

I kept pressing my hand to the wall. Finally, I was rewarded with a click.

The panels slid aside and I dove through the opening, landing on my knees on soft carpet. I scrambled to my feet, and that's when I realized I wasn't alone in the room.

"He's after me!" I pointed at the secret door.

The surprise on Detective Marquez's face quickly disappeared.

As Hawk Man burst through the opening, she and Officer Rogers swooped in to grab him.

"Connie was chasing me too," I said between gasps as I desperately tried to catch my breath. "She killed Marcie and attacked Jan."

"We know," Marquez said grimly.

Of course she did. Grayson had told her as much over the phone.

She yanked the mask from the man's face.

"Connie's husband," I said, recognizing him from the night he was at the Inkwell with his wife.

While Rogers snapped handcuffs onto the man's wrists, Detective Marquez strode to the door that led out to the hallway. She pulled it open and stepped out of the room.

"Hey!" She sprinted off down the hall.

I darted out the door, just in time to see her tackle Connie, who was making a run for the stairway.

Connie had probably hoped to cut off my escape route. She clearly hadn't expected to be met by the police. I hadn't either, but I was infinitely happy about the surprise. I didn't think Connie and her husband felt the same way.

When I heard the handcuffs click around Connie's wrists a moment later, I sank to the floor with relief, my shaky legs no longer willing to support me.

Chapter 34

The arrest of Connie and her husband took place with the majority of the partygoers none the wiser. Detective Marquez alerted Gemma Honeywell to what had occurred and arranged for the newly arrived police officers to enter the manor discreetly through a side entrance.

When I reached the lobby, Officer Rogers kindly retrieved my shoes for me.

As I slipped them on, Grayson came running into the lobby and took hold of my shoulders.

"Sadie, are you all right?" He turned away, but only long enough to see two police officers marching Connie and her husband down the hall.

"When I realized you weren't in the ballroom, I went looking for you," he continued. "But I couldn't find you anywhere."

Aunt Gilda rushed over. "Sadie, where have you been?" She took in my disheveled appearance. Her gaze slid to Grayson.

"I was chased by Marcie's killer," I said quickly, knowing her thoughts had gone in an entirely different direction.

Her eyes widened. In the next moment, Shontelle, Officer Howes, and Cordelia arrived on the scene. Detective Marquez appeared next, and questions suddenly came at me from every direction.

Fortunately, Marquez took charge and quieted everyone down. She gave my family and friends a succinct summary of what had happened, and then ushered me into the office behind the reception desk to ask me questions.

I explained everything, except the fact that Grayson and I had snooped through the locked drawer in the other office. I made it sound like we decided to explore the manor for hidden passageways on a whim, and had lucked out by finding the hidden doorway in the linen closet. Luckily, she seemed to buy that story.

As I gave her my account of the events, I removed a splinter from my hand and wiggled my sore toes. I counted my lucky stars, knowing I could have endured far worse than a splinter and a couple of stubbed toes.

Once I had answered all of the detective's questions, I met up with Aunt Gilda and my friends in the lobby again.

Aunt Gilda pulled me into a fierce hug. "Please tell me you're all right," she said as she squeezed me tight.

"I am," I assured her. "A little shaken up, but otherwise fine."

When she released me, Shontelle moved in for a hug.

"I'm so glad you're okay," she said. "I never should have let you out of my sight."

I laughed, though a bit shakily. "That probably wouldn't have stopped me from finding trouble." I regarded her more closely. "But where were you?"

"Eldon and I went for a walk in the gardens," she said quietly so only I'd hear.

"And?"

She smiled. "And nothing, but we're going out for dinner next week."

Chapter 35

A week after the masquerade, the sun shone brightly and the birds chirped and twittered in the trees. Standing out on the village green, with the sun warming my face, the events at Shady Creek Manor seemed almost like a bad dream. Almost, but not quite.

At least Connie was in jail now, where she belonged. Her husband was too, though he faced less serious charges than his wife.

I'd had a long chat with Linnea over the phone. She'd spoken with Marcie's family and she believed I was right in thinking that Marcie had learned about the legend of the Vallencourt treasure while doing research for Linnea's latest book. Linnea also suspected that Marcie had wanted to find the treasure so she could help out her parents. Her father had been seriously ill the year before and the family had been suffocating beneath an overwhelming pile of medical bills.

As for Jan, she'd finally admitted that she'd been searching the manor for the treasure after finding the blueprints in the basement. She'd hoped to sell any valuables she found so she could use the money to fund the Happy Paws Cat Shelter.

I gave her a squeeze, happy to know somethi
come from the evening.

Cordelia was next in line for a hug, but then evei
satisfied that I was in one piece.

I clapped a hand over my mouth as a big yawn
Apparently, getting chased by a killer and her hu
more than a little tiring.

Grayson put a hand to my back, concern in his b
"You've been through a lot. Do you want to go home

"Gosh no," I said, tucking a loose lock of hair behind
"I haven't sampled the desserts yet and I'm suddenly *sta*

I didn't know who would end up with the Vallencourt treasure, which apparently consisted of Edwin's mother's jewelry and some valuable rare coins. Would Jan's mother get to share it with Edwin's other descendants? Would the Honeywells have a claim to it because they currently owned the manor?

I'd heard plenty of chatter about the subject over the past week, but I hadn't spent much time speculating on the matter myself. I was too focused on trying to put the recent unpleasant events behind me.

My current activity was helping with that. I was strolling across the village green, hand in hand with Grayson. We'd met up with the intention to plan a *Craft Nation* viewing party, but so far all we'd done was enjoy each other's company. I was still trying to keep a tight rein on my heart, not wanting it to get in too deep too quickly, but I suspected I was fighting a losing battle. It felt too good, too *right*, to have Grayson at my side, my hand in his.

Far ahead of us, over on Hillview Road, Eleanor left the general store, a shopping bag in hand. No doubt she'd be skipping the viewing party. I didn't hold a grudge against her for her opposition, though. I'd found out a few days earlier that her aversion to alcohol stemmed from the fact that she'd grown up with an alcoholic father. Apparently, the family had tried to keep that under wraps, but most people who'd lived in Shady Creek back then knew about it nonetheless.

The sight of Eleanor reminded me of the visit Grayson and I had paid to the museum.

"Did you ever read any of Eleanor's book?" I asked Grayson as we passed through the shade cast by a large evergreen tree.

"Cover to cover," he said, surprising me.

"Really? Was it interesting?" Somehow I had trouble imagining Eleanor writing a captivating book.

"Interesting would be one word for it," Grayson said.

"Meaning?"

"It was dry reading, but she certainly wrote about Edwin Vallencourt in glowing terms."

"How factually correct do you think the book is?" I asked, remembering how Marcie had pointed out what she thought was an inaccuracy.

"That particular chapter, probably not very. I've heard stories about Edwin Vallencourt over the years since I moved here, ones that suggest he wasn't squeaky clean, and she makes no reference to any of that in the book. So I did a little digging of my own."

"What did you find out?" I asked, knowing he'd found something.

"That Eleanor most likely glossed over the facts about Edwin. The rest of the book might be more accurate, though."

"But why would she put Edwin Vallencourt on a pedestal? I would have thought she'd disapprove of a party animal like him."

"That's what I thought too." He drew to a stop and pulled his cell phone out of the pocket of his jeans. "But check this out."

He pulled up a black-and-white photo on his phone. It showed a group of about a dozen young men and women, probably in their twenties and thirties, casually grouped together on the lawn in front of the manor.

Grayson pointed to a man with thick dark hair, his shirt sleeves rolled up to his elbows and his hands in his pockets.

"That's Edwin Vallencourt," Grayson said. "And that"—he pointed to a fair-haired woman, probably a good ten years younger than Edwin, who had her arm looped around his as she gazed up at him adoringly—"is Clementina Winters."

"That name doesn't ring a bell." She didn't look familiar either.

"She's Eleanor's mother."

"Really?" I took another good look at the photo. I couldn't see any resemblance to Eleanor, but maybe when she was younger she'd looked more like her mother did in the picture.

Something else struck me about the photo. "Clementina was in love with Edwin."

"That's what I thought too." Grayson tucked his phone back in his pocket and took my hand again. We resumed walking slowly across the grass. "Clementina came from a well-respected family in Shady Creek, and that photo is the only evidence I could find that she ever had anything to do with Vallencourt, so I suspect it wasn't common knowledge that she spent time with him."

"If she managed to keep the fact that she was in love with him a secret in this town, I'm very impressed."

"I'm guessing it didn't last long," Grayson said. "By all accounts, Edwin went through women like smokers go through cigarettes. And a few weeks after this photo was taken, Clementina married Joseph Hallman."

"A few weeks? I could have sworn she was in love with Edwin from the way she was gazing at him. That's not much time to turn around and marry someone else."

"And seven months after that, Eleanor was born."

I stopped in my tracks. "Hold on, are you saying that Edwin Vallencourt was Eleanor's father?"

"I'm saying it's a possibility."

I took a moment to absorb that information. "Wow. That could explain things. She sure doesn't seem to like anyone saying a bad word about Edwin." I paused. "And yet, she'd never admit that she's his daughter, even if that's the case and she knows it. She's too hung up on being prim and proper to want people to know she was conceived out of wedlock, even though that's not such a big deal anymore."

"My thoughts exactly," Grayson said.

"Although, I wonder if she'd bring herself to admit it if it meant she'd get some of the treasure." I considered that for half a second. "Who *does* get the treasure? The Honeywells or Edwin's heirs?"

"I'll leave that for the lawyers to figure out," Grayson said.

"Good plan," I said. "Maybe we should keep our theory about Eleanor's parentage to ourselves. The town would have a field day gossiping about it."

"Probably for the best," he agreed.

"Instead, I guess they'll keep gossiping about us, for now anyway. Half the town has been, you know."

Grayson laughed. "I know. It's hard to miss."

"It doesn't bother you?"

His grin didn't fade. "Not really. In fact"—he stopped walking—"I say, let's really give them something to talk about."

He pulled me close and kissed me, for all the world to see.

And I didn't mind one bit.

Recipes

Milky Way Gargle Blaster

8 oz root beer
1 oz cream
1 oz vanilla vodka

Put some ice in a glass. Add the cream. Add the vanilla vodka and root beer. Stir.

Milky Way Gargle Blaster Mocktail

8 oz root beer
1 oz cream
½ teaspoon vanilla extract

Put some ice in a glass. Add the cream. Add the vanilla and root beer. Stir.

Yellow Brick Road

1 oz limoncello
4 oz yellow lemonade
4 oz lemon-lime soda

Put ice in a glass. Add the ingredients and stir.

The Malt In Our Stars

2 oz blended Scotch whiskey
1 tbsp freshly squeezed lemon juice
6 oz ginger ale, chilled
Lemon for garnish

Fill a cocktail shaker ¾ full with ice. Add whiskey and lemon juice. Shake and strain into a glass. Top with chilled ginger ale and garnish with lemon. Optional: Serve over crushed ice.

The Red Cabbage Of Courage

Salad:
½ medium head of red cabbage, chopped
¼ cup slivered almonds, toasted
¼ cup sunflower seeds, toasted
¼ cup sesame seeds, toasted
one package (approx. 100 grams) ramen noodles, crushed
(keep seasoning packet for dressing)

Dressing:
¼ cup rice vinegar
¼ cup vegetable oil
1 tbsp soy sauce
⅛ tsp black pepper
one packet ramen seasoning

Toast the almonds, sesame seeds, and sunflower seeds in oven at 350° for seven minutes.
Crush the ramen noodles.
In a large bowl, combine all salad ingredients.
In a small bowl, whisk together all dressing ingredients.
Toss the salad with the dressing.

Serves 6.

ACKNOWLEDGMENTS

I'd like to extend my sincere thanks to several people whose hard work and input made this book what it is today. I'm truly grateful to my agent, Jessica Faust, for helping me bring this series to life, and to my editors, Martin Biro and Elizabeth May. The entire Kensington team has been fabulous and I love the beautiful covers the art department has created. I'm also grateful to Samantha McVeigh, Larissa Ackerman, and the rest of the publicity department for all their hard work. Thank you to Jody Holford, Sarah Blair, the Cozy Mystery Crew, my review crew, and all my wonderful friends in the writing community.

Keep reading for a special sneak peek of the next mystery in
Sarah Fox's bestselling Pancake House Mystery Series!

A ROOM WITH A ROUX
A Pancake House Mystery
by
SARAH FOX

*Pancake house owner Marley McKinney takes a break from
the Flip Side for a romantic getaway. But soon, instead of
mixing batter, she's mixed up with murder . . .*

Marley and her new husband, Brett, need some quality couple time before the holiday madness, so they drive up into the mountains of the Olympic Peninsula to charming Holly Lodge. Before long they're enjoying snowshoe excursions, hot chocolate, and cuddling in front of a roaring fire. Despite some barely concealed marital tension between the owners of the lodge, they're finally able to unwind . . .

Until one morning when they notice a glove sticking out of a snowbank outside of the lodge. Inside the glove is a hand connected to a frozen corpse buried beneath the snow—lodge owner Kevin Manning has been murdered. Presented with a stack of suspects and eventually stranded at the lodge by a blizzard, Marley has to catch the coldhearted killer before someone else gets iced . . .

Look for A Room with A Roux, *on sale January 2021*
from Kensington Books!

Chapter 1

Fluffy snowflakes swirled down from the gray sky, hitting the windshield a split second before the wipers whisked them away. I gripped the edge of my seat as my husband, Brett, steered his truck around a tight turn. Driving along winding mountain roads made me nervous at the best of times. The winter weather only added to my anxiety.

Ahead of us, the road straightened out, bordered on both sides by tall, snow-covered evergreens. I relaxed into my seat, relief allowing me to finally enjoy the view. It was the day after Thanksgiving. Winter had arrived early on the Olympic Peninsula and although there was only frost on the ground in the seaside town of Wildwood Cove, up here in the mountains, more than a foot of snow had already fallen. It had covered the world in a beautiful white blanket and it made me think of the upcoming Christmas season—when I wasn't worrying about the driving conditions.

Brett glanced my way as we continued our gentle ascent along the straight section of road. "We're almost there. You okay?" He knew I wasn't keen on mountain roads and hairpin turns.

"Yes," I said, glad that was now the truth. "All good."

A painted wooden sign caught my eye at the same time as Brett flicked on the left turn signal and said, "This is it."

Excitement pitter-pattered through my stomach. I'd been looking forward to this getaway with Brett ever since we'd booked our stay at Holly Lodge a few weeks earlier. After our wedding in August, we had a short honeymoon in Victoria, British Columbia, but ever since our return, we'd both been busy with work. I knew Brett wanted this time alone together, without any distractions, as much as I did.

Brett followed the curving driveway that led through the trees. After a few seconds, we emerged from the woods and got our first look at Holly Lodge. I'd seen photos of the place on the Internet, but the pictures didn't do the building or its setting justice. The lodge looked cozy and welcoming, and was nestled in the middle of a winter wonderland.

Although Holly Lodge was small in comparison to many other hotels, that was partly why Brett and I had chosen it. We wanted a quiet getaway without any crowds, a place where we could focus on relaxing and on each other. It certainly seemed like we'd come to the right spot. The lodge resembled a large log home rather than a hotel. It had two stories and a covered, wraparound porch. Warm light lit up the windows on the ground floor, sending a welcoming glow into the gray afternoon.

White twinkle lights lined the edge of the roof and the porch railing. Greenery also decorated the railing, and a large wreath hung on the front door. The effect was festive and inviting.

Holly Lodge sat in the middle of a woodland clearing, but as Brett drove around the side of the building to a small parking lot, I caught a glimpse of a frozen lake through the trees.

"It's beautiful here," I said as Brett pulled into a free parking spot. "And it looks like we'll get the peace and quiet we're after."

There were five other vehicles in the parking lot aside from ours, but even if the place was fully booked, I figured it would still be relatively quiet for a vacation destination.

"Peace and quiet and alone time," Brett said, leaning over to give me a kiss.

I smiled. "That's a definite yes to the alone time."

We climbed out of the truck and I shivered as the cold air stung my cheeks and the light wind cut through my clothes. Snowflakes still swirled down from the sky. I tipped my head back so all I could see was the falling snow and the leaden clouds. I stuck out my tongue and caught a fluffy flake on it, feeling like a kid. Already I was more relaxed than I'd been for weeks.

I joined Brett on the other side of the truck as he unloaded our suitcase, and together we headed along the shoveled pathway that led to the lodge's front door. Before going inside, we wiped our boots on the welcome mat.

Brett grinned and gently brushed a hand over my curly hair. "Snowflakes," he said by way of explanation.

"You've got some too." I stood up on tiptoes so I could return the favor.

We brushed off our jackets as well and then entered the lodge. As soon as we stepped inside, my breath caught in my throat. I stood there in the foyer, with Brett by my side, gazing around us. Once again, the photos I'd seen online didn't do the lodge justice. Straight ahead of us was a reception desk with a closed door behind it, but my attention was drawn elsewhere.

To the left was a dining room and a staircase with a carved wooden banister, and to the right was a lounge. Both rooms featured gleaming wooden floorboards and exposed beams. I took a few steps to the right to get a better view of the lounge. A massive stone fireplace dominated one wall of the room, a fire crackling away behind the grate. The lounge stretched all the way to the back of the lodge, where floor-to-ceiling windows provided a stunning view of the lake. Cozy armchairs practically called out to me to settle into one and enjoy the warmth from the fire. With the snow falling outside the windows, the interior of Holly Lodge was picture-perfect and fit for a magazine.

We'd definitely chosen the right place for our getaway.

"It looks great," Brett said quietly into my ear.

I slid an arm around his waist and leaned into him. "I'm so glad Patricia told us about this place."

Patricia Murray was a friend of mine who ran a bed-and-breakfast two doors down from our beachfront Victorian. She and her family had spent a couple of weekend getaways up here at Holly Lodge in the past and she'd recommended it to us when we mentioned we were planning a short vacation in the mountains. I couldn't have asked for a better spot.

Although I was itching to explore the rest of the lodge, Brett and I approached the reception desk. I thought we'd have to ring the bell for assistance, but before we had a chance, a woman emerged from an office behind the desk.

"Hello, and welcome to Holly Lodge," the woman said with a smile. She was tall and striking, with high cheekbones. She wore her short hair in glossy finger coils and moved with the grace of a dancer. "I'm Rita Omondi-Manning, one of the owners. You must be Mr. and Mrs. Collins."

I still wasn't quite used to the fact that I was now a Mrs., but the reminder put a smile on my face.

"That's right," Brett replied. "Brett and Marley."

"Did you have a good trip up the mountain?" Rita asked.

"It wasn't bad, considering the weather," I said. "It's such a beautiful place you've got here."

Rita's dark eyes lit up as she smiled again. "Thank you. I do love it. And I'm glad we're able to share our little slice of mountain paradise with our guests."

I told Rita that we'd heard about Holly Lodge from Patricia Murray, who'd highly recommended it.

"You know Patricia?" she said.

"We're neighbors and good friends," I replied.

She asked how Patricia was doing, and I filled her in briefly. Then Rita turned her eyes to a computer screen and tapped a few buttons on the keyboard. "We've got you in room five, up on the second floor. It has a lovely view of the lake."

"That sounds great," Brett said, and I voiced my agreement.

She handed over two keys, each one on a wooden keychain with a number five carved on it. "The dining room is open for breakfast from six until ten, for lunch from twelve to two, and for dinner from five to eight. You'll find a credenza in the dining room, where there's always tea, coffee, hot chocolate, and a few snacks available. There's a hot tub out back, and if you'd like to try snowshoeing or cross-country skiing, just let us know. We have plenty of equipment available."

We thanked her and headed for the staircase, Brett carrying our suitcase. On our way up the stairs, we got a better view of the dining room, and I noticed a man with graying dark hair sitting alone at a table, reading a newspaper, a mug with steam rising from it on the table in front of him. I assumed he was another guest, but he was the only one we encountered on our way up to our room.

The second-floor hallway was silent and deserted, all of the guest-room doors shut tight. Brett unlocked the door to room five and pushed it open before stepping back to let me go in first.

"Holey buckets!" I exclaimed as I entered the room. "This is gorgeous!"

Our room was located at the back of the lodge and, just as Rita had told us, it offered a beautiful view of Holly Lake. Beyond the lake was a higher mountain than the one we were on, barely discernible through the falling snow, its peak shrouded in clouds.

The room itself was almost as impressive as the view. I removed my boots and left them on the mat by the door so I could explore without leaving damp footprints on the hard-wood floors or rugs. I ran a hand down one of the carved posts of the king-size four-poster bed that took up one half of the room, knowing I'd sleep well that night. Matching nightstands flanked the bed, and a chest of drawers and a small desk, made from the same type of wood, sat against one wall.

The other side of the room featured a small sitting area with a loveseat, armchair, television, and gas fireplace. A rustic but tasteful credenza was home to a kettle and an empty ice bucket. When I opened the cupboards, I discovered a mini fridge, two drinking glasses, two mugs, and an assortment of tea bags. A doorway led off the sitting room to a tiled bathroom with a shower stall and a soaker tub.

"It's pretty amazing," Brett said, gazing around with appre-ciation as I returned to the middle of the room.

"It's perfect."

I picked up a glossy brochure that was lying on the bedside table. It was about Holly Lodge and the activities available on-site and in the surrounding area. I sat on the edge of the bed and took a closer look at the brochure while Brett unpacked a few items from our suitcase.

The last page of the brochure featured information on the history of Holly Lodge, which had been built thirty years ago on the site of an old cabin that had stood by the lake for nearly a hundred years before it had become so derelict that tearing it down had been the only real option.

"Hey," I said to Brett as I read the next paragraph. "Appar-ently this place has a ghost."

"Holly Lodge is haunted?" Brett asked. "Wait—I think I saw something about that on the website. It's supposed to be the ghost of a woman, right?"

"Henrietta Franklin," I confirmed. "But it's Holly Lake that's haunted, not the lodge itself."

Brett sat next to me and put his arm around my shoulders. "We've got a good view of the lake from here, but somehow I think we'll be too distracted to notice any ghosts outside the window."

He kissed me in a way that almost made me forget what we were talking about.

The brochure slipped from my hand and fell to the floor. When I retrieved it a moment later, I returned it to the bedside table.

"I think you're right," I said, picking up our conversation where we'd left off. "But I doubt we'd see the ghost even if we weren't distracted."

I didn't know for sure if ghosts existed or not, but I figured most ghost stories were just that—stories. My experience with a supposedly haunted house in Wildwood Cove had led me to believe that more firmly than ever.

"That's probably true," Brett agreed, "but it makes for a good tale to tell the guests."

I couldn't argue with that.

As I got up from the bed, my attention strayed back to the view, and I wandered over to one of the two large windows.

Brett joined me and wrapped his arms around me from behind. "What do you want to do first?"

"Walk down to the lake? I wouldn't mind stretching my legs after the ride up here."

"Sounds good."

Neither of us made a move toward the door. I leaned into Brett, still enjoying the view from the window.

"I'm glad we decided to do this," I said.

"You're not worrying yet?" There was a note of gentle teasing in his voice.

I smiled. "Not quite yet. It helps that the Flip Side will be closed while we're gone."

It wasn't easy for me to leave the pancake house in other

people's hands. Not because I didn't trust them; all my employees were excellent and my mom was always willing to step in to help out when she was in Wildwood Cove, but I didn't like to burden anyone with my responsibilities on top of their own. I also wasn't keen on leaving our pets, even for a few days, but they were in good hands.

My mom and her husband, Grant, had come to Wildwood Cove for Thanksgiving and now they were staying on at our house to look after our goldendoodle, Bentley, and our orange tabby cat, Flapjack. I missed the animals already, but I knew they'd be fine with my mom and Grant, so I was determined to keep my worries at bay and focus on enjoying myself.

After another minute of soaking in the view and each other's company, we put our boots back on and headed downstairs. Rita was no longer in sight, but a man with chestnut-brown hair stood behind the reception desk. His face was tanned and weathered, as if he spent a lot of time outdoors. He had his attention fixed on the computer screen, but he raised his eyes and smiled when he heard us coming into the lobby.

"You must be our newly arrived guests," he said, coming out from behind the desk. "I'm Kevin Manning."

He offered his hand, first to me and then to Brett. As we shook, we introduced ourselves and assured him that we were settling in well so far.

While we chatted, a woman descended the stairs from the second floor. She had a pale complexion and dark hair that was tied back in a messy bun. She wore glasses with purple frames and a thick sweater with a long black skirt.

"How are you doing this afternoon, Lily?" Kevin asked the woman as she reached the bottom of the stairs.

"Very well, thank you." She held up a paperback novel that she had with her. "I'm going to get in some reading time in front of the fire."

"I'm hoping to do some of that myself this weekend," I said.

I'd packed a mystery novel that I'd started reading two days ago. I was only a few chapters in, but the story already had me hooked.

"Lily," Kevin said, "Brett and Marley are our latest guests." He addressed us next. "This is Lily Spitz. She's an author as well as an avid reader."

"That's cool," I said, intrigued. "What genre do you write?"

"I've been writing romance for several years, but I've branched out into mysteries as well."

The phone on the reception desk rang, so Kevin excused himself to go answer it while Lily, Brett, and I headed into the lounge.

"I'll have to check out your books," I said to Lily. "I love mysteries."

A hint of pink showed on her cheeks. "I hope mine won't disappoint."

"I'm sure they won't."

After exchanging a few more words, Brett and I left Lily in the lounge and headed out the back door onto a large deck. In the summertime, it would be a great place for outdoor dining, if the bugs weren't too bad. The view was incredible and the air fresh, if a bit cold at the moment. A stairway led down to a shoveled path. The main part of the walkway stretched toward the lake while a branch to the left led to the hot tub, currently not in use.

The hot tub was tempting, but we bypassed it—for now—and made our way down to the frozen lake. The gray afternoon was already fading toward dusk, and lights glowed in three houses on the far side of the lake. Those dwellings were the only other buildings in sight aside from Holly Lodge. The relative isolation added to the tranquility of our location.

As we stopped to take in the view from our new vantage point, I noticed snowshoe prints along the shore, leading into the woods that surrounded most of the lake.

I pointed them out to Brett. "It's been years since I last had a chance to go snowshoeing. We should go tomorrow."

"We should," he agreed. "We might be able to trek all the way around the lake."

I liked that idea, and I could already picture us enjoying mugs of hot chocolate upon our return, either while snuggled up in our room or in front of the log fire in the lounge. We were going to have a great time at Holly Lodge.

The more the light faded from the gray sky, the more the temperature dropped, so we didn't linger by the lake. As we were about to head back up the path to the lodge, Brett put a hand on my arm to stop me and pointed into the trees to our left without saying a word.

My breath caught in my throat when I realized what Brett had seen.

Two beautiful deer stood at the edge of the forest, standing perfectly still, their eyes on us. With the snow falling softly and with the backdrop of snowcapped evergreens, the scene looked like it belonged on a Christmas card.

Brett and I stayed as still as possible, not wanting to scare the deer. After a few seconds, however, they abruptly turned away and bounded gracefully through the snow, quickly disappearing into the forest.

I smiled and took Brett's hand as we returned to Holly Lodge. Our vacation was off to a perfect start, and I didn't think anything could possibly ruin it.

Chapter 2

Brett and I weren't quite ready for dinner when we got back to Holly Lodge, so we decided to try out the hot tub. I was glad I'd thought to pack a swimsuit and flip-flops. There were two fluffy robes hanging in the closet in our room, so we pulled them on for the trip downstairs. When we passed through the lounge again on our way out the back door, the fire was still crackling and popping away, but Lily had disappeared and there were no other guests in sight. Outside, the snow had stopped falling, and darkness had settled over the mountains.

As we made our way down the path to the hot tub, I questioned the wisdom of our decision. We could have stayed inside and enjoyed a hot drink by the fire before dinner. Instead, we were about to turn into icicles. Or I was, anyway. Brett seemed completely unaffected by the cold. He was as relaxed as he would have been if we were out for a sunny stroll on the beach. In stark contrast, my teeth chattered and I tried to pull my robe more tightly around me, but it didn't do any good. The cold air cut right through the fabric and nipped at my bare legs.

"How can you not be shivering?" I asked Brett as we turned off the main path.

"We've barely been out here five seconds," he said.

"That's long enough to turn into a Popsicle."

He laughed. "Want to turn around and go back?"

I glanced over my shoulder at the lodge, its windows glowing with warm light. We were far closer to the hot tub than the lodge now, and steam was rising from the water, visible thanks to the string of lights hanging above the small deck.

"Too far," I said through chattering teeth.

I picked up my pace and hurried up the three steps to the hot tub deck. I wasted no time dropping my robe and climbing into the water. I let out a sigh of happiness and relief as the hot water enveloped me, instantly banishing the chill that had been working its way into my bloodstream seconds before.

Brett stepped into the water and sank down onto the bench next to me. "Better?" he asked.

I scooted closer to him and rested my head on his shoulder. "Much."

My muscles relaxed more and more with every second spent in the hot tub. Around us, the world was perfectly still and quiet. With my back to the lodge, it was easy to pretend we were in our own private world, alone in the wilderness.

"This is perfect," I said as my eyelids grew heavier.

Brett settled an arm across my shoulders. "You're not thinking of giving up beachfront living, are you?"

I smiled, hearing a note of teasing in his voice. "Never."

"Good." He kissed the top of my head. "But this is a great getaway spot."

"It really is," I said with a happy sigh. "I've never thought of having a hot tub before, but now I'm wondering if we should get one."

"Do you really think we'd use it enough to make it worthwhile?"

"Maybe not," I conceded, thinking about our busy schedules. "We'll just have to make the most of this one while we're here."

"That sounds like a good plan."

Time passed, but I barely noticed. Brett and I spoke in low voices now and then, but mostly we relaxed and enjoyed the soothing heat of the water and each other's company.

"Getting hungry?" Brett asked after a while.

"Mmmm."

"Is that a yes, or an 'I don't want to get out of the hot tub'?"

"Both," I said.

He leaned closer, as if about to share a secret. "I don't think they serve dinner out here."

A sleepy smile spread across my face. "You're probably right."

I decided it was time to force myself to get out of the water, though I didn't relish the thought of how cold I'd feel in the seconds before I could get my robe back on. Before I could make a move, however, the sound of approaching voices stopped me.

"Have you thought any more about my offer?" It was a man who spoke, but I didn't recognize his voice.

Brett and I twisted on the bench so we could get a look behind us. Kevin Manning was trudging along a path that came around the side of the lodge, illuminated by a floodlight mounted beneath the eaves. He was wearing jeans and a red-and-black plaid jacket, a hat pulled down over his ears. A broad shouldered, middle-aged man kept pace at his side. I was pretty sure it was the same man I'd seen in the dining room earlier.

"I don't need to think about it." Kevin's voice was gruff and laced with irritation.

Brett and I stayed still and quiet, not wanting to interrupt the less-than-friendly conversation. Fortunately, the men didn't notice us and continued along the path toward the lodge's back steps.

"I think my offer is more than generous," the broad-shouldered man said.

Kevin stopped abruptly at the base of the steps. "I don't need your generosity. I'm not giving up Holly Lodge, in whole or in part."

The other man continued as if he hadn't heard Kevin. "It has so much untapped potential."

"I've got my own plans for expansion," Kevin grumbled. "I'm not interested in selling."

With that, Kevin stomped up the stairs and disappeared into the lodge. The other man watched him go, only following once Kevin was out of sight.

"Real estate developer?" I guessed.

"Sounds like it could be," Brett said. He stood up, water dripping off his body while steam rose up around him. "I'm definitely hungry now."

Reluctantly, I followed him out of the hot tub, trying to brace myself against the impending unpleasantness. Getting out of the water wasn't as terrible as I expected, until a gust of icy wind blew past us. I tried not to let out a squeal of discomfort as the cold air bit at my wet skin, but I wasn't quite successful. I tugged on my robe as quickly as I could, hoping it would shield me from the wind.

Brett didn't seem as bothered by the wind, but he still didn't waste time pulling on his robe. As I tied the cord of my robe tightly around my waist, I noticed someone else nearby, this time heading up to the lodge from the lake. I couldn't see the man's features, but he appeared to have a thin build, despite the bulk of his winter clothing. If he noticed us, he gave no indication.

Brett and I made our way along the pathway. I was glad for the lights that lined it. Every last hint of daylight had disappeared now and it would have been hard to see where we were going without lights to dispel the darkness.

By the time we turned onto the main path, the man up ahead of us was already climbing the steps to the lodge. The door to the lounge opened, spilling warm light out into the dark evening.

Lily stood framed by the doorway. "Ambrose!" she called out. "Where have you been? I was getting worried!"

Whatever his response might have been, it didn't reach my ears. Lily ushered him into the lodge and shut the door behind him.

We hurried up to the deck and into the lounge, relieved to get inside. The wet ends of my hair had felt like they were starting to freeze on the walk back, and my fingers and toes had been on the verge of going numb. Lily and Ambrose had disappeared, and the room was empty as we passed through it, but I could hear quiet voices coming from the dining room.

Now that I'd left the soothing comfort of the hot tub behind, I realized that I was hungrier than I'd thought. Upstairs in our room, we dried off and changed before heading back down to the main floor of the lodge. When I was three steps from the bottom of the stairway, I drew to a halt, forcing Brett to stop behind me.

Hushed, angry voices floated toward us. I recognized Kevin's voice and I was pretty sure the other one belonged to Rita. After a second or two, I realized that they were in the office behind the reception desk. The door stood open a crack, letting their argument seep out into the lobby.

"This is my lodge just as much as yours!" Rita's anger was unmistakable. "You can't do anything without my say-so."

"You're holding us back." Kevin's words were just as heated. "We could do so much more with this place if you'd just give my ideas a chance."

"People come here because it's quiet, because it's *not* busy," Rita shot back. "I won't let you destroy this place. I'm not going to let you take away what I've worked so hard to build."

"*You've* worked? What about me? I've been breaking my back here for years!"

"This is supposed to be a partnership." Rita sounded close to tears now. "You always disregard anything I have to say."

Brett stepped down next to me and put a hand to my back.

By unspoken agreement, we descended the remaining stairs as quietly as possible and made a beeline for the dining room, leaving Kevin and Rita's angry voices behind us. I exhaled with relief once we could no longer hear them. I wished we hadn't overheard the argument. Kevin and Rita probably would have wished that too if they'd known their voices had carried beyond the office.

Three other guests were sitting in the dining room when we arrived. Lily was at a table with a man I figured was Ambrose. He matched the build of the man we'd seen outside. He and Lily both appeared to be around thirty, just a few years younger than me and Brett. At a neighboring table was the man I'd seen reading a newspaper before. I took in the sight of his broad shoulders and decided he was definitely the man who'd been outside with Kevin earlier.

"Ah," the man said when he spotted me and Brett. "New guests. Come to enjoy the winter wonderland?" He stood up as we approached, and Brett and I shook the hand he offered. "Wilson Gerrard," he said by way of introduction. "Mostly of Seattle, though I like to get around."

Brett and I introduced ourselves, both to Wilson and the other two guests.

"This is Ambrose," Lily said with a bright smile, indicating her companion. "He's a renowned poet." She practically glowed with pride.

Ambrose pushed his wire-framed glasses up his nose. "I'm not sure about renowned, but I will admit to the poet."

"Are you both from Seattle too?" I asked them as Brett and I sat down at one of the free tables.

"Originally," Ambrose said, setting a cloth napkin on his lap, though he had no food in front of him yet. "I moved to the peninsula a couple of years ago. Lily lives in Seattle. That's where we met and became friends."

"We became well acquainted through various writing events

around Seattle and realized that we're kindred spirits." Lily beamed at Ambrose. "Isn't that right?"

Ambrose didn't have a chance to respond before Wilson spoke up.

"Writers on vacation?" He seemed amused by the idea. "Isn't your whole life a vacation? Typing a few words and then staring out the window, waiting for inspiration to hit?"

Lily's smile faded and flinty annoyance showed in her eyes.

Ambrose didn't appear impressed either. "Actually, that's not—"

Rita swept into the dining room, her arrival cutting off the conversation. That was probably for the best, judging by Lily and Ambrose's expressions. Wilson seemed oblivious to the feathers he'd ruffled.

"Everyone's here," Rita observed with a smile. She picked up two menus from an unoccupied table and handed them to me and Brett. "Can I get you something to drink to start?"

We both requested water. I was still thinking about a mug of hot chocolate, but I decided to leave that until later so I could enjoy it by the fire.

"I'll be right back with your drinks," Rita said. Then she addressed the others. "And I'll check on your meals."

She disappeared into the kitchen. Wilson produced a cell phone from his pocket and focused his attention on the screen. Ambrose and Lily talked quietly together at their table, no longer appearing so irked by Wilson's comments.

Out the back window, I could see that snow had started falling again, thickly this time, the flakes illuminated by the lights on the back deck. That made the lodge seem even cozier, and the flickering votive candles on our table added a touch of romance.

Brett reached across the table and I gave him my hand.

"Anything catch your eye?" he asked.

I smiled at him. "Definitely."

He grinned and squeezed my hand. "I meant on the menu."

I'd forgotten all about the menus. "I knew that."

"Sure, you did."

Still smiling, I slipped my hand from Brett's and turned my attention to the list of available meals. It was fairly limited, but that wasn't surprising considering the small size of the lodge.

As I read over the options, Rita returned and placed two glasses of ice water on our table. We thanked her and she disappeared into the kitchen again, returning a moment later with two plates of food, which she delivered to Ambrose and Lily's table.

She fetched another plate from the kitchen and placed it in front of Wilson. As she headed our way, I closed the menu, having finally decided what I wanted. Brett ordered the butter chicken while I requested the quinoa-stuffed bell peppers.

Rita took our menus and headed for the kitchen once more.

"I hope Flapjack and Bentley aren't missing us too much," I said.

I was itching to send my mom a text message to ask how things were going, but I'd purposely left my phone up in our room. I didn't want anything distracting me from my time with Brett.

"I'm sure they're doing just fine," Brett said. "You know your mom will be spoiling them, and Grant loves taking Bentley for long walks."

"I know. I'm sure they're having a great time."

Brett must have sensed the residual worry lingering in my mind. "We can text them later to make sure."

I nodded and pushed my remaining worries to the back of my mind, determined to stay in the moment and enjoy every minute of our vacation.

A short while later, Rita brought out our meals, setting the plates in front of us. Delicious smells wafted up to greet my nose, and my stomach grumbled in anticipation. We thanked

Rita and started in on our meals. Right from the first bite, the food didn't disappoint.

Rita had only taken a few steps away from our table when Kevin appeared from the lobby.

"Is everyone enjoying their dinner?" he asked the room at large.

We all assured him that we were.

He slid an arm around Rita's shoulders. "If there's anything you need, just let me or my wife know. We want to make sure your stay at Holly Lodge is as comfortable and enjoyable as possible."

Rita gave him a loving smile and Kevin returned it before they parted ways, Kevin heading back toward the lobby and Rita disappearing into the kitchen.

I couldn't help but wonder if they were really on such good terms as they had appeared to be a moment before. Maybe they had hot, short-lived tempers and had already put their argument behind them, but somehow I had my doubts. There had been such a bitterness underlying their angry words, and I couldn't help but think that their loving smiles hadn't quite reached their eyes.

Maybe I was wrong, but I had a sneaking suspicion that the apparent affection they'd shown a moment ago was nothing more than an act.